To Ben —

Great to meet a fellow Mount Vernon resident!

5/19/25

Also by John Adam Wasowicz

*Daingerfield Island*
*Jones Point*
*Slaters Lane*
*Roaches Run*
*Gadsby's Corner*
*Hazel Falls*

# SPITE HOUSE

John Adam Wasowicz

*To David Clark*

## SPITE HOUSE

Copyright © John Adam Wasowicz, 2024

All rights reserved under International and Pan-American copyright conventions. No part of this book may be reproduced, stored in a retrieval system, or transmitted in any form—electronic, mechanical, or other means—now known or hereafter invented without written permission from the publisher. Address all inquiries to the publisher.

Publisher: John Adam Wasowicz
Editor: Charles Rammelkamp
Graphic Design: Ace Kieffer
Cover art: Alex Herron Wasowicz
Author photo: Aron Wasowicz

This is a work of fiction. Names, characters, places, and incidents are products of the author's imagination or are used fictitiously and are not to be construed as real. Any resemblance to actual events, locales, organizations, or persons, living or dead, is entirely coincidental.

Alendron Publishing LLC 2024
3005 Wessynton Way
Alexandria, VA 22309

Distributor: Itasca Books, Inc.

ISBN: 979-8-9880480-2-2

Printed in the United States of America

"Hell is empty and all the devils are here."
William Shakespeare, *The Tempest*

# One

Roxie Neele lived in a spite house.

Hers was not the famous Hollensbury Spite House on Queen Street, the envy of the neighborhood. Rather, it was one of the three lesser known spite houses that coexisted with Hollensbury in Old Town.

The Hollensbury Spite House's Wikipedia page threw a little light at Roxie's place, referring to its location in the 400 block of Prince Street, its measurements (7' 9" wide), the date of construction ("sometime before 1883"), and the name of the original owner ("most likely" Samuel Janney).

Roxie didn't own her spite house, which was last purchased by the O'Leary family in the '70s. She felt the O'Learys should convey ownership to her for caring for the place for so many years, and was resentful toward them for not doing so.

These days, Roxie's spite house drew more attention than any other residence in Old Town, which engendered jealousy in some quarters. Cars crawled by and drivers stole a peek while passengers gawked at the house. Some passersby peeped in at the windows. Film crews shot newsreels. Old Towners snapped pictures and posted them online.

In fact, there hadn't been this much local activity on social media since the last Rose Bud murder.

It would be nice to say that all the attention was the result of some good fortune, but, regrettably, that was not the case. Roxie had been arrested for fatally poisoning her neighbor, Trudy Vine. Alexandria Police Officer Joey Cook arrested Roxie and carted her off to jail.

Roxie was a resident of the big house tonight. The width of her tiny cell was roughly equivalent to that of her spite house, a thought that brought her no comfort and didn't make her feel the least bit at home.

Roxie's spite house sat cold and empty in her absence, an orphan in a neighborhood of brightly lit and cheerfully inhabited townhomes. If other townhouses in the neighborhood envied the attention that Roxie's house attracted today, her spite house was jealous that it remained unoccupied while the other houses bustled with life.

Although Roxie's spite house was constructed between two regular size domiciles, most spite houses were built at the entrances of alleys or other spaces to obstruct the normal flow of traffic. They acquired the "spite" designation because they were constructed to "spite" the free flow of commerce and irritate the neighbors.

Spite houses were around long before tiny houses became fashionable and before home decor magazines began publishing the skinny on how to furnish narrow spaces. Spite houses were unwelcome residential dwarfs, nothing more than a clump of bricks thrown in an alley or walkway between two normal size dwellings. Install a door and tack up a window and presto! A spite house was born.

They were as adorable as a doll house or as ugly as the wrinkles on Cybil Shawl's face (more on that later).

But enough about spite houses.

Let's duck around the corner and look in at the law office of Mo Katz, Esq., at 221B Wales Alley. Our story opens lightheartedly, comically almost, if murder can be thought so, though the tale will soon turn mournful as the menacing murder spree of Rose Bud comes into focus.

# Two

Since departing the U.S. Attorney's Office the previous year, Mo Katz had settled into a cozy solo law practice.

If he'd wanted, he could have been a partner with one of the white collar law firms along the K Street corridor in D.C.

That was the typical landing spot for a former U.S. attorney, either that or a governor's mansion.

Katz held the position of U.S. attorney for six years across two administrations, which was testimony to his apolitical nature. Both liberals and conservatives applauded his professionalism, a rare feat in the age of polarization.

He never planned to leverage the federal job for something else down the road. All he ever wanted to do was fight the good fight. And he still did, just from a different angle.

He opened a small law office in Old Town Alexandria handling misdemeanor and felony cases in criminal court, family law cases, and some civil litigation. Lots of people came to him when they or their kids got into trouble with the law or with their spouses or business partners.

Mo was tall and attractive, with mahogany skin, wiry hair graying at the temples, and sharply chiseled facial features.

He was content with his station in life, due in large part to his current domestic life, which was defined by three females: his partner Abby Snowe, her college-aged daughter Shayne Duncan, and six-year-old Katie Fortune.

Abby was Mo's wife in every respect except the one that resulted in a ring on the fourth finger of her left hand. They shared a townhome on Harvard Street. Mo owned it but Abby was the one who transformed the house into a warm and comfortable home.

Something was always baking in the kitchen. The joint living/dining room had an antique table in the center beneath a bright chandelier and sofas and chairs nestled around a bay window. Plush Oriental carpets covered the hardwood floors. Plants sat on small tables and windowsills. Photos, etchings, and artwork of Old Town — depicting the waterfront, King Street boutiques, the Masonic Temple, and Christ Church — adorned the walls.

The kitchen table was square like a card table. None of the chairs matched. Two had high backs, one folded, and the fourth was a stool.

Katie owned the stool.

A section of newspaper was always open on the table, usually *The Wall Street Journal*, *The Washington Post*, *The Washington Chronicle*, or *The New York Times*, though both Alexandria's *Zebra* newspaper and the *Alexandria Times* took up space from time to time.

Mo and Abby's commitment to one another was strengthened by twists of fate that had brought Shayne and Katie into their lives and transformed them into a family.

Katie was the daughter of Tony Fortune and Maggie Moriarty. Tony was murdered on the Georgetown towpath the night of Katie's birth in November 2017. Maggie overdosed four years later. Before she died, Maggie left a note asking Abby to care for Katie.

The following year, Shayne showed up on the front stoop of the townhouse. She was the daughter Abby had given up for adoption when she got pregnant during senior year in high school.

Raised in Wisconsin, Shayne transferred to Georgetown University, where she played varsity basketball. Shayne had her own place near school but spent most weekends in Old Town with Abby, Katie, and Mo.

Although neither Katie nor Shayne were Mo's biological children, he loved them both.

In his heart and in his soul, he knew that love was the single most important force in the universe. Life was filled with vices, vindictiveness, petty jealousies, and cruel animus. By giving his unconditional love to Abby, Katie and Shayne, he received love in equal measure. And that was enough to sustain him.

*P*eace and love were all the fashion this time of year, or so they said. It was early December, and Mo was meeting with Helena Delacroix. She explained she was soliciting his assistance on behalf of Roxanna "Roxie" Neele, who'd been arrested for fatally poisoning her neighbor, Trudy Vine.

According to news reports, the murder weapon — or weapons — was a six-pack of cupcakes liberally laced with rat poison. *The Washington Chronicle* newsfeed explained the situation as follows:

**WHO POISONED A BELOVED NEIGHBOR?**

Monday, December 4
by Tom Mann, editor and publisher.
© The Washington Chronicle

When Trudy Vine, 66, collapsed unexpectedly last week along the waterfront at the base of King Street, people immediately suspected foul play.

She had been in excellent health, having finished third in last month's Turkey Trot along the George Washington Parkway.

An autopsy has revealed what people feared, namely the presence of poison in her system, leading to the conclusion that she had been murdered.

Sources tell The Chronicle that Vine had visited the home of Roxanna Neele earlier in the day and Neele reportedly served her cupcakes.

Hearing the unverified rumors, Alexandria Police Officer Joey Cook investigated the matter, questioning Neele at her spite house on Prince Street.

According to Cook, Neele admitted to murdering Vine.

The veteran officer took the suspect into custody, earning commendation from the community for his effort.

Neele is being held at the Alexandria Detention Center.

It's unclear whether she has retained counsel or will be represented by the public defender.

"It's all so horrible," said Helena Delacroix, a friend of both the suspect and the victim. Dayton Longmire, an accountant and financial advisor to Vine, said, "We've lost one of the good ones."

Yesterday, a search warrant was executed at Neele's home.

Police removed cooking equipment, mixing bowls, cupcake ingredients, spoons, and baking trays from the residence, along with trash bags believed to contain empty boxes of rat poison.

Several years ago, Neele was charged with assault and battery of a fellow Alexandrian. Although she was convicted by a judge in district court, the charge was dismissed in circuit court. The circumstances surrounding that case are unknown.

When told about the current charges against Neele, no one expressed sympathy.

"That woman's just a crazy old bat," said one neighbor who asked not to be identified.

No trial date has been set for the case, which will be prosecuted by Deputy Commonwealth Attorney Dash Low.

---

"Nobody has a good word to say about Roxie," Helena acknowledged to Mo, fidgeting with her glasses as she spoke. She'd put them on, take them off, place them on a bookcase, and then retrieve them from the shelf.

"What compelled you to come to me?"

"She said you're the only person in the world who could help her."

"You've spoken to her? She asked you to visit me?"

"That's right," Helena said. "She called from the jail. For full transparency, she paid me to come here."

His gut told him to steer clear of the case. It was a weird crime with a preposterous murder weapon, namely a poison cupcake, and an implausible outcome. *Could ingesting a small amount of rat poison in a bite-sized item really kill you?* Furthermore, the suspect was poorly regarded in the community, and "poorly regarded" was putting it mildly. An anonymous source told *The Chronicle* that she was batshit. That could have been anyone and probably conveyed the sentiments of everyone.

Plus he had a nagging feeling that something wasn't right about Roxie soliciting him to serve as her counsel.

"Did she say anything else?"

"No," Helena said. "But if you're asking whether she has some ulterior motive, I think she might. I just don't know what it is."

They sat silently studying one another. Then, looking somewhat disoriented, she asked, "Why am I here?" She glanced around. "Oh, yes, for Roxie. Poor Roxie!"

"Are you okay?" Mo asked.

"Yes, of course. I think maybe it's my blood sugar. Anyway, when she called me to see you, she said she'd never hurt Trudy. She said she loved her."

"Would you do me a favor? Write down what Miss Neele said to you." Mo handed a piece of paper to her. "Please date and sign it."

Helena put on her glasses, scribbled on the paper and handed it back to him. She then removed her glasses and put them back on the shelf. He opened the desk drawer, slipped the note inside, and closed the drawer.

"What are you going to do with that?" she asked.

"I'm not sure," he confided, "but it's better to have it and not need it then to regret not having it if it's needed."

She nodded in agreement. Then that disoriented look reappeared.

"No reason for you to stay any longer," Mo said helpfully. "I appreciate your stopping by."

It was already late afternoon. He still had people waiting to see him. On top of that, he'd promised to join Abby and the girls for dinner at a restaurant.

"Are you going to take the case?" Helena asked, once again focused.

"I'll consider it," he lied. The answer was no, but that would have required further explanation.

He escorted her to the front door, where she removed her jacket from the coatrack, and he assisted her in putting it on.

As they parted, Helena added, "She told me that you once pursued a wrongful case against her. She said she was innocent of the charge. She said this is your chance to make up for it."

*Ah, yes*, he thought to himself. *The case referenced in the article.*

"She said it had something to do with an assault."

Mo nodded as he bid farewell. Then he checked the appointment list and ushered the next prospective client into his inner sanctum.

As he did so, a knock on the door was followed by the reappearance of Helena, who asked: "Did I leave my car keys here?" She plunged a hand into her coat pocket. "Oh, no, sorry. Here they are! Sorry to bother!"

The day ended with no further disturbances, although, when he made himself an espresso after the last new client of the day left, he discovered a pair of glasses on the bookshelf. He concluded Helena either owned a second pair of glasses or had wondered why everything appeared blurry during her drive home.

Assuming she'd be back in a day or so to pick up the glasses, he left them in the reception area.

Mo sauntered upstairs to the conference room. He checked the time as he didn't want to be late for dinner. Still, he needed a moment to travel back in time and revisit his previous encounter with Roxie.

How long ago had it been? And what was it even about?

# Three

The case was *Commonwealth v. Neele*.

A woman had appeared on a cold January evening at the magistrate's window with her nose bleeding, a shiner beneath her left eye, scratch marks on her cheek and forehead, and a scraped chin.

The victim recounted how she'd been assaulted by Roxie along Washington Way, a micro park adjacent to an alley on N. Pitt Street.

The victim said she was sitting on a bench in the park minding her own business when Roxie approached and accused her of having an affair with a local politician. Concerned for her safety, the woman got up to leave, at which time Roxie struck her, inflicting the injuries on her face the clerk was staring at through the magistrate's window.

The magistrate issued a summons for Roxie to appear in court to answer to the charge and took photos of the victim as well.

The case folder sat unattended until the day of trial when junior Assistant Commonwealth Attorney Mo Katz, assigned the district court docket, got it as part of the day's caseload.

To avoid trial, Mo approached Roxie's attorney, Jimmy Wolfe, the dapper dean of the defense bar, and proposed a 30-day suspended term in exchange for a plea and an agreement to take an anger management course.

Jimmy dismissed Mo's proposed plea agreement. "She's innocent," he announced. "Your witness is a total whack job. She did this out of jealousy and spite toward Roxie."

The case proceeded to trial. Mo called one witness, the victim.

Jimmy invoked the rule on witnesses, requiring witnesses to remain outside the courtroom until called to the stand. Mo thought it odd, since the victim was the only witness in the case-in-chief.

The victim testified verbatim to the facts as previously provided to the magistrate.

Mo introduced the photos of the victim's facial injuries taken by the magistrate, as Jimmy stipulated to their admissibility.

Jimmy asked the victim no questions on cross-examination. After the prosecution rested, Wolfe announced that his witness, Cybil Shawl, was outside in the hall and needed to be sworn in to testify. Mo objected on the grounds that he had no advance notice that Cybil would be called to the stand. The judge overruled the objection.

Cybil took the stand. She was a tiny woman of indeterminable age, with pale, wrinkled skin. Clothes hung on her so haphazardly that she appeared almost stylish, and her matted gray hair clung to her scalp like mud.

Cybil said she contacted Jimmy Wolfe when she learned that Roxie had been charged. "I couldn't stand to see an injustice done to that poor woman," she said, alleging that the victim paid her to inflict the wounds that subsequently caused the magistrate to issue the warrant against Roxie. "She wanted me to mess her up real good," Cybil told the court.

She said Cybil paid her $200 on the day of the incident.

To rebut Cybil's story, Mo excused Cybil and recalled the victim to the stand for redirect examination.

Under the rule on witnesses, the victim had been excluded from the courtroom during Cybil's testimony.

"Do you know a woman named Cybil Shawl?" Mo asked when the victim returned to the witness box.

"No," she answered, her voice indicating contempt and annoyance.

"She claims you paid her to plant bruises on your face."

Jimmy objected. "The prosecutor is testifying," he complained.

The judge upheld the objection and admonished Mo.

Mo rephrased the question. "Did you pay anyone to assault you on the day in question?"

"Did I *what*?" she replied, incredulous. "I was attacked by that woman sitting over there, Roxie Neele." She pointed a shaky hand at the defendant. "She struck me repeatedly. I certainly didn't make this up by paying someone else to mutilate my face. Why on earth would I do something like that? What do you think I am, a masochist or something?"

After Mo finished redirect, Jimmy stood and ambled to the witness box. He placed his elbow on the front of the box. "You're sure you don't know Cybil Shawl?"

"I'm sure."

Jimmy jingled change in his pocket, turned his back to the witness, and sauntered over to the defense table where he picked up a photo that lay face down on the oak table. He pressed it against his stomach and turned back toward the witness.

"Let me repeat the question: Are you sure you don't know Cybil Shawl?"

It occurred to Mo that the victim had never actually seen the woman who called herself Cybil Shawl. Mo had given her a person's name and she'd answered that she was unfamiliar with it — the name, not the person. *What if the victim knew Cybil by another name? Or what if the victim knew Cybil but didn't know her name?*

Mo stood. "Your honor, I ask that the woman in the hall be returned to the courtroom and that the witness be asked whether she can identify that woman."

"I'm not going to permit that," the judge replied curtly. "You should have requested an in-court identification before you asked the witness whether she knew Cybil Shawl." Then, to Jimmy, the judge said pleasantly, "Proceed, counselor."

"But, your honor," Mo pleaded.

"Don't quibble with me, Mr. Katz," the judge rejoined. "The problem with your office is that you're clogging up the docket with a lot of frivolous cases."

"My case is anything but frivolous," complained the victim.

The judge struck his gavel. "My chambers," he snapped to both counsel. Flapping the sleeves of his gown, he rose and exited brusquely, Mo and Jimmy trailing behind him.

Let it be known the judge envied Katz, having correctly marked the young prosecutor as a talent at the beginning of a long and distinguished arc.

Furthermore, the judge relished any opportunity to disrupt Mo's trajectory, perhaps foolishly believing that you could run interference with a person's rightful destiny.

"Mr. Katz," the judge said, "this is a 'he said/she said' case and, without corroborating evidence, there is no way you can sustain a conviction." Technically speaking, it was a "she said/she said" case but Mo got the point and remained silent.

"Your performance in this case has been amateurish," the judge continued. "Didn't you see what was coming? Mr. Wolfe set a trap and you fell into it. Now you have to live with it."

Turning to Jimmy, the judge said, "I've long admired your tactics, Mr. Wolfe."

It bears mentioning that the local bar association selects candidates who are qualified to sit on the circuit court and the Virginia General Assembly normally confirms a jurist from that list. Jimmy was dean of the defense bar and his brother-in-law was a respected member of the Virginia House of Delegates and chairman of the Judiciary Committee.

Having given the lie to justice being blind, the threesome returned to the courtroom.

"You may continue your cross-examination," the judge said. Jimmy then showed the witness a photograph previously sitting on the defense table. The photo showed two women standing beside one another.

"Do you recognize the two women depicted in this photo?" Jimmy asked.

She sputtered words that didn't form a sentence.

"I offer the photo as evidence to be part of the record," Jimmy said. "It depicts the victim and Cybil Shawl in conversation, with the victim handling a bundle of bills to Ms. Shawl. No further questions."

"The defendant's exhibit number one will be admitted…," the judge said, hesitating to glance at Mo, "…without objection."

"With the court's indulgence," Mo said politely yet sternly. "I *do* object. The defense hasn't laid a foundation. Who took the photo? When was it taken? It can't simply be admitted into evidence because he's offered it."

"There's no need to lay a foundation," the judge replied dismissively. "And unless you have another objection, I'm going to admit it over your objection. Let's end this charade."

Mo considered his next move.

"Why don't we unpack the evidence," Mo said to the victim, still on the stand, "beginning with the other woman in the photograph. Do you recognize her and, if so, who is she?"

"She's a homeless person who wanders up and down King Street pulling a suitcase as though she was heading for the Metro to go to Reagan National Airport. I don't know her name. I occasionally feed her. I also have given her clothing."

She studied the photo. "I'm not sure but some of the clothes she's wearing in this photo might be ones that I've given her."

"Did you ever give money to her?" he asked.

"I was always reluctant to give her money because I was afraid she'd spend it on drugs or alcohol," replied the witness. "I didn't want to be an enabler. I felt clothes was a wiser bet. But yes, on one occasion I gave her money."

Mo placed his index finger pointing to the upper right corner.

"Do you know when this picture was taken?" She looked at the photo and then at him.

"It was March," she replied. "St. Patrick's Day weekend. You can tell by the Irish flags flying from the street lamps."

"Objection, relevancy" hollered Jimmy. "Who cares when they met? The point is they knew one another."

"Actually, the date is extremely relevant," Mo countered. "The defense witness testified that money was exchanged the day of the incident, but this photo was taken *after* the alleged incident occurred. The crime occurred in January. This photo was taken in March."

While Jimmy and the judge milled over the purported timeline, Mo said, "Your Honor, I'd like to recall the defense witness." The judge sent the bailiff to fetch her, but the woman who'd identified herself as Cybil Shawl was gone.

The case closed with the uncertainty of a dangling chad on a Florida ballot in a presidential election. It was anyone's guess how the court was going to decide.

*T*he attorneys proceeded to closing argument.

"The victim in this case alleges that she was assaulted by the defendant," Mo said. "The defense counters by claiming the victim actually paid another party to beat her so that she could press false charges against the defendant.

"At first, it appeared nearly impossible to know who's lying and who's telling the truth. And, for that reason, the case appeared likely to be dismissed.

"But then we learned that the defense's sole witness lied under oath. We know that because the photo shown by defense counsel of the victim and the other woman was taken after the date of the assault. We can conclude that the picture was part of an elaborate hoax concocted by the defendant to escape punishment.

"The trick played on this court is in fact the best evidence of the defendant's guilt. The lie has been exposed and her deceit is her undoing."

The judge glared at Roxie in disgust. "I've heard enough," he said. Not pausing to allow Jimmy to present a closing argument, he said to Roxie, "Please stand."

"Your honor," Jimmy began, reminding the judge of his right to make a closing argument.

"Sit down," the judge instructed. Then, focusing on Roxie, he said, "If I am to believe the prosecution, you devised a sinister plan to win an acquittal. You mercilessly and brutally attacked the victim. Then, when you were charged with assault, you concocted a scheme to create the appearance that the victim was the perpetrator of the very crime that you had committed against her.

"And believe the prosecutor I do."

He scratched his head. "What sort of twisted, demented person would do something like this? It's diabolical and fiendish. And more than a little weird. Therefore, Roxanna Neele, I find you guilty of assault and battery and sentence you to 12 months in jail: 6 months for assaulting the victim and 6 months for lying to me. Court is adjourned." The judge flung his gavel contemptuously across the bench and retreated to chambers.

"I'm innocent!" Roxie screeched. "The prosecutor twisted the facts and you bought it! How stupid can you be?"

# Four

*A* word about Roxanna "Roxie" Neele.

Fifty years ago, all she had was a high school education and a couple of bucks in her pocket when her parents departed to points unknown, leaving her to fend for herself without any family other than a baby on its way.

Most people live in the present. Not Roxie. The present was too painful, as was the past. So she escaped to the only place she could find refuge: the future.

This is not to say she had the imaginative genius of Jules Verne or Isaac Asimov, but she did possess the foresight to see Old Town not as it was but as it could be and, fortunately for her, as it became.

Back in the '70s, the waterfront was nothing spectacular, cluttered with steel-sided warehouses best suited for the wrecking ball. The condition of retail shopping deteriorated the further one proceeded up from the river. And it was hard to believe that a Metro line at the foot of the Masonic Temple would bring new life to upper King Street.

While a lot of traffic passed along Washington, Patrick, and Henry Streets, it was almost exclusively commuter traffic between Fairfax and Prince William counties and the District of Columbia, with few of those commuters stopping to shop or dine in Old Town. It was difficult to imagine those cars parking in driveways in Old Town in a bustling inner city.

The coal power plant in Old Town North seemed destined to remain in operation forever, spewing ash in the surrounding area with coal trains stopping traffic along the George Washington Parkway as they lumbered along the tracks to the generating station.

Roxie saw beyond that.

She knew the old coal-fired power plant was destined to close. Sooner or later, the city's primary newspaper wasn't going to need those huge print shops at Robinson Landing and elsewhere along the waterfront. Once the Metro station got situated, hotels and restaurants would prosper and commercial and retail establishments would blossom.

And while she didn't foresee a pandemic, she sensed something big was going to happen some day and people would settle in Old Town instead of passing through on their way to someplace else called home or work in the D.C. or in Fairfax County.

Gentrification — a rarely used word in those days — was already in her mind if not in her vocabulary.

As a result, she leveraged every penny in her possession and forsook every luxury to buy real estate.

She opted for public transportation over owning a car, dispensed with air conditioning in the summer, and opted for a wood-burning stove in the winter. Borrowing a page from the Suze Orman playbook, she never ate out. She also mended old clothes and cut her own hair. Another quirk: She went to church daily.

When the future came knocking — at that intersection of opportunity and preparation — she was ready. She had four little green houses and a red hotel on every square of the board game.

Why she chose to rent a spite house and live a Spartan existence was an enigma. She was the wealthiest landlord in Old Town and a real estate mogul in the truest sense of the word. Perhaps it was symbolism.

It came as a surprise to everyone when Roxie's name turned up in *Alexandria Living Magazine* as one of the ten wealthiest people in Alexandria. Most readers thought it was a misprint or a case of mistaken identity.

*That* Roxie Neele?

Others assumed it was dumb luck. She must have inherited the money or won the lottery. Nobody gave her credit for having done it entirely on her own.

After all, Roxie didn't fit the bill. She was ordinary, nondescript, average.

Of course, if she had exuded the airs of the rich and famous, she would have been ridiculed as being pretentious and ostentatious.

She never made any effort to conform to her standing. Rarely did jewelry adorn her, except for the tiny baubles that ran down her left ear like a constellation of stars.

If someone had observed her closely, they would have recognized a self-awareness in this strange woman who drew strength and satisfaction helping those who suffered from addiction and self-loathing.

As she aged, her neck sagged, her eyelids drooped over her eyes, her wrinkles multiplied, and her teeth chipped and yellowed. She didn't spend a penny on plastic surgery or cosmetic dentistry. Her hands appeared red and coarse. She lost circulation in some of her fingertips but never lost her grip on things. She continued to cut her own hair and, from the looks of things, not particularly well. She continued to purchase her clothes at second-hand stores, often the ones in buildings she owned along King Street. And she still ate at home and darned her socks.

A woman of her means could have dressed like royalty and thrown parties for everyone on the street, but not Roxie. She just existed in a tiny spite house, which was something like living in a shoe.

The only thing that was grand about Roxie was the size of her annual giving, but you'd never know it because her donations were always made anonymously. Truth be told, many local charities, health clinics, education centers, and entrepreneurial endeavors owed their survival to her.

Charities came to depend upon the arrival of the anonymous checks as the days ticked down toward the end of the calendar year.

Ironically, many of the people who headed these institutions were the same ones who berated her in private conversation.

"I don't know how that woman can be worth more than a dime," said one unknowing recipient of her largess. "She doesn't have any academic background to speak of."

"She's never worked in any reputable financial institution," said another. "She's completely unqualified to handle a portfolio in excess of a few thousand dollars, let alone millions. I wouldn't trust her with my kid's savings account."

"Roxanna Neele is a cultural Neanderthal," commented a third person. "She has no savoir faire. I'll bet she's never been to the Kennedy Center, let alone the Met. The woman wouldn't know high culture if it bit her on the neck!"

They all laughed at Roxie as they rushed to check their mail to see if the end-of-year holiday checks had arrived.

# Five

Wearing a gray herringbone top coat with a blue scarf wrapped around his neck, Mo strolled briskly down Union Street past Robinson Landing.

He hadn't forgotten about dinner with Abby and the kids. He even called to let her know that he was on his way, though there was no answer.

Not that long ago, a huge warehouse filled the block he passed along the waterfront, he recalled. It was composed of sheet metal without any windows, resembling a gigantic sardine can. After it was torn down, a magnificent townhome development took root and the entire area had been transformed.

Combined with the addition of new restaurants and a promenade that extended along the city's waterfront, the vista rivaled anything else along the East Coast, including Newport, Charleston, and Savannah.

He reached Windmill Hill Park and walked through Wilkes Tunnel. He hadn't been able to shake that old assault and battery case from his mind since Helena Delacroix had mentioned it. Her words came back to him: "She told me that you once pursued a wrongful case against her. She said she was innocent of the charge. She said this is your chance to make up for it."

*What in God's name was she talking about?* he asked himself. *Innocent? Give me a break.*

He cracked that case because Jimmy committed an error introducing a photo that revealed an inconsistency in the case. The sequence of events had been wrong. And then there were the problems with the witness's identity. The entire defense wobbled. And once it began to wobble, it crashed.

Roxie had been guilty as sin.

Mo ducked inside the corner pastry shop and ordered a coffee. Then he summoned an Uber and walked to Washington Street. His ride soon appeared, and 15 minutes later, he had finished his coffee and arrived at the city jail.

After passing his bar card and driver's license to the deputy on the other side of an opaque glass wall for routine inspection — a mere formality, as everyone in the system knew him — Mo boarded an elevator to the fourth floor. There, he passed through two heavy metal doors — one closing before the other opened along a narrow passageway — and finally entered an octagon-shaped room with a high ceiling.

It was like a space capsule somewhere far removed from Old Town Alexandria, except he wasn't wearing an astronaut's suit.

Few people not associated with the judicial system in some way had ever been in this space. Most didn't even know it existed, since the jail was a nondescript building in the Eisenhower Valley, hidden at the end of a dead end street at the outskirts of a burgeoning urban enclave.

The smell was somewhere between a laundromat and an auto repair shop. No natural sunlight existed; the only illumination in the room came from the buzzing overhead neon lights. The Spartan furnishings consisted of a couple of grubby plastic chairs and a metal table screwed to the floor.

A door on the opposite side of the room clicked open and a diminutive woman wearing an orange jumpsuit walked into the room. She was older and smaller than the woman Mo remembered from the assault case.

"I wasn't sure that Helena was going to persuade you that this was worth your time," she said bluntly as she approached him, the table between them.

"It was when she reminded me of the case we had together."

She cocked an eyebrow as if to ask whether the ploy was

effective.

"It brought me here," he replied.

*True that*, she thought triumphantly. She'd gotten him here. But could she hold him?

Mo wasn't an especially big guy — 6 feet tall but slightly built, reedy almost — yet he hovered over her like a giant.

Her jumpsuit was a couple of sizes too big and she was practically swimming inside of it. The pant legs puddled at her feet. The effect made Roxie look even smaller than she was, like a kid doing dress-up from their parent's closet.

They sat down in the plastic chairs, the kind better suited for an elementary school classroom. Roxie fit perfectly in hers, which was yellow. Katz settled against the edge of a red chair, tilting forward and spreading out his legs to get comfortable.

"How're you holding up?" he asked with sincere concern.

"I can't complain," she shrugged. "The quarters are larger than my home."

"Well, I'll get straight to the point. I don't think I can take your case."

"What'll it take?" she countered, undeterred. "Money? I have plenty." Desperation echoed in each word. "Please don't expect me to say I'm innocent and ask whether you can get me out of a jam. It's not like that. It's not like that at all, which is why I *really* need a good lawyer."

Despite his best effort, Mo was already in trial mode. It couldn't be helped. He asked himself how Roxie would present to a jury. While his instincts told him to resist the case, he was already assessing it with the end in mind. Some habits were hard to break.

"I killed her," Roxie volunteered. "And I'm not sorry. Trudy was a pain in the ass. I'm not sorry and I don't feel that I should be punished."

She sounded incredibly honest, which was rare. Most clients

didn't share the truth with Mo, particularly when they were guilty. Either they lied or they clammed up.

"You realize we don't have any agreement as to confidentiality," Mo reminded her. Since no attorney-client relationship existed, Mo wasn't obligated to hold her confidences.

"I'm not worried," she said.

"Like I said, I don't think I can take your case," he repeated.

"So why are you here if not to sign up as my counsel?" she asked smugly.

"That other case," he answered. "The one where Jimmy Wolfe represented you. That's what compelled me to come. I never felt I understood everything that happened. Maybe you can fill in the missing details now."

He waited.

She sighed, then gave in. "I was this close." She held her thumb and index finger an inch apart. "I should have been acquitted. You used my own exhibit against me. You raised questions about the veracity of the surprise witness. You even turned the judge, who was clearly in Jimmy's pocket at the outset of the case."

As she spoke, her hand clenched into a fist.

"Do you want to tell me about what really happened?" he asked. "I never could figure out the truth from the falsehoods."

"There was no falsehood," she replied. "Only truth. You just couldn't see it."

*Mo* turned, jarred by the sudden sound of metal clanging against metal as the door snapped open.

A sheriff's deputy entered the room. She was short and thick, almost as wide as she was tall. "Everything okay?" she asked, hitching the belt of her holster with her wrists.

"We're fine, Deputy Davis," Roxie said curtly.

Ignoring Roxie, the deputy, Marcia Davis, looked squarely at Mo, arms akimbo. She needed to hear it from him.

"We're fine," he repeated, except in a different tone, less abrasive, warmer, and more appreciative.

"Okay." The deputy pointed her thumb at Roxie. "This bitch doesn't deserve someone like you. She's trouble. We treat her accordingly. Sometimes she isn't allowed exercise. She should just rot in this place."

Snickering at Roxie, she added, "If I had my way, she'd eat like a dog, served scraps in a corner and chained with a collar."

Turning to Mo, she smiled. "Holler if you need anything, Mr. Katz."

"Will do," Mo said. His face emitted no sign of the fact that he found the deputy's comments rehearsed.

The steel door popped open and slammed shut in Deputy Davis's wake.

Roxie said, "Some of the clientele resent me, as does most of the management. They're constantly running interference to disrupt my mood."

Mo nodded.

"She's just one more Nurse Ratched in the joint," Roxie added. "At first it rankled me, then I learned to adapt. Being denied an occasional meal is a godsend. The food here sucks. And exercise isn't all it's cracked up to be."

A warm feeling inhabited the room and Mo sensed a strange alchemy brewing in an invisible caldron.

"If I took your case, which I'm not, I couldn't put you on the stand to claim innocence," he said. "You can't lie under oath. You understand that?"

She lowered her head and raised her eyes. She waited for him to speak next, but he didn't say anything.

"Look," she said, "The evidence in this case is weak. I entered a not guilty plea at my arraignment and I intend to take the case to trial.

"I got charged because there's past animus between Trudy and me. Everyone knows it. They'll claim it was the motive. I need an attorney who is shrewd enough to navigate through the nooks and shoals, or shoals or crannies, or whatever, to get me acquitted.

"I have no intention of testifying. I don't lie. But this case isn't strong enough to hold me."

Mo looked at her blankly, concealing his curiosity.

"So how do we get started?" she asked.

He smiled. "The first thing I have to do is consult bar counsel to be sure I can represent you. After all, I did prosecute you once upon a time."

Roxie replied, "I called the state bar and posed a hypothetical where an attorney prosecutes a person and years later defends that same person for another crime. There's no conflict of interest so long as there's no connection between the facts in the cases, which there is not in this case."

"That was presumptuous," Katz said.

"I didn't want you to get into any ethical trouble," she said. "So are we good?"

"I'm not going to take your word for it," he said. "I'm still going to contact the bar and, assuming it passes muster, I'll consider it."

"What's your initial prognosis?" she asked.

"Trudy ate cupcakes at your house around 11 in the morning. Soon afterwards she died of rat poisoning. The timing and forensics are going to be important. If there are traces of rat poison in the pots and pans taken into custody, that's incriminating evidence. The bad relationship between the two of you is a complicating factor.

"But it's a weak case. A bitter relationship with a neighbor is hardly grounds to be charged with murder. 'Beyond a reasonable doubt' is a pretty high standard. I don't see it here."

There was something else, which Mo hid from Roxie.

He doubted rat poison placed inside cupcakes consumed in a single day could be fatal. If he was correct, it meant something other than the fact that a jury wouldn't find Roxie guilty of murder. It meant she couldn't be guilty, period. *And if it was impossible for Roxie to have poisoned Trudy, then what was going on?*

The overhead humming of the light intensified.

"Do we want a jury trial?" she asked.

"You're jumping ahead of yourself," he laughed. "I still haven't said I'll take the case."

"Hypothetically."

"In your case, I prefer a jury," he reflected. "A judge might be more disposed to find you guilty. A jury, on the other hand, might be more easily swayed that the evidence isn't sufficient. And, with a jury, all you need is one juror favorably disposed to hang the jury and deny the prosecution a victory."

He glanced at his phone, noticed the time, and remembered he was supposed to be at dinner with Abby and the kids. Wrinkles formed across his forehead like lines of sheet music.

"What is it?" asked Roxie.

"Nothing," he lied.

"Let's continue tomorrow. You look like a person who needs to be somewhere else."

"Do you mind?"

"Not at all. If you agreed to represent me, I'd be honored."

Mo lifted the wall phone and waited for a deputy to pick up on the other end. A moment later, he was in the elevator going down to the lobby.

*S*hortly after Roxie returned to her cell, Deputy Davis visited. With a magician's sleight of hand, a $50 bill materialized and found its way into the deputy's waiting palm.

Deputy Davis grinned slyly. Truth be told, she would have done it for free if Roxie had asked politely. *Mo effing Katz*, she thought to herself.

Back in the day, that bastard put her brother Freddie in prison for dealing drugs in the Berg. Nowadays, those same drugs are either legal or considered part of a public health crisis. That conviction broke poor Freddie. Today he was living on the street or under some bridge.

Deputy Davis wasn't sure what game Roxie was playing with Mo effing Katz but anything that messed with him was fine by her.

Standing outside the jail in the bitter cold that inhabited Old Town after the sun had set, Mo called another Uber. While he waited, he used his phone to check the public record on the outcome of Roxie's old assault case, which had been appealed from the district court to the circuit court. He'd lost track of the case, which was retried as he'd departed the prosecutor's office and gone into private practice

The public record showed the case was dismissed on appeal because the complaining witness never showed up.

At that instant — the very instant that a $50 bill greased the palm of Deputy Davis — Mo recounted the interaction in the attorney-client room.

The deputy's hostility was intended to portray Roxie as a sympathetic character. *But what if that scene was staged?* he asked himself. *After all, it seemed rehearsed as it unfolded. Assuming it was staged, was that a reason to drop the case or an incentive to pursue it?*

Inside the jail, Roxie had a premonition that Mo saw through her ploy but that it actually worked to her advantage by enticing him to take the case.

Mo's phone rang as he closed the app. He glanced at the number. "Hey, Sherry," he said to Deputy Police Chief Sherry Stone. "What's up?"

"He struck again," she said, referring to an active serial killer in Old Town nicknamed Rose Bud by the media. "It's the fourth time since Valentine's Day."

His eyes tightened to small slits as he contemplated the implications.

# Six

*Diary entry from February 13, ten months earlier.*

I'm not much of a romantic. Maybe that's part of my problem. I have to go online to figure out how to set a mood.

As it turns out, scented candles haven't gone out of style.

An article I read recommended soft touches: background music, preferably violins; rose petals and tiny red hearts strewn on the floor leading to the bedroom or bathroom; satin sheets on the bed; bath bombs in the tub.

This Valentine's Day I'm going to make my move. I'll blindfold her and envelope her in a warm embrace. We'll make sweet love. Afterwards, we'll lie in bed, our heads against the headboard — the one we pounded against the wall incessantly! I'll have an ashtray on my chest, we'll smoke cigarettes.

Where can I find tiny paper hearts? Would a variety store sell a blindfold? Perhaps I should go to a lingerie shop. I bet they've got the perfect something. Does 7-Eleven still sell cigarettes? And what about bath bombs? Who sells those?

Maybe I'll just buy these things tonight from a street vendor at one of those pop-up stores in Old Town.

The truth is, I don't know anything about anything. I just bury myself in my work. It's rewarding, sure, but I'm not really getting ahead. People don't acknowledge my value. The powers that be hold me down. They're jealous of my superior talents.

But enough about work. Let's talk about love. First I'll woo her; then I'll wow her; and finally I'll win her!

# Seven

As Sherry spoke, Mo felt an ominous sense of *déjà vu*, reminded of her phone call last year from Hazel Falls about the discovery of skeletal remains along Hooes Run.

"People are becoming afraid to leave their homes," she said, pulling him back to the here and now. "It's like the pandemic. What's worse, it's almost Christmastime."

This year the city had been plagued with four sexual assaults and murders, although, as Sherry explained, this one was different. The victim was still alive, though barely. Dead or alive, however, things like this didn't happen in Old Town. And the year wasn't over.

The first murder occurred in the victim's apartment. Patricia Sakkara was in the second month of a two-year lease in Old Town, having moved to Alexandria to take a job on Capitol Hill with Don Lotte, a newly elected senator from her home state.

Her parents were proud of her getting a job working for a senator. They helped her move. Two months later, they returned to identify their daughter's body and return home with her coffin.

*No parent should ever have to go through that*, Mo thought, shuddering at what he'd do if anything ever happened to Katie or Shayne.

The second incident occurred in early June and involved a woman named Rachel Adores. And the third victim, Lina Dobbs, was murdered on Halloween.

Immediately after Lina's death, her father, Lance, a widower, moved to Old Town and started *Enough Is Enough!*, a nonprofit dedicated to assisting families who'd lost a loved one to violence. Some people envied him for finding so much meaning in life, regardless of the fact that the source of inspiration was his daughter's death.

All of the victims were in their twenties. The M.O. was the same. The women were blindfolded and found strangled in a room with red rose petals strewn about like leaves in a forest. In one case, it was the bedroom. In another, the bathroom. The third time, a study. Two of the murders occurred in the women's apartments; one was in a hotel room.

Candles, incense, bubble baths, and wine were found at the crime scenes. The first murder suggested the items were intended for an actual sexual interlude. However, beginning with the second crime, the scenes appeared staged. The candles and incense weren't lit. In fact, the candles were still in their wrappers. No evidence existed that anyone had splashed in the bubble bath. And the rose petals strewn about the body seemed the equivalent of a maniac's business cards.

The media started to call the murderer Rose Bud, a name coined by Tom Mann in stories that appeared in *The Chronicle*.

Odd thing was, there was no evidence of consensual sex or rape in any of the cases. And the assailant had been meticulous in covering up his presence. There were no fingerprints or identifiable DNA that could have led to a suspect. No witnesses had seen the man enter or leave the women's apartments or hotel room. The police were stymied.

Despite the depraved nature of these crimes and the attendant pressure to solve them, some police departments in other metropolitan areas resented the attention the Alexandria Police Department was receiving when all they heard about were citizen complaints and threatened budget cuts.

"Curtis helping out?" Mo asked.

Curtis Santana was Sherry's best friend with benefits. They'd been together six years. He would have proposed long ago if he thought she'd accept. But Sherry was afraid the magic would stop if she committed to a relationship and therefore she brushed the issue aside every time he raised it.

"Yeah," she said.

Curtis had left the U.S. Attorney's Office last year at the same time as Mo. He had his old P.I. business going, with most of his private investigations connected to Mo's current cases. However, Sherry persuaded the police department to hire him to assist in catching the perpetrator.

She believed an outsider would offer a fresh perspective since the department wasn't making any headway.

A lot of people resented Curtis's selection. Some considered it a conflict of interest, putting the deputy chief's significant other on the payroll. Others didn't like an outsider, period, regardless of whether or not he was sleeping with the deputy. It implied the police department was deficient.

And some people simply didn't like Curtis. He'd always been a smartass who didn't follow protocol.

Some people said that Stoner (Sherry's nickname that derived from her reckless youth) and Santana deserved one another, though not in a good way. Stone was a bitch and Santana a bastard, at least in the eyes of their detractors.

As much as Mo liked both of them, he didn't think putting Curtis on the police payroll was a good idea either. "You're asking for trouble, and sooner or later it's going to find you," he had warned her.

"Got any leads?" he asked now.

"I'm at the crime scene," she said. "It's off Slaters Lane."

As soon as she gave the location, Sherry felt sure Mo winced. He'd lost a senior prosecutor there in an attack on Easter Sunday in 2019.

"Sorry," she said, immediately recalling the pain of that case.

"It's all right," he said.

Truth was, memories lingered on every street corner. That's

what happened with the passage of time. The past stuck around. Most of the memories were good. Many were sweet. A few hurt. Some hurt a lot.

Handling a murder case wasn't easy. Most homicide detectives burned out in a few years. The ones who stuck around got jaded. Mo knew Sherry wanted this investigation solved. It was getting to her because it consumed Curtis and that ran the risk of interfering with their relationship.

She needed to solve it. She was feeling vulnerable, and that was one of the things she couldn't share with Curtis, so she put it on Mo.

"At least she's alive," she said.

"Is she expected to recover?"

"One can only hope."

The implication wasn't lost on either of them. If the victim recovered, she would be able to identify her assailant and the nightmare that confounded the police and frightened the community would end.

As soon as he hung up, Mo called Abby. He was still standing outside the jail, having lost track of time. "Where are you?" he asked. "I'll come right over."

"Don't bother at this point," she replied curtly. "It's late. We're almost finished. We'll be home by the time you get here."

"I'm sorry," he said, tucking the scarf around his neck into his topcoat while wondering if she would bring him some leftovers. He was starved.

"No you're not," she said irritably. "With you, it's work first. Always preoccupied. Well, you can have at it. We're leaving. You'll have the place to yourself and you can keep whatever hours suit you."

The Uber pulled to the curb. He sighed heavily, his cloud of breath escaping into the cold night air. *Leaving?* What was that about? "I'm sorry," he said again. "I seriously lost track of time." No one was listening. The line had gone dead.

# Eight

**Diary entry from February 15.**

*I don't know what happened.*

*It started out like I imagined it would. Then something went inexplicably wrong. I wasn't prepared for that. Once it veered off course I didn't know what to do.*

*She started to laugh. At me. A mean laugh. Mocking. Wicked. Condescending.*

*Stop it! I insisted. Don't ridicule me. Shut up!*

*If she'd reacted the way she was supposed to, this never would have happened.*

*I can't write about this now, despite the fact that it's part of my assignment.*

*I have to blot it out. It's too gruesome. I mean, that wasn't me! That was someone else!*

*It was her fault.*

*She laughed at me.*

*Didn't she realize who I am?*

*I control a lot of people in this city.*

*I get my way.*

*I've built a mousetrap. I've snared several people. Here's how it works: I discover something embarrassing about them. I promise to hide their secret. Then I bury it just deep enough — like a shallow grave — so I can reach down and bring it back to the surface when I need a favor.*

*I would have shared my designs with her. She would have been impressed. Maybe she would have become my accomplice.*

*But no. Instead, she laughed.*

*At me!*

*Here's an odd twist. Despite how this turned out, I feel the night couldn't end any other way. The evening seemed oddly scripted, like I was playing a role, one for which I am well cast.*

*Teacher said to keep a diary to help us understand our feelings, but I don't know if it's helping.*

# Nine

When Mo got home, Katie was already upstairs in bed. Shayne was sprawled out on the sofa in the living room with her eyes closed listening to music pulsating through her earbuds. Through the kitchen window, Mo could see Abby sitting in a chair on the back patio bundled in blankets and wearing a balaclava pulled down to her eyes and a heavy wool sweater. She was sipping from a wineglass.

A lit candle shone on the center of the patio table, its flame flickering as though it was shivering in the cold.

Mo opened and scanned the refrigerator, grabbed a Port City lager, and headed for the patio, beginning to peel off the bottle's label like a scab as he opened the sliding glass door and greeted her.

They kissed.

"What's this talk about leaving?" he asked, sitting opposite her.

She flipped a strand of yellow hair over her shoulder. "I got tickets earlier today. That's what I wanted to share with you over dinner. Too bad you were so preoccupied. We're going to Wisconsin."

"Who's we?"

"Shayne, Katie, and me." Then she dished: "Shayne's *mother* calls her daily. She's turning into one of those helicopter parents. Shayne can't stand it. She's a grown woman. We have to go to Madison and straighten this out."

She raised her glass and sipped some wine. "We have to settle this thing through a face-to-face conversation. I don't want to make it confrontational, but we need boundaries.

"As soon as Shayne finishes one more exam — she's studying for it now — we're jumping on a plane and going to Madison. I figure it's better taking Katie with us than leaving her with you. She needs a lot of attention, and God knows what that's asking from you."

She added sarcastically, "I hope you can find the time to take us to the airport. If not, I'll call for a ride."

"Yes, of course," he said, resting the beer bottle on the slate patio. By now he'd rubbed off most of the label, which stuck to his fingertips. "I hope it works out to everyone's satisfaction."

"Everyone's satisfaction isn't the preferred option in this case," she corrected him. "The only person whose satisfaction matters is Shayne's. I'm going to make sure of that."

He looked at his fingers and rubbed at the damp bits of paper embedded in his nails.

"What?" she asked.

"It sounds a little…." He was unsure how to finish the sentence. *Disingenuous* might fit, but he edited out that word as he completed his sentence. "…ironic."

"What do you mean by that?"

"Your statement that you're going to make certain that Shayne's satisfied with the outcome," he answered. "It sounds like you're the one who needs to be satisfied, that's all."

"Speaking of irony, I'll tell you what's *ironic*. What's *ironic* is that Mo Katz is a very non-confrontational guy outside the courtroom. When he's inside, he can be a total son of a bitch. But when he's outside, he avoids a fight."

"I think that's unfair," he said, though he really knew it to be true. "I just don't want to assert myself in this equation. It's not my battle."

"I'm her fucking mother, Mo," Abby replied. For a woman who rarely used the F-word, this signified to Mo that she was deeply affected by the state of affairs. "I'm also your partner and I deserve your support. You're supposed to be in this fight with me.

"I know Shayne's independent streak. It's in our DNA, hers and mine. That woman in Wisconsin doesn't know anything about that. Nobody is going to clip Shayne's wings, and sure as hell no one in Wisconsin. I'm not jealous or protective or anything like that."

"Yeah," Mo said. "Listen, it's just not my place."

"This *is* your place," she responded angrily. "You're really her father. You have a say in all of this."

*How many glasses of wine has she had?* Mo wondered.

Shayne's biological father was deceased. He was a year older than Abby and was attending the University of North Carolina at Chapel Hill when they met. He died when an overcrowded rooftop platform collapsed at a frat house.

Mo certainly didn't see himself as a father figure. Shayne had entered their lives only a couple of years ago. Sure, he loved her, but he wasn't assuming a role that was never assigned to him.

"Okay Abby, whatever you say." Mo said, rising from his chair and grabbing his beer in one fell swoop. "Don't stay out too long. It's cold."

He went inside and scoured the refrigerator for something to eat. He didn't need this. He didn't even understand it. All he was thinking about anyway was Roxie Neele and what was behind her solicitation of Mo as her counsel in the Trudy Vine case.

# Ten

Curtis hadn't departed the crime scene despite the fact that the victim had been transported to Inova Alexandria Hospital, where she lay in a coma after having been left for dead.

The media had called it a night with the exception of Tom Mann of *The Chronicle*, who was somewhere nearby biding his time to corner Curtis.

Having been responsible for penning the name on everyone's lips, Mann was deeply invested in the case. The name came to him almost as soon as he'd heard the details of the case. Rose Bud: a sicko ("bud") who sprinkles rose petals at the scenes of his murders.

He thought it was clever. So did the rest of the press corps, who resented him for it.

The police thought the romance stuff — the hearts, candles, incense, flowers and bubble bath — was simply evidence of a good time gone bad. Some of them weren't even convinced it was the work of the same murderer. They thought it might be a copycat created by media hungry for a story that grabbed eyeballs and ignited the public's worst fears.

The fact that Tom devoted so much ink to the case confirmed that suspicion.

Curtis knew otherwise. Maybe the first murder wasn't premeditated, but the others were. The second time the killer struck, it was blood lust. Murder was the main attraction. The red roses and other accoutrements were his signature. The killer set the scene *after* the crimes were committed. Rose Bud wasn't after companionship.

Curtis didn't scare easily but he was scared now. A madman was on the loose. And the madman would kill again and again until he was stopped.

He walked around a scene, studying it, over and over, trying to get inside of the head of the sicko, and looking for little clues.

He looked for patterns, and one pattern he found was books. A lot of books. Based on his investigation, all of the victims were voracious readers. And at least a couple of them were amateur writers.

While the local police were interviewing the usual suspects — men convicted of sex crimes in the area — Curtis was looking for someone with a literary bent.

Before he departed the latest crime scene, Curtis scouted the area to be sure that Tom didn't confront him. The last thing he needed was a tape recorder in his face and a request for a comment. Yet, as he successfully avoided Tom, Curtis sensed their paths would cross in the coming days in connection with the case.

# Eleven

*D*on Lotte was a little bit jealous. After all, *she* didn't have to deal with the fallout. She was dead. How convenient.

*She* had been Rose Bud's first kill.

He'd met Patricia at a campaign rally in Lexington two years earlier. He recalled her long blond hair and her tight turtleneck sweaters. He remembered the adoring expression on her face as he spoke to crowds at political rallies.

Those speeches were nothing more than stump speeches filled with the same empty promises and false bravado that he'd used for over a decade to build a political career that had propelled him from the state legislature to the House of Representatives and, now, to the lofty U.S. Senate chamber.

She'd broken off an engagement with some sweetheart to move to Washington to be beside him. In turn, he promised he'd leave his wife, Dominique, soon. They just needed to keep their relationship under wraps for a little longer, he said.

She said it pained her to wait, but he had the antidote. As he told it, there was an outside possibility he'd be selected as a vice presidential running mate. That was enough for her to bide her time: the thought that someday she would be standing beside him on the stage, perhaps at a national convention, waving at adoring crowds, surrounded by the candidates on the ticket.

"What a fool," he muttered aloud. Didn't she suspect he was a philanderer? Hadn't she realized he was just stringing her along? And what was she thinking when she put herself in harm's way, getting herself killed and potentially jeopardizing his career and aspirations to grab the ring?

"Senator!"

He turned. An aide had obviously been calling his name repeatedly. He just hadn't heard it.

"It's your wife."

He groaned.

She was threatening divorce. He contemplated the implications. There would be alimony, accusations, headlines, and headaches. The media would have a field day. He'd lose a share of his daddy's inheritance, which was eminently unfair, since it belonged to him and served a valuable purpose in funding his political career.

He took the phone as the aide departed and closed the door to his office in the Hart Senate Office Building. "What is it, Q?" he asked impatiently.

"An investigator called," she whispered. "Some guy named Carlos Santana." Others had made the same mistake, referring to the P.I. as though he was the famous guitarist. "He wanted to talk to me about that girl who died earlier this year. She was in a writing workshop with me."

That was news to him. "What did you say to him?" he asked.

"I didn't say anything," she answered. "I said I hardly knew her. The fact we were together in a writing workshop and that she worked for you was coincidence."

Of course, it wasn't. Dominique had enrolled in Henry David McLuhan's writing workshop to keep an eye on Patricia. Dominique kept tabs on all of Don's girlfriends. Some might say she stalked them. Patricia Sakkara wasn't the only one that Dominique followed. Trudy Vine was another.

"Did he ask anything about me?"

"I told him you're a very important person and you can't be disturbed because you're up on Capitol Hill working on important legislation to help our nation," she replied, sounding like a dutiful wife.

Silence ensued; tumblers turned inside each of their heads. It was weird that this Santana guy was asking questions now, months after the incident. Why couldn't the police just catch Rose Bud for his current transgressions instead of digging up the past?

"Maybe this isn't the right time for a divorce," he suggested.

"Maybe so," she agreed. Then, "What time will you be coming home tonight?"

"Soon, darling," he replied. "Soon. I promised to stop by a picture gallery on my way home." He hesitated. *Was that tonight?* "On second thought, I'll be home shortly. I think there's only one more floor vote."

She knew otherwise. The chamber had recessed for the remainder of the day. Members of Congress had rushed to pack their bags and depart Capitol Hill for the winter holiday. The important affairs of state could wait.

# Twelve

When Mo returned the next time to visit Roxie in the detention center, he brought a contract setting the retainer and hourly rate for his representation. Despite some reservations, he had decided to take her case, primarily out of curiosity than anything else.

Curtis had cautioned against it with a wry text message: Curiosity killed the Katz.

After he removed his coat and they got situated in their plastic chairs, Mo asked Roxie to walk him through the case. He offered simple instructions: "Start at the beginning."

"There was knock at the door," Roxie said dramatically. "Trudy stood there with a box in her hand.

"I was baking cupcakes. It was during the Capps Cupcake Competition. I wasn't a finalist but I was inspired by the excitement in the community. I asked her if she wanted to come in."

Mo could picture the scene: Roxie wearing an apron over a worn T-shirt and baggy pants. Her short sloppily-cut hair would be uncombed and her hands would be dusted with flour. The tiny house would be filled with a sweet aroma.

"Why did you invite her inside?" he asked. "I thought you hated her."

"I despised her," Roxie agreed. "But she came in. She'd come over to complain about a house in disrepair on the other side of the street. And now that she had crossed my threshold, I felt I could punish her for her past treatment of me."

"Go on," he said, although doubtful of her explanation.

"I invited her to sit down and have some freshly brewed coffee. While she was drinking it and yakking about her complaint, I opened the pantry and surreptitiously scooped some rat poison from a burlap bag. I pretended it was flour, and mixed it in a fresh batch of cupcake batter."

She smiled sinisterly.

"While she sat unsuspectingly a foot away, I poured the batter into the pan and put it in the oven. Then I poured myself some coffee, splashed a tad of bourbon in the cup, sat beside her, and waited."

Katz eyed her skeptically. "You're telling me that you decided to kill her on the spur of the moment? And for no reason other than the fact that you despised her?"

"People destroy one another when the opportunity avails itself," Roxie replied defensively. "It happens all the time. I think we're always filled with spite and envy. You can get shot for winning a swimsuit competition. It doesn't take much. I'm just a victim of the times in which we live."

Mo controlled the urge to roll his eyes and motioned with his hand for her to continue.

"When the timer went off, I put on some baking gloves and removed the pan from the oven. I placed the pan on top of the oven to cool. Trudy commented about how sweet the cupcakes smelled and about how eager she was to eat one."

Roxie chuckled.

"I figured the sweetness was caused by the rat poison. I told her that she could have her fill as soon as the cupcakes cooled a little."

Like a co-conspirator, she leaned closer to Mo and lowered her voice. "She had no idea that I'd lit a fuse to a time bomb and placed it on the stove. I was looking at her and thinking to myself, lady, you are in for a surprise."

Roxie lowered her head. Her dark eyes were riveted on something invisible in the room. She wiped the corners of her lips with her fingers.

"Once the cupcakes cooled, I lathered them with butter. I fed three of them to her, like giving cyanide pills to an unsuspecting victim. I refilled her coffee so she could wash them down and settle in her stomach."

She raised her head and rolled her tongue over a thin lip line. Then the tongue disappeared and she puckered her lips like a serpent. "A few minutes later, I gave her three more, the pig."

She looked like a witch hunched over a caldron, rubbing her coarse hands and relishing the moment.

"Right after she left, I wiped the counters down with paper towels and bagged them with the cupcake pans. Then I raced down to Jones Point, where I threw the bag into a dumpster. I thought I'd left no evidence of any rat poison anywhere in the kitchen."

Mo considered her statement. "You know they always sweep an area after a crime looking for evidence that might have been discarded. That includes trash bins, manhole covers, and mail boxes, assuming there are any on street corners these days."

Roxie nodded despondently. "As it turned out, they found all that stuff and carted it away."

"What about the poison in the pantry?"

"I left it there. Otherwise, I thought it'd look suspicious. A lot of people have rat poison in their house. Rodents are pretty common in some of these old houses. I got a few mouse traps down there too, including a couple of heavy-duty ones."

She snorted. "I once caught a rat in a mousetrap. He dragged that damn trap around on his back and buried himself in some boxes by the furnace. He thrashed about for three days before I felt it was safe to take him outside and throw him in the trash can."

Mo thought about the basement of his Harvard Street house. He rarely went down there. It was dank and dusty. He was pretty sure there were some mice in the wintertime.

Moving on, he asked, "At no time did you confess to any crime?"

"That's right," she nodded.

"What about when you were taken away in the cruiser on the night of your arrest?"

"I didn't say anything, despite what that cop, Joey Cook, says. He made up that confession. All I've done is deny it. There's no admission on my part, except, of course, to you."

She straightened her shoulders, smacked her lips, rubbed her chin, and raised her eyebrows. "There you have it."

Mo rubbed his forehead. "Why did you tell me you committed the crime when we first met?"

He asked that question because her story was thin. *Was she covering up for someone else's crime? Did she have an accomplice? Why had she volunteered her complicity so quickly on the day they first met? What was her motivation? Was she playing a game and, if so, why?*

"I wanted to see your reaction," she said. "I'm a student of faces. You didn't flinch. In fact, you appeared surprised and relieved. I assume most clients aren't as forthcoming.

"A good attorney is useless if you can't share the truth. Right now, you're the only person standing between me and the gallows. If I'm not honest with you, I might as well climb those stairs and greet the hangman."

He laughed. "I do tell clients I can only help them if they share the unvarnished truth with me."

"It's a game," she said insightfully. "Outcomes aren't preordained. You can beat the system by playing by the rules. You just can't break 'em." She didn't say *fatta la legge, trovato l'inganno*, (every law has a loophole) but she might as well have. She was singing to the choir.

As he departed the jail, Mo reflected on their conversation. His instincts told him to remain vigilant. Roxie wasn't to be trusted. She was playing some strange game of three-dimensional chess, ingratiating herself to him for some sinister reason. She was feeding poison-laced cupcakes to him, figuratively speaking.

# Thirteen

When Curtis wasn't working on the Rose Bud serial murder case, he assisted Mo with Roxie's defense. A day after Mo's visit with Roxie, they sat in the law office's conference room comparing notes.

It appeared to be an odd dichotomy. On the one hand, Curtis was tracking down a killer; on the other hand, he was looking for ways to help an accused murderess.

Curtis didn't see any inconsistency, despite the seemingly contradictory roles. He believed Roxie was innocent. Like Mo, he also sensed a connection between Roxie's case and the Rose Bud murders, though the nature of the link eluded him.

During his investigation, Curtis found that Trudy had been a bit of a scoundrel herself. She'd had a habit of accusing people of things they hadn't done and then extorting money in exchange for stopping the false rumors.

For example, in one instance, Trudy falsely claimed her mail had been stolen by a neighbor. As evidence, Trudy posted a doorbell video of the neighbor standing on her stoop with a handful of her mail. Though the neighbor claimed Trudy had asked her to check the mail, the narrative was damning. As a result, the neighbor paid Trudy $1,000 to remove the post and cease spreading the falsehoods.

In another instance, Trudy claimed a motorist had rear-ended her car, causing damage to the vehicle and injury to her spinal cord. She had a photo of the motorist inspecting her car. The motorist argued that Trudy had asked him to look at the car, claiming someone else had struck her parked car. Regardless, Trudy threatened to go to the magistrate and swear out a warrant unless the motorist paid her $2,000, which he reluctantly did to make her go away.

"Trudy Vine gave dozens of people a motive to kill her," Curtis informed Mo. "She was like an artist who painted pictures of people with horns and pitchforks and then blackmailed them to erase the false characterizations. It's easy to imagine one of those people killing her."

"It's worth considering," Mo responded unenthusiastically.

"There's something else," Curtis divulged. "The day that Trudy died was the same day as the Capps Cupcake Competition. Trudy was a contender for the prize."

The Capps Cupcake Competition was a tradition in Old Town, as popular as Thanksgiving Day treks in Del Ray or down the George Washington Parkway. It started following the death of Claudia Capps, who ran the Old Town Cupcake Coliseum until she died at 90. Loyal fans of the confectionary created an annual competition to preserve her memory and ensure that sugary treats wouldn't disappear from the landscape like the Cupcake Coliseum.

While it was intended as a kind-hearted event, the competition became cutthroat. People sabotaged one another's entries. They posted lies online that bakers had paid professionals to prepare their entries. In fact, the competition had nearly been canceled the previous year.

"Because Trudy was a contender for the crown, maybe someone killed her out of spite," Curtis said. "It's happened before in cases involving beauty contests and cheerleading competitions. Someone lets their emotions get way out of control and, before you know it, there's a murder."

"Yeah," Mo replied, "Both are good defense strategies. Either one could divert attention from Roxie and create sufficient doubt in the mind of one or more of the jurors to result in a hung jury.

"Both scenarios provide a motive to kill Trudy, and each one is plausible. Since Trudy was blackmailing people, any one of her victims could have become so enraged as to strike against her to silence her. And you're right about people becoming insanely jealous about simple competitions. The ends to which people aspire know no bounds. Murder is certainly in the mix."

"I'm not saying that any of those people actually did it," Curtis said. "I'm just saying…"

"I know what you're saying," Mo interrupted.

On more than one occasion, Mo had diverted a jury's attention away from his client by turning the spotlight on an alternative theory and, as a result, on other individuals. This approach rarely resulted in an outright acquittal, though it did in some cases. More often, the strategy split the jury, with some members dismissing the tactic while others embraced it.

In the end, it was a self-serving maneuver to create a reasonable doubt in the jury's mind and to prevent the jurors from unanimously agreeing that the prosecution had proven its case beyond a reasonable doubt.

Mo rarely used the ploy to aid an innocent client.

"I just don't know that we need to go down either of those roads in this case," he said. "I'm actually thinking of a slightly different tactic." Mo then transitioned to the other case that consumed Curtis's time and asked, "How's Rose Bud going?"

"Not well enough," he replied. A tempest was brewing inside Curtis's head. "I don't want this to end up like the Colonial Parkway murders," he murmured. He referred to unsolved murders of several couples between 1986 and 1989 near or along the scenic road connecting Jamestown, Williamsburg, and Yorktown. "I don't want this to go unsolved. I don't want additional victims. And I don't want Old Town to be remembered as the place where something like this happened."

"Any leads?" Mo asked.

"I don't know if I'd call it a lead, per se, but there is an interesting development," Curtis admitted. "He's getting sloppy. This last incident was rushed. Maybe something's spooking him. I'm not sure."

"But you have your suspicions," Mo prodded.

"I think someone's figured out his identity," Curtis opined. The law of percentages supported his hypothesis. There were only so many times a person could get away with something before others divined his modus operandi.

"If the killer thinks he's been exposed, he might feel compelled to go after whoever's figured out his identity," Mo observed.

"Are you suggesting what I think you're suggesting?" asked Curtis.

"I'm not suggesting anything, at least not yet," Mo answered. "I do have my doubts about Roxie's guilt, however, which is why I'm indisposed to pursuing either of the two strategies you just outlined.

"I also think there's something sinister behind Trudy's death and Roxie knows what it is. She's not sharing. I may have to play her game to get to the truth."

# Fourteen

*Diary entry from June 4.*

The fog is ridiculous. It's caused by Canadian forest fires sweeping down as far as Virginia. The weather advisory is like Level 5. Unhealthy. I can smell it this morning. My throat is a little sore too.

I'm staying indoors but it's not only because of the weather. I've got a scratch mark on my face.

That bitch, clawing at me like that.

She invited me over to her apartment after work. I asked if I could get there ahead of her and cook dinner. She welcomed the idea and willingly surrendered her key.

I didn't bother making dinner. I knew in advance what was going to happen. I'm clairvoyant, you see.

When she arrived, I caressed her face and lovingly placed the blindfold over her eyes. I have to admit she seemed a little nervous, even though she didn't resist.

As I squeezed my hands around her soft throat, the blindfold fell to her shoulders. I watched as she stared back at me in disbelief, incredulous as to what was happening.

Controlling a person's life is empowering. When they realize you are squeezing the life out of them, their incredulity is replaced by panic, but by that time it's already too late.

My physical strength overpowered her. I pushed her head against the wall, held a gloved palm over her mouth to suppress her cry for help, and squeezed tighter with the other, cutting off the flow of oxygen.

Afterwards, I inspected my handiwork and immediately got to work. I sprinkled the floor with rose petals as though I was Cupid. I instructed Alexa to play romantic music.

*Here's a playlist you might like: Romantic Strings!*

*(No, they can't trace my voice but it does give those stupid police a better idea of when I was here.)*

*I filled the tub with bubble bath. I lit candles on the window sills, the staircase, and the bookshelves (so many bookshelves). Let there be no doubt as to who was here.*

# Fifteen

Mo strolled through Old Town. The season was reflected everywhere. Crews of city workers had hung holiday lights from trees and lampposts throughout Old Town. Houses were decorated with bright lights and glittering candles. Reindeer and Santa Clauses sprawled on the ground in front of homes in the daytime before being inflated to life-size statues at night. Bedecked trees shone through windows with bright ornaments and glitzy tinsel. A nativity scene adorned a front yard, with a bed of real straw.

Any time of the year this was his preferred stomping ground. It was his single point of reference, where he lived, shopped, ate, and worked. He rarely ventured outside of this defined universe and didn't feel the less for it. He was like an octopus in the ocean and reveled in his environs.

It was a little like that old *New Yorker* magazine cover showing a map with NYC being large and in charge and with very little existing west of the Hudson River. Mo's world was like that, the difference being that his center of the universe was located along the western bank of the Potomac River.

His personal and professional routines had been affected by the pandemic, which made the world smaller for a lot of people. In his case, he retreated to the core. He'd opened a law office in the heart of Old Town about a mile from his residence. The courthouse was almost equidistant between home and office.

He rarely drove anymore, which was okay by him, since he didn't want to run the risk of damaging his newly restored vintage VW Karmann Ghia, even though the vehicle was parked outside on the street.

As he walked, with his long herringbone coat dangling down

below his knees and his scarf wrapped firmly around his neck, he *saw* things, things that are never seen from a car as it whisks up and down streets, such as the sign in the tiny front yard located near Roxie Neele's spite house that read:

> *In This House We Believe*
> *Black Lives Matter*
> *Women's Rights Are Human Rights*
> *No Human Is Illegal*
> *Science Is Real*

Although Mo agreed such signs espoused good intentions, he felt they were too blatantly *politically correct* and, to be honest, in some instances hypocritical for professing virtues that the occupants of the houses where the signs were posted didn't practice.

Mo occasionally walked by Roxie's now-unoccupied spite house on Prince Street during his daily sojourns. He'd check it out as he passed, making sure there weren't any broken windows, graffiti on the door, or trash in the front yard.

He felt confident she would return home soon and he wanted the place to be ready to welcome her.

On this particular day as Mo approached Roxie's house, he glanced across the street and noticed a dilapidated property whose loose slate shingles were perilously hanging close to the edge of the roof, presenting a safety hazard. Also, a stack of bricks leaned away from the house forming a concave patch ready to crash to the ground at any time.

Although scaffolding was erected along part of the house, nothing would prevent the unstable shingles and bricks from falling without warning.

Once he reached Roxie's house, he noticed for the first time a sign planted on the edge of her property that read:

> *In This House We Believe*

*Only My Life Matters*
*Privilege Determines Right*
*Humans Are Alien*
*Science Is B.S.*

As he looked at it, Mo considered whether Roxie went out of her way to appear ornery and irascible.

*Was it possible*, he asked himself, *that she deliberately cultivated a negative image to mask something else?* Maybe she was really tender and sweet on the inside but needed to project that outward prickliness to be left alone, like an attractive holly with spines as sharp as needles. Don't tread on me!

Maybe she was even the equivalent of an obscure Rembrandt hidden among a bunch of clutter at a yard sale.

# Sixteen

Neither Curtis nor Sherry cooked. They reheated. In fact, their kitchen didn't include a stove, just a microwave, a toaster oven, and an air fryer.

The stove was discarded when Sherry renovated the place a few years ago. At the same time, she installed two refrigerators to store precooked meals and carry-out. She also added a wine cooler and two dishwashers, one for dirty and the other for clean dishes.

Colorful plates and bowls, rich crystal and exotic glasses, and handcrafted cups and saucers adorned open shelves for show rather than daily use.

Sherry and Curtis ordered out and ate in. It suited Curtis fine, as he'd never been much of a cook, though he loved to eat.

Now, sitting in the stove-free kitchen, he thought about the Capps Cupcake Competition. He was a big fan of the confectionery. In fact, both he and Sherry attended Claudia's funeral to pay their respects to her baking abilities.

Knowing the competition had taken place at the same time as Trudy's murder, Curtis thought again that any one of a number of people could be responsible for adding rat poison to a cupcake.

The Capps Cupcake Competition was a big deal involving local restaurants, public and private schools with courses in home economics, an adult culinary school, as well as hundreds of local pastry makers throughout Northern Virginia.

One of the reasons the contest was so popular was the $100,000 annual prize money provided by an anonymous donor. And all of the excess submissions were distributed to food pantries throughout the area, providing free treats during the holiday season.

Of course, a competition with such a lucrative award was rife with sabotage. Around the time of each year's competition, there was a rash of break-ins at the homes of the previous year's finalists. Jealous contestants destroyed stoves and pans, stole measuring cups, and spoiled cupcake ingredients by dumping sawdust and gravel on them.

Some mischief-makers even filed false reports with the local utility about the smell of gas on certain streets, occasionally resulting in gas being turned off at particular venues, namely those owned and operated by the city's best restaurants and chefs.

Some bakers even found threats posted on their front doors or sent in the mail reading, "Enter the contest and it'll be your last!" Occasionally, the threats were attached to bricks hurled through kitchen windows.

This was another reason why Curtis was happy that neither he nor Sherry cooked. If they did, they might have gotten involved in this madness. As it was, he was content to just eat their desserts.

As they devoured Chinese take-out that evening, Sherry expressed no shock as Curtis recanted the mayhem surrounding the contest in past years. "It's sad but hardly surprising," she said. "It's the way people are."

Throughout her career, others attempted to intimidate her. And police work exposed her to an ugly side of people, one in which jealousy and envy often led to criminal activity.

Her tires were sliced by cops angry about her career ascendency on the force; dog shit had been dumped on her front step by the families of people she arrested; graffiti had been painted on her car and house by felons released from prison; and she regularly received plenty of menacing letters and emails from Old Town residents dissatisfied with the department's performance.

"People can be vicious and spiteful," she added.

Curtis nodded in agreement.

"Out of curiosity, what's Mo say about the competition occurring at the time of the murder?" she asked as they slurped lo mein.

"He said it's created a large pool of potential suspects and further raised a reasonable doubt as to Roxie's guilt," Curtis replied.

"Whether there's one or a hundred suspects, Mo has serious doubts about Roxie's guilt. You know that, don't you?"

"He's told me that he doesn't believe Roxie and Trudy were frenemies," Curtis confirmed. "He believes Roxie's using him for some ulterior motive."

"What ulterior motive?" she asked, stuffing food into her mouth with a pair of chopsticks, which would go right into the trash instead of the dishwasher.

Curtis shook his head and replied, "You know as well as I do how Mo works. He shares pieces of evidence with everyone but doesn't show the whole cloth to anyone. He looks at things from strange angles and weird perspectives and he finds patterns that elude others. We've seen it before. This is no different.

"If I had to hazard a guess, he's looking beyond Trudy's poisoning, maybe as far as the Rose Bud murders."

# Seventeen

Roxie rested uncomfortably on a lumpy mattress in her tiny spite-house-sized cell. Her head rested on a pillow as thin as a piece of toilet paper as she stared up at the bunk above her. She felt bad for good reason.

She'd misled Katz big time. He had swallowed her story hook, line, and sinker. She didn't expect him to be so gullible.

Worse, he believed *in* her. She knew that he was going to throw himself into this case, heart and soul. In the end, he would probably believe she had betrayed his trust.

Roxie was reminded of a bit of philosophy embedded in a Doris Day song, "Que Sera, Sera." She'd heard the tune last night in a classic she watched on television, Alfred Hitchcock's *The Man Who Knew Too Much*.

In her opinion, Mo was the man who knew too little.

*Too bad. That's life. Hopefully, it'll all turn out all right. What will be, will be.*

She'd never forgiven him for prosecuting her. Granted, it was years ago. But memories died hard. Mo never cared about the truth, she felt. He just wanted to win. *Game on.*

Damn if he didn't pull victory out of the jaws of defeat, a fourth quarter rally in a game that seemed mathematically impossible to win. But that's why they played the game. *Any given Sunday, right?*

That was the reason she selected him for this assignment. She knew he'd figure out who was really responsible for Trudy's murder. When he did that, Rose Bud's identity would also be revealed.

Even if Mo ended up hating her forever, it was worth it. She was acting for the greater good.

She closed her eyes and hoped for the best, at home in her

75-square-foot hovel, 7.5-foot-wide and 10-foot-long spite cell.

She was roused from her daydream by Robyn White, one of two "friends" she'd made in jail. Samantha Ring was the other. Robyn was in the slammer for dealing drugs, although it was a setup by a snitch who got a sweetheart deal for ratting on her. Sam's conviction was for arson. She burned down her ex-boyfriend's apartment as punishment for stalking her.

Neither of the girls were bad, just unlucky, Roxie felt. She swore that she was going to become their sponsor when this thing was over.

"How'd you snag him?" asked Robyn, who wandered into Roxie's cell, which was open.

Mo Katz was a huge deal in the big house. His reputation preceded him. He was either responsible for putting some of the girls in jail back in the day or for saving them in more recent bouts with the law by securing reduced sentences for lesser crimes.

He'd walked both sides of the street; it all depended on whether they encountered him as a prosecutor or a defense attorney. Either way, the result had a lasting impact on their lives.

"My power of persuasion," Roxie answered cautiously. She was careful what she said since jailhouse snitches have been known to testify against other cellmates, even the ones they called their BFFs.

"Mo's good people," said Robyn.

When Katz was a defense attorney years ago — between his stints as a city prosecutor and U.S. attorney — he represented Robyn on a possession charge. He got the case dismissed on a technicality but demanded that she get treatment for her habit. She did. This current charge for dealing was really nothing more than a setup.

"If anyone can bust you out of here, it's Mo Katz," said Robyn. "He's more powerful than a keg of dynamite. Have you seen that man in action?"

"No," Roxie lied.

"Well, girlfriend, you're in for a treat. How he operates in the courtroom is a marvel. The man's a magician."

"Total sweetheart," said Sam, joining the conversation. "Mo prosecuted my ex-boyfriend for beating me up. Thanks to Mo, the piece of crap was put behind bars for 30 days and ordered to stay away from me for a year." Unfortunately, that was then. This time around, she had to take matters into her own hands, which amounted to a book of matches and gasoline poured on a rug in his hallway.

"You both speak fondly of him, but here you are, sitting in this hole with me," Roxie said, sliding out of her bunk.

"If he'd represented me, I guarantee I wouldn't be here," Sam said. "My ex would be back in jail for slugging me instead of me in jail for burning his trashy little digs.

Robyn chimed in with a similar refrain. "If he represented me, that snitch would be doing time instead of me."

"We all know how the system works," Sam said. "A good defense attorney can always find a way to beat the law. You just got to look hard to find it. *Fatta la legge, trovato l'inganno.* That's Mo's saying. For every law, there's a way around it."

Roxie yawned and stretched her arms above her head. She was not counting on Mo Katz only for an acquittal of the charges against her. She expected that miracle worker to save the next girl from getting mauled by a madman stalking the streets of Old Town.

"*D*id you do it?" Robyn asked.

"Of course not," Roxie said. "Trudy Vine was my friend. I'd never poison her."

"Do you have an alibi?" Robyn queried.

"I don't," Roxie admitted. "Trudy had rat poison and cupcakes in her system when she died. I fed her cupcakes and I keep rat poison in my pantry. It sort of adds up."

"Not enough to convict you of a crime, it don't, let alone murder," Sam chimed in. "I'm actually surprised they even charged you on such flimsy evidence. Someone must have it in for you."

"They all hate me," Roxie said. "They'd like nothing more than to see me thrown out of my house and carted off to the penitentiary for the rest of my days."

"Well, I wouldn't worry if I was you," Robyn said. "Mo'll punch more holes into that case than a piece of Swiss cheese. You'll be back home in no time at all."

Roxie studied her two compatriots. She needed to confide in someone and wondered if they were trustworthy. Who knew? She might even need to enlist their help if the unexpected occurred.

*M*eanwhile, Mo checked with Virginia State Bar counsel about representing Roxie, despite the fact that she said she'd checked on her own.

As he surmised, there was no conflict of interest that prohibited him from representing Roxie even though he had previously prosecuted her for a crime. There was no nexus between the two offenses; no quid pro quo had been extracted; and a significant period of time had passed.

To be on the safe side, he notified the trial court and the Commonwealth Attorney's Office about the matter.

No one expressed any concern over the fact that he had previously prosecuted Roxie for assault and battery. In fact, no one even requested any of the details about the case, such as the name of the victim who'd leveled the assault charge against her.

*S*herry called while Mo worked on the case. "Do you handle sexual harassment complaints?" she asked. "I ask because I just got hit with one. It's total bullshit. I mean, I'm the one who's harassed by every man in the department, and even some of the women.

"But it wasn't unexpected. I've been bracing for something ever since we hired Curtis to help with the Rose Bud case. You even warned me. I just didn't see something like sexual harassment.

"It just goes to show they're always out there gunning for you. You can never be too careful, you know."

"I *do* know," Mo replied. "I just finished telling the world that I prosecuted Roxie years ago and that there's no conflict representing her now for a totally unrelated crime."

"Smart," she said. "Except I never knew you prosecuted her."

"Assault and battery," he explained. "I was a young assistant prosecutor for the city. She beat up some woman. A witness lied in the case, claimed Roxie didn't do it, but the judge didn't buy it, even though Jimmy Wolfe had him in his pocket."

"Say *what?*"

"It's neither here nor there. Tell me about your claim. Who accused you of sexual harassment? And, yes, I'll handle it for you. It's not my usual line of work, but I'm not going to leave you in the lurch."

"Thanks," Sherry replied. "And it was Joey Cook."

"That's unbelievable," Mo said.

"Not really," she replied. "He may be an asshole but he's one of the good ol' boys."

The good ol' boys network remembered Sherry as a punk-ass cop who used drugs her rookie year. She would have been tossed from the department if it wasn't for Mo, who represented her during a prior stint as a defense attorney.

Due to his effort, drug charges against her were dismissed, her suspension from the department was terminated, and she was awarded a settlement — all of which galled the old guard to no end.

Since 2019, their criticism had been muted, partly because she was tight with Mo. So long as he was U.S. attorney, members of his clique were a protected class, and she was a member in high standing.

Now, however, Mo lived on the dark side — which was what the ol' boys network called the place where attorneys represented criminal scumbags — and it was time for them to make their move.

The good ol' boys had bided their time and now the message went out, "Take her down."

A whisper campaign got into full swing. She was a lesbian, some said. Santana was her bitch, others scoffed. She didn't have kids and she was not married, they observed. Something wasn't right.

The people spreading the lies, of course, were the ones with *issues*. They were in dead-end marriages; their kids were messed up; and their careers were going nowhere. It was just easier to try to pull her down than to look in a mirror and lift themselves up.

Sherry discarded the rumors. She wasn't one to retaliate either. It was not her nature; she ran her race against herself without regard for who else was on the track or who was putting up hurdles in front of her.

Unfortunately, the rumors didn't seem to hurt her. If anything, her reputation was enhanced.

So, drastic times called for drastic measures.

"Assuming Joey's complaint is B.S., which it is, how did it get through the review process?" Mo asked. "Isn't there a procedure in the department to investigate complaints? Isn't the first step to determine if the claim has merit? Shouldn't there have been mediation or something like that, assuming the claim is legitimate? Why level a formal complaint and make it public so fast?"

"I've been asking myself the same questions," Sherry replied. "It's strange, particularly since Dianna Lox is the ombudsperson for the department handling these issues. There's an entire protocol that she disregarded."

"It sounds as though maybe someone got her to pursue Joey's charge," Mo speculated.

"But who has enough power over an individual to get them to put aside their professional responsibilities and try to hurt me?"

Before Mo could answer, another thought crossed his mind. "Say, wasn't Dianna Lox head of internal affairs at the department? Didn't she get involved in something with Sheriff Malcolm?"

"She got booted downstairs, I remember that much," Sherry said. "It was all very hush-hush. As I recall, there was a short investigation by Richmond. Records were sealed. I never paid that much attention to it."

"Well don't worry about it," Mo said. "Once we get a date for the hearing, we'll look into her background. In the meantime, just do your job. Don't get vindictive toward anyone. That's probably what they want in order to make a real charge stick.

"Plus, maybe something will happen to persuade Joey to change his mind. You never know. But if not, I'll handle the matter for you. If we're lucky, we'll win you another settlement."

The conversation ended, and he got back to work on Roxie's case. It was dark when he prepared to leave his office on Wales Alley.

# Eighteen

"Mister Ka-atz! Mister Ka-atz!"

Dickie Lewis sputtered Mo's name while running toward him. A homeless man of indeterminable age, Dickie roamed Old Town with a battered suitcase. It was impossible to know how Dickie managed to stay clothed and fed, yet he was always freshly scrubbed and cleanly dressed.

To an untrained eye, Dickie appeared to be an out-of-town visitor who'd alighted from the King Street Metro via Reagan National Airport and was headed to his hotel. In truth, all his earthly belongings filled that suitcase as he wandered the streets and alleys day and night.

In the morning, he could be found sitting at a restaurant's sidewalk table sipping a cup of coffee. In the evening, he would find an unoccupied bench along the waterfront and unroll the blanket bundled on top of the suitcase.

No one knew who Dickie's parents were, other than a couple of people who abandoned him at some stage in his life, probably when it became apparent that he wasn't developing like the other kids and was going to be a drag on someone's life for the remainder of his existence.

Mo was departing his office when Dickie accosted him. Dickie pretended their running into one another was coincidental when in fact he'd been standing outside for hours waiting for this moment to intercept Mo.

Dickie was attired in a fashionable array of warm clothes he'd selected from various bins of discarded clothes left in alleyways for the homeless.

"What is it, Dickie?" Mo asked.

Mo knew Dickie, as did most of the locals. He had been a fixture of the community as long as Mo could remember. Mo and Abby even brought Dickie food on occasion, particularly when he'd camped in the small triangular park near their townhouse.

"Where's Rock Anna, Mister Katz?" asked Dickie, a look of deep concern on his face. "Have you seen her? How's she doing?"

The media had already spread the news that the former U.S. attorney had taken Roxie Neele's case. It'd been a topic of debate in every quarter of the city among members of the legal bar and inmates at the local jail, and everyone in between. *Why was Mo risking his reputation for a woman like Roxie?* He'd be wise to find a reason to beg off her case, so they said.

Any expression of interest was tinged by the reality that some people would love to see Mo tumble off his high horse. A large number of local attorneys envied him. After all, he'd moved seamlessly between the public and private sectors, garnering impressive wins as a prosecutor and a defense attorney without sullying his reputation.

Some hoped the worst for Mo. *Wouldn't it be special if the venerable Mo Katz got wrapped up in controversy surrounding his representation of Roxie Neele?*

"She's fine," Mo replied. "Why do you ask?"

"No reason, not really, just wondering," Dickie answered guardedly. "I just haven't seen her lately. She's always been nice to me, that's all. Even though she's got a reputation for being mean, I've never once seen anything but a smile on her face."

"I haven't seen you around much," Mo commented. "Are you okay? You haven't done something that you're not supposed to do, have you, Dickie?"

"No, sir," Dickie replied firmly. "I've been sleeping outside of Rock Anna's house sometimes, watching over the place, picking up trash and other things that people leave in her front yard. I also go to the Friendship Firehouse. I like it there. The fire trucks are cool."

He grinned innocently. "How's Miss Abby doing? And little

Katie?"

"Abby and Katie are in Wisconsin with Abby's other daughter, Shayne," Mo replied. He looked at Dickie, who looked a little tired and hungry. "Say, why don't you join me for dinner?"

After they arrived at the Harvard Street home, Dickie parked himself in a chair on the porch, with his suitcase beside him. Mo encouraged him to come in from the cold, to no avail.

Mo went inside and checked the refrigerator. There wasn't much of a selection, only the basics, including bread, cheese, and butter. *Good enough*, Mo thought, turning on the gas burner over the grill. He searched a cupboard and found a can of tomato soup. In a few minutes, a meal of hot soup and grilled cheese sandwiches would be ready.

While he was making dinner, Mo checked his text messages. One read:

> "I know it's been awhile. You may remember the encounter we had a few years ago. An issue's come up and I need to speak with you. I'll be in touch. R.L."

Encounter wasn't the word Katz would have used. Katz wondered what bad karma had brought Ryan Long, a long-time legal foe, back into his life.

The text was followed within minutes by voices echoing outside.

Mo carried a tray of grilled cheese sandwiches cut diagonally and two bowls of tomato soup outside only to find Ryan standing on the porch with Dickie.

"I wasn't expecting another dinner guest," Mo said, smoothly suppressing his displeasure. He put down the tray on a side table. "Dickie, help yourself," he urged. Then, to the uninvited guest, he said flatly, "Let me go inside and pour another bowl of soup."

"Very neighborly of you," Ryan said, with a sly smile. He was dressed in a pinstripe suit with a silk scarf wrapped around his neck.

A black onyx ring with a diamond set in the center encircled the middle finger of his right hand, which was holding on to the strap of a backpack.

Their quaint exchange couldn't completely disguise the enmity that each felt for the other. Ryan was a headhunter who wanted to add a notch to his imaginary six shooter by taking down people in positions of prominence. He'd had Mo in his sights before.

Mo stood staring coldly at Ryan and Dickie sensed the tension between them. He quickly got up and grabbed a wedge of sandwich, dipped it into a bowl, and plunged the corner of bread dripping with thick red soup into his mouth. Then he moved to the corner of the porch with his sandwich and soup bowl as though stepping outside the ropes of a boxing ring.

Mo noticed a copy of *The Rhythmic Cycle of Life* by Henry David McLuhan sticking out of Ryan's backpack.

Motioning to the book, Mo said, "I'm looking into that case at Roaches Run. A law enforcement officer died. Nobody really investigated it as a possible murder. I think something fishy might have happened with that case."

He was referring to the van that exploded at the waterfowl sanctuary along the George Washington Parkway near Reagan Airport in 2021. The death was deemed a suicide and the case closed.

"You drove to Dulles Airport after the explosion occurred," Ryan said, referring to the Roaches Run case. "It was the same night that Henry David McLuhan boarded a flight for Paris."

Neither of them moved despite being too close for comfort.

Ryan continued, "You accused him of complicity in the death at Roaches Run. Then you let him board the plane. The next thing you did was visit Sherry Stone.

"I think you and Stone entered into a conspiracy of silence as to McLuhan's complicity in the death that occurred at Roaches Run.

Writing it off as a suicide was an easy way to end any speculation about something far more sinister."

Mo stepped back and took full measure of Ryan. Mo's face betrayed no emotion. Yet, from his corner perch, Dickie felt that Ryan had struck a nerve.

"I also think Stone ran a similar calculation last year in connection with the disappearance of a suspect in the Hazel Falls case," Ryan said. "I think the suspect's actually dead and I think she knows what happened to him."

Mo grinned. "I think you've been streaming too many murder mysteries on PBS," he said. "You're losing your grip on reality."

"I don't think so." Ryan shook his head, dismissing Mo's banter. "Both of you were sworn law enforcement officers at the time. You were U.S. attorney and she was deputy police chief for the city. I think you were both involved in a gross miscarriage of justice or two."

"I'd be careful about leveling accusations like that," Mo warned.

"Or what? Are you going to report me? I doubt it. The last thing you want is for anyone to reopen either of those cases. You like the way they ended. They fit your idea of justice. The only problem is that your idea of justice leaves loose ends."

"Watch what you say," Mo said.

Ryan continued, "From what I hear, you're back at it, representing some despicable woman who murdered her neighbor. Oh, excuse me. I mean some despicable woman *accused* of murdering her neighbor. At least it's a benign weapon this time, a cupcake, and not a bomb in a van or a boring device cutting trenches deep underground."

"Don't you talk about Mr. Katz and Rock Anna that way," piped up Dickie from the corner of the porch.

Ryan ignored him. "Still, it amounts to the same thing, which is allowing the guilty to go free because it suits your perverted sense of justice."

"What are you after, Long?" Mo asked coldly.

Ryan let loose his sly smile. "I'm assigned to a special unit with the AG in Richmond looking into a number of cases. I'm adding those two to my portfolio. I intend to break you, Katz. When I'm finished, no one is ever again going to broach your name in a respectful manner."

Ryan despised the fact that Mo was loved and respected by cops and criminals alike. He wished he'd received half those accolades. Looking at his prey, Ryan saw that his jabs connected, despite Mo's best effort not to appear nonplussed. *As Mike Tyson said, everyone has a plan until they get punched in the face.*

"Sorry I can't stay for dinner," Ryan said. He hesitated, then added, "I could, of course, be persuaded to cease my investigation in exchange for an amicable arrangement between the two of us."

Mo said nothing.

Ryan continued. "I don't dig any further. In exchange, you are *on call*, so to speak, to provide me with privileged information when the need might arrive. It might involve one of your clients or concern a certain court case. Or I might need you to run interference for me on one thing or another."

He got nothing but a glare from Mo in response.

Ryan turned and retreated down the walk until he reached the sidewalk along Harvard Street. He stopped and glanced back at Mo.

Mo's eyes turned fiery red, or at least they appeared so to Dickie.

"Get away from my house and stay away," Mo said sternly.

Ryan shrugged and slunk away into the dark night.

"The-the nerve," Dickie stuttered as Ryan disappeared in the shadows. The two then sat down on the porch and ate in silence. When they finished, Dickie thanked Mo for the meal and vanished with his suitcase.

# Nineteen

The next day, the unexpected occurred, a carjacking in broad daylight. The driver crashed the car on Slaters Lane and then raced down the street toward the river, taking refuge by the Transamerica sculpture. Reportedly, he was armed.

Joey Cook responded as the first officer on the scene. He wasn't a patrol officer any longer, having been relegated to inventory evidence in the property room years ago for running a scam to fix bogus traffic tickets, so he didn't have any business being there. Yet, as he explained later, he was close to the scene when the dispatch went out and did what any officer would do under the same circumstances.

Sherry Stone was similarly nearby and raced over. She and Joey took up a position behind a dumpster. The carjacker fired in their direction when she hollered for him to surrender.

"We should rush him," Joey said excitedly. "I can sneak up behind him."

"No," she replied wisely. "We should wait for backup and proceed cautiously. Nobody's in danger." Cool heads should prevail.

As Sherry radioed for more assistance, Joey dismissed her advice and ran out from their cover. A barrage of bullets greeted him, sweeping him off his feet and tearing holes in his uniform. Fortunately, the bulletproof vest he wore stopped a bullet from hitting any vital organs.

Nonetheless, he collapsed from the impact, and his body lay splayed on the ground. The next shot might strike his head and blow it up like a watermelon.

Sherry rushed toward his motionless body, pointing her firearm with her outstretched hands and firing as she advanced. The carjacker popped up behind the sculpture and returned fire.

A black-and-white screeched to the scene. Then a second. And a third. Uniforms flooded the street and began firing on the carjacker.

Sherry dropped to one knee and checked on Joey's condition. Meanwhile, the uniforms rushed toward the carjacker, who lay on the ground wounded in the exchange of fire with Stone.

Joey opened his eyes in disbelief. "You?" he groaned. "For me?"

"You'd have done the same for me," she responded.

But in fact, he would never have stepped into the breach to save her. In fact, his actions in this instance were reprehensible. Not only did he put a fellow officer in harm's way, but he compelled her to use deadly force in a situation where such action was preventable.

"Yeah," he mumbled, "I would have."

An ambulance arrived to transport Joey to the hospital for observation. As he was carted off, he whispered, "I owe you."

*U*pon hearing of the carjacking, Mo immediately called Sherry.

"That took guts," Mo said when she answered the phone. It wasn't the first time she'd demonstrated extraordinary valor. "Especially considering the person for whom you risked your life."

"It wasn't totally for naught," she replied. "It resulted in a reversal of fortune. He's dropped his complaint. Apparently it's the first thing he did when he got to the hospital. I won't be needing you after all, or at least not for helping me out of this jam."

"That's wonderful news," Mo said. He knew the complaint had preyed on her, and the withdrawal was like a weight lifting from her shoulders. "It's the least he could do. After all, you saved his life."

"He's still an idiot, despite the fact that he dropped the complaint."

"I don't know why he even responded to the call. He was way out of his league."

"I have a theory," she said. "The circumstances were similar to those surrounding Roxie's arrest. Joey didn't have any business getting involved in that case either. He was way too quick to the scene. And he seemed overzealous about proving himself a hero."

"Points well taken," Mo reflected. "I had a similar thought myself."

Sherry never mentioned that she hadn't been wearing a vest when she rescued Joey.

# Twenty

*O*ne time zone away, in Wisconsin, a woman spoke to a door.

"You need to get away from her," Martha said. "Abby Snowe may be your birth mother but she isn't your friend. She didn't love you the way I do. You need to get away and stay away."

A moment earlier, Shayne had run to the bathroom and locked the door. She had to get separation from this woman who professed love for her.

This woman was her mom, not her real mom, but the mom who'd raised her, the woman who had the most entitlement to be called mom, except for the fact that this woman wasn't her actual birth mother.

Part of her wanted to cry. Another part wanted to smash the mirror. She bowed her head over the sink.

That's when she spotted it.

*It* was some kind of an insect, tiny, green, with wings like cellophane, maybe a quarter of an inch long, about the size of a large speck of lint, alive, with a body and legs, eyes, and those translucent wings.

She grabbed a piece of toilet paper to lift the insect out of the sink.

To Shayne's surprise, the little insect flew up in a series of loops, like a miniature circus plane, landed in her palm, and crawled along the edge of her finger. Given the size of the creature and the size of her finger, Shayne figured it would take about a minute to reach the tip.

She unlocked the door and opened it, and moved past the woman who professed unconditional love for her. The woman stepped aside for Shayne and the little bug that continued crawling along her finger.

Shayne opened the back door, then the storm door and, leaning forward, raised her finger, blew on it, and the insect fluttered away into the black night.

"What in God's green acre are you doing?" Martha asked with exasperation.

Shayne stepped into the night, headed in the same direction as the insect.

*M*o put in a call to Roscoe Page, the information technology guru hunkered down in Tysons Corner running an IT empire.

Page combined his private sector work with special projects for clandestine national and international intelligence agencies. Ever since the Daingerfield Island caper in 2017, he'd slipped in and out of projects undertaken by Mo and his entourage.

"I need a special favor," Mo said when Roscoe answered, which was code for something outside the normal boundaries of law enforcement.

"Name it."

"I need to search a database operated by the state inspector general's office."

The ensuing silence was characteristically brief. Roscoe knew the request would never have been made if it wasn't vitally important, particularly since the requested hack was illegal. "And what are we looking for?" he asked.

"Not what, but who," Mo replied. "I'm looking for reports that were prepared by a particular person of interest."

"You mean reports buried in the bowels of the system that are difficult to locate and impossible to open?" Roscoe asked. "Reports that were buried deliberately to avoid detection and that might be used for nefarious reasons, such as to bribe the parties who are the subject of those reports?"

"That's precisely what I'm looking for," Mo admitted.

"I have an idea what you might be up to," Roscoe said, "and I'm only too happy to oblige. Who is the person of interest?"

"Ryan Long."

Roscoe wasn't surprised by the name Mo gave him. He'd heard some rumors about strange goings on and concluded the inquiry was tied to those rumors. "The man with the black onyx ring," he said, referring to the piece of jewelry that everyone seemed to have noticed.

"None other than," Mo replied.

"You realize you're playing with fire," Roscoe warned his friend. "Both you and Sherry are on his radar. I hope you're looking out for something more than your own self-interests."

# Twenty-One

Someone had planted a new sign in Roxie's front yard that read:

*A Spiteful Person*
*Lived in This House*
*Now She's in Jail*
*Because She's a Louse.*

No one took credit for it but everyone got a kick out of it, particularly those with signs on their own lawns about kindness and goodwill to all.

Dickie stared at the sign. He wanted to tear it down but was afraid he'd be charged with destruction of property. That's the last thing he needed, he reckoned. He was already trespassing, technically speaking, because he was standing in Roxie's front yard.

She was not really a bad person, he said to himself, just a little off her rocker. *But wasn't everyone?*

He felt he knew Roxie better than others and that the truth about her ran contrary to the myth. Her fortune in real estate wasn't the consequence of dumb luck. She was the best educated and hardest working woman he'd ever met in his life. And she gave liberally to local charities and foundations.

As he turned away from her house, something caught Dickie's attention. The door of the unoccupied house undergoing renovation across the street was ajar. He headed in its direction. Scaffolding had been set up along one side of the house. He walked up the porch steps to the door. Maybe he could use the toilet while he was here. He had to go and didn't want to take any chances in the bushes outside Roxie's house. With his luck, he'd be charged with urinating in public *and* destruction of property.

Sometimes he felt as though an upside-down horseshoe hovered over him.

As he stood on the porch with his suitcase, a bunch of slate tiles slid off the roof. The movement caused part of the unsteady pile of bricks to topple over as well. The slate and brick avalanche fell perilously close to where Dickie had been standing before he ascended the steps.

Looking at the sharp shards of slate and the heavy red bricks, he quickly ducked inside to find a bathroom. Maybe he could even take a shower.

*L*ate that night, Dickie sat on his rump in the alleyway, his back against the brick side of Friendship Firehouse and his suitcase leaning against him. He was freshly scrubbed and smelled like a rose. After his shower in the abandoned house, he'd found a fresh set of warm winter clothes in one of the bedroom drawers. They were big but he figured he'd grow into them.

Suddenly, without really knowing how, Dickie found himself inside the old fire station.

Friendship Firehouse had been a real firehouse a hundred years ago, before Old Town became Old Town. It was the city's first fire station, one of the first in the Commonwealth of Virginia if not the United States of America. Now Friendship Firehouse was a museum, with old fire trucks on display, including one built like a carriage with huge wooden red wheels and thick spokes and gold trimming, pretty enough to carry Cinderella to the ball.

Dickie moved from one fire truck to another, climbing rungs of ladders, pulling fire hoses, spinning wheels, and finding old firefighters' hats and placing them on his head, one atop another.

*A*t nine the next morning, the police responded to complaints about noise at Friendship Firehouse. They found Dickie inside and promptly placed him under arrest.

He said he'd innocently fallen through a wall but there was no evidence of that. However, a window had been pried open and it appeared to be the more likely point of entry.

He was charged with breaking and entering and taken to the jail. He was not unhappy about it; maybe he'd see Rock Anna.

As word spread of Dickie's arrest, speculation grew that he might be Rose Bud. It was fueled by people who disliked Dickie. He was a nuisance, they said behind his back. Forget about political correctness, which was only expressed in the public arena where words like "mentally challenged" were used. In the privacy of homes and online chats, Dickie was demeaned and referred to in words that were definitely not politically correct.

# Twenty-Two

*Diary entry from July 23.*

*I*'ve identified a rising star in my writing group. She was in our spring seminar and she's back this fall. It's taken time for others to recognize her talent, but I took note of it right away. I have an eye for talent; I see it every time I look in a mirror.

This girl can write. She shared with me a couple of her diary entries online. That was bold, since I don't show myself on the screen or participate in class. I'm not sure what drew her attention to me, though I suspect it has something to do with one gifted person sensing the presence of a kindred spirit.

Our writing instructor assigns us a single word and then gives us 10 minutes to write down our thoughts about that word. He's a strange guy and, to be honest, he's not a particularly good writer. His claim to fame is "The Rhythmic Cycle of Life." I checked it out. I got about 10 pages into it and stopped. I don't advise anyone to bother reading it. It's rubbish.

Yet his teaching technique is intriguing. It causes self-reflection. If you give me a word and ask me to write a paragraph about it, I'm going to write things that are in my wheelhouse. That reveals things about me. And it gives me new ideas.

One idea I'm toying with is writing a manifesto. I'll provide my thoughts about how to improve life. I'll get it published so that others can gain knowledge from my insights.

Anyway, back to the girl.

I invited her out for a drink. She turned me down. She said that something happened to her and she doesn't like going out. She didn't want to talk about it.

I went online and did a Google search. It turns out she was arrested *for DWI a few months ago. The case got dismissed on some technicality. Small wonder. Her dad hired Mo Katz to represent her.*

*I can't stand Katz. He is a menace. He has his own system of justice. At times, he lets the guilty go free. The same is true of Sherry Stone. I'm going to break both of them. Katz first.*

# Twenty-Three

Mo's phone rang. The area code was 608. He guessed it was Madison, Wisconsin, and answered it right away.

The first words out of Abby's mouth — even before "hello" or "how are you?" — were "they hate me."

She was sitting in a rocking chair on a porch outside a country store that had an attached cafe. Inside, Shayne and Katie were finishing dinner with Shayne's adoptive parents, Martha and Gus Knudsen.

Abby kept an eye on them through the window, fearful they'd hear her conversation and rip the phone out of her hand. The moment she left the table, Shayne's other mother — the pretend mother, as Abby silently referred to her — started fawning over Katie. Abby instinctively knew the plan: Pretend mother was going to win over young, impressionable Katie to score points with Shayne.

"It's so sad," she continued. "I really wanted to find common ground. But they treat me like the enemy."

Right now, 1,000 miles of separation felt pretty good to Mo. He didn't want to get in the middle of things. He'd have to side with Abby and he wasn't sure she'd be right on all accounts.

"What exactly are they doing?" Mo asked.

"It's all petty stuff. But over time it accumulates like flotsam."

"Give me an example," he said, envisioning debris piling up in some far corner of a faraway sea.

"It's hard to pinpoint. She's controlling and possessive, but in a discreet and Machiavellian way. She pretends to care, but it's all about getting her own way."

Ironically, while Abby was a sensitive and caring person, Mo knew she was also a bit of a control freak herself.

As a probation officer, she went the extra mile to help clients who teetered on the edge of life's precipice. She was their advocate and their angel, helping them comply with court-ordered counseling in order to assimilate into mainstream society. But her care and feeding of the dispossessed and alienated came with a price tag: You followed her rules or she cut your lifeline and returned you to jail.

To Mo, it was beginning to sound like a typical court case where no one was right and the truth lay somewhere in the middle.

"Everything I do is wrong," Abby complained. "She's questioned my intentions in coming to Wisconsin. She blames me for stealing her daughter. She thinks that I should have rejected Shayne and refused to build a relationship with her.

"I can't believe it, Mo. Shayne's my daughter. This woman has no right to tell me that I shouldn't have a relationship with my own kid. It's hurtful.

"She's jealous that Shayne feels closer to me than to her. And she's trying to hurt me because of it."

Katz had his own complicated relationship with his parents. Families were like that. He wasn't anxious to become involved in Abby's feud.

Mo sat in the kitchen. It was dark and cold, and lonely. No lights were on, except for the digital clocks on the appliances, which provided their own eerie glow to the room. Normally, this was the nerve center of the house, with Abby making a dish, Katie running around, and Shayne popping in and out unexpectedly. Now it felt like a room on life support.

"It's probably hard for her too," Mo said.

"Whose side are you on?" Abby asked, annoyed.

He meant Shayne in his comment but she obviously thought he was siding with the pretend mother. That in itself told him something.

"I'm always going to be on your side, but look at it from the other side," he said. "She raised Shayne. She's known her for 20 years. She's invested. Now, suddenly, someone else is stealing all of the affection. She's probably hurt.

"And, worse, she knows that she can't compete with you. You're the biological mother. In the end, no matter how much resistance she puts up, you win."

"I can't believe you're saying that," Abby replied. "I don't treat her with any disrespect."

Silence inhabited both ends of the conversation.

Then Abby resumed, "She's jealous of me because she can't have children of her own. All of her kids are adopted. She's envious that I had the courage to have my baby when I was a teenager. She'd give anything to be able to assume my role."

"Maybe the two of you need to hit the reset button," he advised.

He got up and walked to the back of the house where he grabbed his coat and scarf, opened the patio door, and slipped outside.

Abby was talking nonstop.

He slid into one of the white wicker chairs on the patio, placed the phone on the patio table, turned on the speaker, and stared up at the stars. When she finished with her tirade, he changed the subject by saying, "I miss you and the kids."

"I can't wait to get back," she confessed. Then, almost as an afterthought, she added, "How's work?"

"I took Roxie Neele's case."

"You did *what?*"

"The evidence isn't very substantial," he continued. "In fact, it's hardly grounds to hold her. They charged her more out of malice and spite than hard evidence. I'm looking forward to trying the case in a courtroom. It'll be fun to be on the other side for a change."

"Is she guilty?" Abby inquired. His idea of a good time, she knew, was matching wits against friends and beating them at their own game.

He didn't answer.

"That means either that she's guilty or something's fishy about the case and you can't pass it up," she said.

"You know I can't talk about the case," he said.

"Well, I hope you lose the case if she's guilty. Successfully defending a murderer is akin to cheating the grim reaper."

"Criminal defendants never walk away unscathed," Mo replied. "Even if they prevail in a courtroom, consequences catch up with them."

"If you say so," Abby replied sarcastically. "You know I don't share your view about karma and all that stuff."

Mo's basic philosophy was that you got as good as you gave. If you lived your life treating people honestly and fairly, then everything worked out for you, he felt.

If you didn't, there was no hope.

Abby's perspective was different. She'd seen too many bad things happen to good people. Fate seemed random and not related to how you conducted your own life, as she saw it.

"Well, listen," she said, "I have to go. The others are coming. Love you."

"Love you, too."

He went back inside, put down the phone, shed the coat and scarf, grabbed his tablet, and returned to a chair to read news headlines, sports scores, and stock closings.

While he was reading, an insect landed on the iPad and paddled across the lit screen. He took his eyes off the words he was reading and studied the bug. "Where did you come from?" he inquired. It was hardly larger than a capital O. He blew a burst of air across the screen. The bug didn't move, seemingly impervious to gale-force winds.

Mo had a mind to squash it but instead allowed the tiny creature to move freely about the screen like an ice skater gliding across a rink.

Strangely, he thought about Shayne.

The phone rang again. He reached over and grabbed it, somehow expecting it to be Shayne.

"Mr. Katz, it's Mallorca Cannon. I hope you don't mind my calling."

He remembered Mallorca, who he'd represented in a DWI when he first returned to private practice. She was the daughter of a fellow attorney. He hadn't charged any fee and had managed to get the case dismissed on a jurisdictional technicality.

"Of course not. What's up?"

"I'm not in trouble or anything like that, if that's what you're thinking," she said. "It's just that I think I'm being stalked by someone and I wanted to get your opinion, especially since that Rose Bud character is out there haunting the community."

"Go on," he said.

"I'm participating in the McLuhan Writers' Workshop. Last summer, I interacted with one of the other writers. He wrote that he really liked my work, which I shared with him. He asked if I wanted to go out with him. I said no."

As she spoke, she became increasingly agitated.

"I got the feeling he was following me online. I've delayed calling you, expecting it to stop. But it hasn't. It's creeping me out. My dad said I should call you for advice."

"This can be serious," he said. "Do you know his name?"

"Not his full name," she replied. "He doesn't come to the class — he's always online. He goes by Damian. That's the name that appears below his screen."

"Okay. As soon as we end this call, I'll contact Curtis Santana, who's assisting the police department with the Rose Bud case," Mo said. "In turn, he'll notify the police. They may want to assign a special detail to you."

"Do you think I have anything to be afraid of?"

"I don't know, but you shouldn't be taking any chances," he advised.

"Thanks," she said. "For the record, I haven't touched a drop since the night I got stopped."

*M*o scheduled an online conference call to include Curtis, Sherry, Henry David McLuhan, and Tom Mann.

Mallorca's phone call disturbed him. The person she'd identified as Damian might be Rose Bud. It was impossible to know. But if there was one thing he'd learned from the criminal justice system it was that every tip needed follow-up because the one that mattered most was always the one that failed to be investigated.

Plus, he had a nagging feeling that he knew the identity of the serial killer. It was someone who could claim dominion over others, the kind of dominion that had been attempted on his doorstep the other night.

# Twenty-Four

*Diary entry from July 30.*

A vicious storm cut through Northern Virginia yesterday afternoon. I think it's the consequence of this indomitable heat. Trees toppled and flooding was reported all over the place.

But I've got something far more important on my mind than the weather.

When I enrolled in Henry David McLuhan's writing class at the beginning of the year, he encouraged us to write down our emotions and our experiences. It allows us to make sense of things that happen to us, he said.

It's proven to be valuable advice and I'm glad I followed it. It's given me a window in time to look back on some of my past actions and evaluate my thoughts and feelings.

If I didn't have this record, I wouldn't be able to chart events as clearly as I'm able to do.

I just have to be careful that this diary doesn't end up in the wrong hands. When you think about it, I'm effectively writing my own death sentence.

Imagine me: Rose Bud.

I'm a celebrity.

Except, unlike most celebrities, I have to hide my identity.

Now I know how Ted Kaczynski must have felt.

I remember in September 1995 when The Washington Post published the Unabomber's "Industrial Society and its Future." Kaczynski, whose identity was unknown at the time, promised to stop killing people if the paper printed his work.

I read an article about him last month that said the mad ideas *expressed in his manifesto are now mainstream.*

*I should consider doing something along those lines, i.e., contact the media to publish my work. Maybe I'll offer to stop the killing in exchange for seeing my work in print.*

*Is that mad?*

*I don't think so. I'm going to find a way to get my work published before the year is over.*

# Twenty-Five

Henry David McLuhan's creative writing workshop took place at the Lyceum, the city's cultural center. Most participants attended in person, while only a few were online.

Today, three online cameras were turned off, hiding the students' faces. The names below the blank screens read Curtis, Damian, and Mallorca.

Curtis knew all of Rose Bud's victims were bookworms, one of whom briefly participated in Henry David's classes. Therefore, Rose Bud's initial contact with at least one of the victims could have begun in this class.

Henry David cleared his voice. "Disenfranchised," he announced, enunciating the word slowly.

Henry David had a novel approach to writing. He called it "dropping ink," as though he was Timothy Leary dropping acid.

As Henry David explained to his students, a single word on a page could spread across the paper like a splash of ink, spontaneously forming an image that hadn't been sketched in advance.

He had his students imitate his art form.

"Ten minutes," he reminded everyone.

They knew the drill.

Students scribbled in their note-books or tapped on their laptops, phones, and tablets.

Today's word was actually a gift to Curtis. Henry David used a word that might prod Rose Bud, if he was participating in the class, into revealing his identity, or at least that was the plan.

Curtis didn't know about the plan until an hour ago. "I appreciate you," he mumbled to himself as he observed the students following Henry David's instruction and putting their thoughts into words.

Appreciation was not a word that Curtis would normally have assigned to Henry David. They had a natural aversion toward one another. Curtis believed Henry David shared a secret with Mo and Sherry about the Roaches Run case to which he would never be privileged. And Henry David believed Curtis had no business handling the Rose Bud case given the P.I.'s relationship with the deputy police chief, which he believed created a disqualifying conflict.

Yet, in this case, a common bond existed between them. They both wanted to catch Rose Bud and end the terror that choked the city. *The enemy of my enemy is my friend.*

"*T*ime's up."

Henry David waited a few more minutes and then asked, "Who wants to go first?"

"I will," Mallorca announced. She turned on her camera, revealing a luminous visage: pale complexion, blue eyes and full lips filled in with black lipstick. All surrounded by lustrous red hair. She put a poem in the chat. It read:

> *i am dis*
> *Appointed and dis*
>
> *Enfranchised, dis*
>
> *Illusioned by your appropriating*
>
> *my Life.*

She read it aloud, pausing at the end of each line, her voice lingering like a piano key pinned down to provide every filament of sound until it faded away.

"Interesting structure," Henry David said. "Enfranchised and appointed are both actual words, while illusioned is not. You separated 'dis' in two instances without actually disturbing actual words, but created dissonance in the third instance.

"Or," he paused, "should I say dis-sonance," imitating her recital. Everyone laughed.

"Tell us about your poem," he implored her.

She said, "My poem comes from my heart. All my life, I've felt marginalized. I try to be a good person and see the best in others. But it seems as though everywhere I go people are jealous of me and want to put me down. Some think I'm too precocious. Others think I'm too pretty. It's weird. All I want to do is fit in. But I can't."

"Welcome to the party," said Henry David.

Mallorca smiled. "It's important how you position words," she said. "A poem's structure is an organic thing that exists in all forms of composition, including sound and appearance as much as thought and feeling."

As she spoke the room grew so quiet it seemed as though some of the group had stopped breathing.

"Words are vessels," she continued. "They're laden with meaning. We might look up the definition of a word, but its definition is only part of its meaning. Words like love, fear, hope, despair, and faith mean lots of things to us but the meaning of those words is not necessarily the same to everyone.

"Words have universal application, some say, but they also have unique meaning to different individuals. Love may be soothing to you and melancholy to me."

*I love you!* Rose Bud thought silently, watching and listening on his computer.

"Thank you for sharing," Henry David said when she finished. "It's never easy opening up and sharing, and I appreciate it whenever you or others in the class do so. So, who wants to go next?"

Dayton Longmire, who'd been in the class for the past year,

avoided eye contact with Henry David and the others. He preferred to keep his thoughts to himself.

Lance Dobbs raised his hand timidly. He had begun attending classes after his daughter's death in an effort to better understand her.

"You have the mic," Henry David said respectfully.

Lance rose from his seat, holding a tablet in front of him.

"Being disenfranchised means looking in from the outside," he read from the screen in a voice that sounded as familiar as Jimmy Stewart's.

Then he looked up. "For me, it came with the death of my daughter, who was taken from me too soon by an unknown evil person who still crawls around the streets of this community."

He cleared his throat as emotion welled up inside him.

"You're on the *inside* when things are running normally. You're moving with the herd. No one notices you and you really don't notice anyone else.

"But once disaster hits, you're thrown off your orbit and nothing can ever be the same. The routine is forever altered. Circumstances beyond your control catapult you into the void. When you look around, you're now on the *outside* looking in."

He put down the tablet.

"To be disenfranchised is to become unmoored from the things that bind us. Poor health and the loss of a job can trigger it, though you might recover from either of those. You don't recover from personal loss," he said as his voice began to quaver.

The emotion overtook him and tears started rolling down his cheeks. "I miss Lina so much," he choked out. "I quarreled with her too much while I had her, never realizing I could lose her. Since her death, I've tried to learn about her world to better understand her. It's why I moved to Old Town. This class was one of her favorite things.

"Without her, I've lost meaning in life. *I'm* disenfranchised.

103

And there is seemingly no way out for me, no way to get back inside a world that is normal and routine."

Mallorca set afloat a red heart that fluttered over the screen.

Five minutes later, Rose Bud launched a message of his own.

*E*nsconced in his makeshift office in the attic that offered views of quaint Prince Street below, Curtis opened the text message from *The Chronicle's* Tom Mann, which read: "Check your email. I just received an anonymous message. I forwarded it to you."

Curtis switched from the screen depicting the workshop and its participants to a screen showing his emails. He found Tom's communication and opened it, which contained a message sent within the last five minutes.

*People don't know what it's like. They might talk about it, but they don't actually feel it. At least not like me.*

*I've never fit in, no matter how hard I've tried.*

*The average person thinks someone is disenfranchised if they aren't the right color, haven't got the right heritage, or don't have enough money or a good enough education. And they assume the problem can be remedied by affirmative action, whatever that is, public housing, education vouchers, and reparations.*

*Wrong.*

*All wrong.*

*Disenfranchisement is a state of mind. It's knowing you're different from everyone else, that you don't belong, that you never did and never will, that you're an outcast, and that you don't relate to anyone or anything. No amount of political, economic, or social engineering can fix that. Once you're damned, there's no way out.*

*Publish my Manifesto and the killing will cease.*

Shortly, the writer would make arrangements to drop it at Dark Star Park.

"*T*onight was pretty incredible," Henry David said as he

wrapped up the writing session. "Two writers shared their definition of the word disenfranchisement. Both provided a fresh interpretation. Yet, in a way, they shared the same theme.

"Words are charged with emotion, like Mallorca told us. String together a bunch of those words and you capture a thought. Put that thought into print and you create a shared experience. Bundle thoughts into chapters and you have told a story.

"I encourage each of you to delve further into the recesses of your own minds. As I've said repeatedly, keep a diary. Track your actions. Transfer your experiences and your thoughts into words. You'll find that you'll be recording life as it passes by us and, hopefully, making sense of all of it."

Then he added, first speaking to the camera, "Thank you again, Mallorca, for sharing." And to Lance, in the room, he said, "Maybe your journey to walk the path of your daughter's life will bring you back inside. I hope so. If it's any consolation, you're *in* our hearts tonight."

"*It's* him," Tom observed an hour later on the conference call with Mo, Curtis, Sherry and Henry David, as they discussed the anonymous email.

"Rose Bud wrote that email while he was attending Henry David's workshop," Sherry said.

Curtis nodded, buried in thought. "I wonder how long Rose Bud's been participating in the workshop?" he asked. "Maybe he's been following Henry David's instructions and chronicling his murders. If he maintains a journal and if we can find it, we'll have the evidence to put him away forever."

"But who is he?" asked Sherry.

"The person whose video was turned off," said Henry David with certainty.

"Or someone in the classroom," added Curtis. "We can't discount anyone, not even Lance or Mallorca. Everyone is a suspect."

"There's another possibility," Tom suggested. "Maybe this is pure coincidence and nobody in the workshop is guilty of anything."

"Regardless," Curtis said, "we need to track the identity of Damian, the guy whose video was turned off. Do you have a last name for him, Henry? Any other identifying information?"

"He gave a last name of Smith. I don't believe I have an address for him. My recollection is that he left cash in my mailbox when he signed up for the workshop."

"Well, that's too bad, but we need —," Curtis began.

"Let's hold on a minute," Sherry interrupted. "We don't have sufficient cause to launch an investigation to determine his identity. He has to make the first move."

# Twenty-Six

"*I*'m calling for Mo Katz."

The screen on the phone showed the area code 608.

"Speaking," he replied.

"My name's Martha," said the woman. "Shayne's mother. I'm calling from Madison, Wisconsin."

*Actually,* Mo thought, *the pretend mother,* but he kept that to himself.

"Is everything okay?"

"No," answered Martha. "There's been an accident. That silly girl has gone and injured herself pretty bad."

"What happened?"

"She said she was going out for a bike ride," Martha explained. "I don't know what ever possessed her. It was the stupidest thing I've ever seen. The girl's got no sense. The bike needed fixing. It was in terrible shape. I'd told Gus a dozen times to take it to a repair shop.

"I warned her. She was looking for trouble. Maybe she felt compelled to get away from us. She's been acting very uppity, if you know what I mean. Like a city girl. I'm sure you do, know what I mean, that is.

"Anyway, by the time she got to the base of the driveway, she'd gone head over heels over the top of the bike and landed on her back. She managed to break her leg, injure her back, and twist her neck.

"It was a good thing Gus was here at the time. He was able to load her into the back of the truck and rush her to the hospital. Poor thing might have died in our driveway if he hadn't been there to render assistance."

"That's terrible!" Katz said. "Where is she? Can I talk to her?"

"She's in surgery."

Neither spoke. Mo realized he was holding his breath.

"She's going to have to stay with us for a little while," Martha continued. "The doctor isn't going to let her travel right away, no matter how desperately she wants to leave and how much we want her to be gone.

"Of course, Shayne has to get back to school. She can't take off time to take care of Abby. I'll have to do it. Gus and me. And that means taking care of that little nuisance, Katie, too. She's a handful."

Mo suddenly realized she was talking about Abby, not Shayne, as he initially thought. A burst of adrenalin shot through him. After a pause to collect himself, he spoke. "I appreciate what you're doing for Abby and Katie," Mo said, feeling a need to placate her. "And Shayne." He added, "Are you at the hospital now?"

"No," Martha replied. "Gus stayed. I've got my hands full with the rest of the kids. There's more than just Shayne and Katie, you know. We've got our own."

Mo wondered if he was supposed to drop everything and rush out to Wisconsin. After all, Abby chided him for failing to take her and the girls to dinner the other night. And he barely redeemed himself by taking them to the airport.

"No need to come out here," Martha advised before he could reply. "Abby told me earlier that you're not one to pitch in. Work comes first for you, above all else. But don't worry. Everything's under control. You'd just make a nuisance of yourself if you did come. We'll let you know how the surgery goes."

"You're sure?" Mo asked, ignoring the insult.

"I don't ever second-guess myself, Mr. Katz. Yes, I'm sure. Goodbye."

*D*ayton Longmire, Trudy's erstwhile accountant who'd been quoted in *The Chronicle* as saying "we've lost one of the good ones" when informed of her demise, wished he hadn't started small.

If he'd begun by siphoning off large chunks of assets, then

maybe his conscience would have told him to stop. Or he might have been caught in the act. Either way, this mess would have been avoided.

This mess was the false accounting of assets in Trudy Vine's stock and bond portfolio.

In his defense, who would have imagined that the stock market would rally at the end of the year? Every day brought new S&P 500 and NASDAQ records. While 401(k) investors cheered, Dayton bemoaned the news.

The portfolio he managed for Trudy had grown exponentially over the past weeks, fueled by the Magnificent Seven, the tech stocks that fueled the rally. Yet the spreadsheet he stared at did not reflect that reality and only showed meager gains.

He had siphoned seemingly undetectable pieces to his own account. Now he faced a reckoning. The numbers he'd sent her a few hours before she died — which sat unopened in a spreadsheet attached to an email addressed to her — would show the lie.

And it would provide a motive for murder.

As if that wasn't bad enough, he was beholden to the person who had uncovered his prior mismanagement of service funds held by the Commonwealth of Virginia.

He prayed for a way out before it was too late.

# Twenty-Seven

*T*hat evening, Ryan Long received an unexpected call.

He'd been working late. The floor of the office building in Potomac Yard where he worked was deserted and dark save for his desk lamp and light from his computer screen. Ryan relished being left alone; he did his best work when others weren't disturbing him with their idle chatter.

"I've got dirt on Mo Katz," said the caller.

Since Ryan had dropped hints that Katz was engaged in unspecified nefarious activities, it was hardly surprising for him to receive an unsolicited call.

"Who am I speaking to?" he asked, "And what sort of… information…do you possess?" He hesitated using the word, dirt, though he hoped she had some.

"My name is Lucy Dallas. He made a pass at me in the elevator in the federal courthouse," she said. "I think he might have been drinking."

"Did you create a record?" he inquired.

"I'm telling you now. Isn't that good enough?"

Ryan disregarded her impertinent response and asked, "Did he touch you?"

As he asked the question, Ryan quickly conducted an online search of her name using the criminal history database in his office. Though she did not have any criminal convictions, she had been charged with stalking in the past and ordered to stay away from an ex-boyfriend. Complaints had also been filed against her for falsifying her personnel record.

"He might have touched me," said Lucy. "I'd feel more comfortable coming to your office to discuss the matter personally with you."

That sounded tantalizing but dangerous, particularly given her background, and Ryan was no one's fool.

He rose with his cellphone in hand and walked the length of the hall. Overhead motion lights ignited as he cut briskly through the shadows that crisscrossed the corridor.

In his mind, red lights flashed. Caution was the order of the day. After all, a great deal was at stake. He knew or suspected of incidents where the hunter became the hunted and he didn't want to get snapped by that mousetrap.

*Am I paranoid?* Ryan asked himself. He had reason to be. He couldn't trust other people.

He knew Curtis Santana and the Alexandria police were desperately trying to solve the Rose Bud murders. Was he a suspect? Was this call related to that investigation?

Furthermore, he'd made an enemy of Mo Katz and it was possible that Katz would attempt to compromise his investigation.

Finally, there was the Trudy Vine murder case.

"Why did you *really* call me?" he asked.

"Quit being so cautious. I'm not going to bite you. When do you want to meet?"

Long replied evasively, "Let me check my schedule and I'll get back to you in a day or two." He preferred meeting on neutral turf. And he contemplated a maneuver that might intrigue Tom Mann of *The Chronicle*, a man he anxiously wanted to meet.

Almost immediately after Ryan hung up with Lucy Dallas, Tom's phone rang. The ID showed the incoming call was from Ryan Long, a state auditor or investigator who habitually called him with story ideas that were really nothing more than vainglorious efforts to get his own name in print.

Tom reluctantly answered the call.

"I just spoke to a woman who swears she was sexually assaulted by Mo Katz," Ryan claimed without preamble. "She called me out of the blue. I've arranged to meet her. I'd like you to join me and do an exclusive."

"You haven't met her?" Tom reacted in surprise.

"I'd like you to hear it unvarnished, raw, and unrehearsed," explained Ryan. "Maybe you'll be sufficiently impressed and run with it. Will you? Publish a story about it?"

Tom laughed. "That's like asking if I'd eat a fish before you catch it. First, let me hear her story. If it's credible, I'll need corroboration. I always contact the other side for comment, so I'd reach out to Katz for his side of the story as well."

"In other words, it's not as simple as listening to someone and then running with the story."

Ryan decided to employ a hardball tactic. "Are you afraid of Katz? Does he have something on you?"

"No, no, it's nothing like that. It's just unusual for someone to call me with dirt on Mo Katz. I don't think it's ever happened before. But, sure, I'll meet with her."

It worked.

"Good," Ryan said. "Oh, one more thing. I heard Rose Bud contacted you."

"Where'd you hear that?"

"The police department leaks like a sieve," Ryan laughed. "But please don't ask me to give up my source."

"Very funny, but I'm really not in a position to say anything," Tom replied.

"The police don't seem to be getting anywhere," Ryan lamented. "Same with the P.I. helping them who is, by the way, Sherry Stone's boyfriend. Talk about a conflict of interest, huh?"

Tom remained silent.

"If you ask me," Ryan said, "the whole bunch of them is crooked and need to be exposed by someone with your kind of journalistic integrity."

"About this woman —," Tom interjected.

"Okay, then," said Ryan. "I'll try to set it up for tomorrow. I'll be in touch."

Cilia Roosevelt stood in the doorway to Ryan's office. He started, unaware that anyone else was on his floor.

He wondered how long she'd been standing within earshot and what she'd heard.

"I didn't know you were still working," he said.

Hardly anyone was in the office anymore, day or night. Since the pandemic, the return to work policy in the public sector had languished. Up and down the floor of the building, cubicles were routinely vacant and offices with blank monitors were unoccupied. It was almost like a post-apocalyptic scene from a movie.

"I've only been here a few minutes," she said. "Not long enough to hear anything scandalous, if that's what you're thinking."

"Oh, no, no," he replied. "But I'm glad you stopped by because I have a job for you. It's very hush-hush. I hope you're up for it."

Cilia nodded her acquiescence. She was anxious to gain a promotion.

"I'd like you to visit an inmate in the women's detention center up the street and record a conversation."

"You want *me* to wear a wire?" Cilia exclaimed.

She wondered whether Ryan had permission for such an undertaking but was reluctant to ask for fear the offer might be withdrawn. She was jealous of others who'd been given plum assignments. Cilia figured this was her chance to climb the ladder. Even if it wasn't sanctioned — and she was pretty sure it wasn't — she was doing his bidding and he was in a position to help her achieve her goals.

*So, if something went awry, they were in it together,* she told herself. *Right?*

Furthermore, Cilia knew Ryan possessed compromising

information about her, namely an old drug charge that Cilia assumed had been expunged from her record. She had answered no when asked on an employment application whether she'd ever been charged with a drug-related offense. She'd almost forgotten about it when Ryan had brought it up.

That was six months ago, before he began asking her for favors.

"Of course, it's your choice whether you want to help me," Ryan said. "There's no obligation on your part."

"I'm always willing to help out in an investigation, even if it's risky," she said.

"I was hoping you'd say that. Unfortunately, I can't go into further detail right now. I wasn't expecting to see you and I have another urgent commitment. I'll be in touch soon enough."

# Twenty-Eight

Shortly before visiting hours ended, Roxie was summoned from her cell for a meeting with her attorney, which left her wondering why Mo was making an unannounced visit late in the day.

Her question was answered when the metal door sprung open and Jimmy Wolfe greeted her.

"Well, this is a surprise," she said without enthusiasm. She hadn't entertained a thought of him since he'd represented her for assault and battery years ago, and that wasn't a favorable one.

His once ruddy complexion had turned pale and his face was gaunt. His magnificent mane of white hair had thinned and turned yellow, like snow on which a dog had peed. And his once statuesque physique had shriveled to a fragile and slightly bent frame.

"It's been a while," she commented.

He wasted no time on niceties. "What do you think you're doing?" he growled.

"I'm sorry?" she replied.

"Don't act so surprised," he replied. "You know what I'm talking about. What do you think you're doing getting Mo Katz involved in this case?"

She cocked a menacing eye in his direction. "You're a fine one to come here and ask a question like that. You did a horrible job representing me. I was innocent of that A&B charge. Did you expect me to ask you for your help again? No way. You got beat up in the courtroom, so naturally I turned to the guy who pummeled you."

Having conjured up the old case, she couldn't stop talking about it.

"You'd won the case. The judge was eating out of your hand. Yet you managed to pull defeat out of the jaws of victory. Maybe you're jealous that Mo is handling such a plum case. After all, a lot of people would like to have the notoriety of representing me in court. Maybe you're afraid he'll steal the mantle from you as the best defense attorney in Alexandria.

"You lost that mantle a long time ago, Jimmy. Everyone knows it except you. Wise up."

He sighed. Was it simpler back in the day or was he just impervious to the emotional weight of it all? He wasn't sure.

He felt as worn down as he looked. He had an appointment with a urologist tomorrow. His PSA numbers were increasing. Death seemed to be encroaching, throwing him off balance, interrupting his train of thought, to the extent the train ran at all.

He sat down heavily in the red plastic chair. She remained standing. In an odd twist, she appeared to have dominion over him.

"I admit I should have done a better job for you," he said. "Mo outfoxed me. Maybe he intimidated me. At any rate, I never expected him to turn a sow's ear into a silk purse."

"As angry as I was at the time, I grudgingly admired the man," said Roxie. "As much as he hurt me, I will never forget that day. He was a magician."

"Is that why you've asked for his help? Is it that or something else?"

Roxie didn't answer.

"Have you told Mo about Trudy Vine?" Jimmy prodded. "Does he know who she is? Are you going to deal squarely with him? Or are you planning to set him up?"

Roxie answered in a firm tone. "You have no right to inquire about my motive. Despite what others say, I am an honorable woman. I play my own game but I play it for a noble purpose."

Jimmy looked at the tiny woman swimming in an orange jumpsuit. He doubted his resolve to influence her decision. He *was* jealous of Mo and he had grown to doubt his own ability.

He rubbed his brow. "Did you ever hear from or see Cybil

Shawl after the trial?"

Roxie answered, "She's a good woman. She came forward to abate the lie. Mo Katz inferred that she gave false testimony. I wish she hadn't run off that day. If she'd stayed, the result would have been different."

Roxie scrunched her face with displeasure. "You should have let me testify. That was a tactical error."

"You would have come across as a liar," Jimmy replied.

"Whose decision was it?"

"It was yours, of course," Jimmy said, though he made it for her.

"You still think I beat her up, don't you?" Roxie hissed. "After all these years, you still don't believe I was innocent. The truth is a hard thing to see, I suppose. We twist it so often we don't see it when it's staring us in the face."

Jimmy shook his head. "I shouldn't have come here tonight. Nothing has changed. You're the same old woman you were then, only older."

"Don't beat yourself up," she chided. "It's a waste of time. You're already washed up."

# Twenty-Nine

***D**iary entry from November 1.*

*L*ast night was devilishly divine.

I dressed as Hemingway, complete with white beard. She called me daddy. The girl was effed up. We laughed and laughed. When the night was over, I laughed last.

I felt less a novelist than a playwright, a master of the three-act play.

The first act was the seduction, getting her in my grasp, innocent and helpless, believing that everything is okay. Believing in tonight, tomorrow, and the day after that.

(What a sap.)

Act two was the murder, the instant when romance and enjoyment turned to disbelief and horror. No more tomorrows.

Act three was the signature line: staging the candles, incense, bubble bath, and rose petals. Ah, those ubiquitous rose petals!

Unfortunately, someone is threatening to end my fun. She claims to know I'm Rose Bud.

I don't know whether it's a lie or not. From what I've deduced, she's a bit of a con artist herself, having faked crimes and bribed people to enrich herself.

Still, I can't take chances. I'll have to find a way to kill her. Slowly. Without suspicion. I'm not sure how. But it'll come to me. Maybe I'll walk into a store and someone will give me an idea.

# Thirty

There was a loud slam at the front door of the Harvard Street townhouse.

"Hey!"

Shayne stepped inside carrying a backpack, which she dropped in the foyer. She wore a black puffy coat and purple gloves, which she discarded beside the backpack.

"I'm home!"

"When did you get back?" Mo asked, rising from the desk where he'd been strategizing Roxie's case.

Shayne rushed over, clung to him, and suddenly began crying.

"That good," he said sarcastically, referring to Wisconsin. He had heard from both Martha and Abby and knew that Abby's surgery had gone well and she was on the mend. So he knew Shayne wasn't crying about that.

He was out of his depth. Hugging had always been awkward for him. He was more effective at arm's length. He carefully disengaged himself and led Shayne to a chair beside the desk. Then he sat down facing her.

"I'm being marginalized," she sniffled. "I have two mothers. Both of them want exclusive rights. Neither is giving me the support I need. I'm angry and frustrated, and lost."

He tried to redirect the conversation. "Are you hungry as well?" he asked. "Do you have school work to complete while you're here?"

"No," she replied. "I just want to talk. Is that okay?"

Mo took a deep breath. *Maybe it was all right*, he thought.

"I usually avoid moments like this," he confided. "I'm uncomfortable sharing my feelings or having people share their personal feelings with me. I can handle it professionally, but not personally.

"If truth be told, my growing up wasn't all that different from yours. My parents wanted to avoid steeping me too deeply in either of their families. As a result, I scratched the surface of both of their cultures but never really got immersed in either one.

"I'm adrift and have been adrift all of my life."

"You don't seem that way," she said. "In fact, you impress me as a person who really has his shit together. I mean, you empathize with people." She sniffled again, wiping her nose on her sleeve. "I've seen it. You're wonderful that way."

"I'm empathetic because I'm emotionally crippled, if that makes any sense. And a lot of that has to do with having been marginalized all my life too."

"You're not marginalized, Mo. You're the center of the universe. Everyone admires you."

"Maybe that's how it looks from the outside, but not in here," he said, pointing to his chest.

They both reached for each other, then stood and hugged each other tightly. Then they both started to laugh as they pulled apart.

"Neither of them is doing it deliberately," he counseled, referring to Abby and Martha. "They just don't know any better. It's your responsibility to teach them it's okay for them to suffocate you with love.

"It's not going to kill you. In fact, it's the opposite. It's going to enable you to breathe."

"How can you be so sure?" she asked. "I mean, I want to believe what you're saying. It's just so hard. And I feel so responsible."

"The last thing you should feel is responsible," he said. "You didn't create this situation. And, to be honest, when I listen to Abby and then listen to you, I think you might be the only adult in the room. So don't be hard on yourself."

*Mo* made spaghetti from a can for dinner. The remains of a

fresh loaf of Italian bread sat on a wooden board, torn on both ends. Crumbs adorned the table like confetti. Red wine, barely touched, floated in two bowled glasses. They actually preferred ice water, so a perspiring pitcher sat beside the bottle of wine.

Shayne picked up their conversation where they had left off.

"I don't want to hurt either of them," she said. "But it can't go on like this. It's like the War of the Roses except they're both more like sunflowers. I want to make both of them happy but I can't and it's making me miserable."

"It's not easy being in the middle," he consoled her.

"What would *you* do in my situation?" she asked.

Trying to appease warring factions and find middle ground had been a part of his personal and professional life since, well, forever.

"You can't choose sides," he said. "You're allowed to give both of them a place in your life, aren't you?"

"I don't think you understand," she said. "*I* want us to coexist with each other. *They're* the ones that don't. Each one of them claims me as her own. There's no room for a threesome."

Mo said, "Actually, right now, it's just the two of them. You've removed yourself from the equation by returning to school. What if you stay out of the picture and force them to rely upon one another without you in the picture? Instead of trying to solve their problem, make them solve it themselves. It's like putting two people who disagree in a room, locking the door, and refusing to let them out until they find a shared solution to the problem."

Shayne smiled slyly. "That's genius."

"Actually, maybe it's already happening," Mo observed. "They're both out there in Wisconsin now. Who else do they have other than themselves? Katie, yes, but she's just a kid. They really only have each other."

Shayne still looked unsettled.

"What's the matter?" Mo asked.

"I'm not going to lie," she said. "Having both of them fight over me gives me a feeling of self-worth. It's going to be hard to extricate myself from the battle. Part of me likes being the center of attention."

"That's an interesting observation," he said. "You have a pretty good sense of self. Most people wouldn't recognize something like that about themselves. But try to set aside your own feelings, whether or not those feeling are partly selfish, and see what happens."

After they finished dinner, they did the dishes together. Mo rinsed the plates and the pot, and Shayne placed items in the dishwasher.

Afterwards, Shayne started to head upstairs to her room. She paused on the stairs.

"It's not what I expected you to say, about my mothers, I mean," she said. "I expected you to take sides with Abby and tell me to listen to her because she's my birth mother. I just thought your allegiance was with her."

"I love Abby but that doesn't mean I'm compelled to support her positions on everything," Mo said. "I don't adopt a position to conform to her point of view and I don't expect her to do that for me.

"Look at it from a legal perspective," Mo continued. "Both Abby and Martha have rights. If one of them sued to be able to see you, a judge would grant the request and tell them to work out the details between themselves."

"Is that how you see the world, through a legal prism?" Shayne asked, leaning on the banister with one foot on the staircase.

"Yeah," he admitted. "Maybe it helps keep me grounded."

She lingered. "Can I ask you something totally off-subject?" She waited for him to nod his approval. "Have you ever wanted kids of your own? I mean, you're a great father figure but…"

"Yeah, sometimes I think it might be cool to have my own kids." He started to say that he and Abby had started in earnest but that their progress was interrupted by the unexpected arrival of Katie and Shayne into their lives. But he didn't want that comment to be misinterpreted.

"You and Katie filled a void in Abby's life and you both enriched mine," he said. "I'm content with that. It's more than a lot of people have. It brings its own unique responsibilities."

Mo thought of the tragic demise of Katie's parents, Tony Fortune and Maggie Moriarty. And while he never knew Shayne's father, he could sense the essence of him in her. Her father had been a star athlete and academic whiz kid who died about a year after Abby gave Shayne up for adoption.

As if reading his thoughts, Shayne asked, "Did you know my father?"

Katz shook his head. "No, that was before my time. I'd never been to the D.C. area until law school. My decision to sit for the Virginia Bar was totally random. I didn't meet your mother until I got a job as an assistant commonwealth attorney in Alexandria."

"When did she tell you about me?"

Mo reflected. "When you love someone, you share secrets that you don't divulge to other people, secrets about the events that shaped your life and made you who you are. Abby told me that she'd given up a baby girl for adoption during her senior year in high school. She said she felt she didn't have a choice at the time, but that she's regretted it a million times over."

"Did you ever encourage her to find me?" Shayne's hands held the bars of the staircase as though they were strings on a harp.

"I neither encouraged nor discouraged her," Mo replied. "It wasn't my place."

Shayne straightened her posture, stepped to the foyer, and leaned against the wall. "You two have a pretty special relationship," she said. "My parents — my other parents — always try to control one another. They tell each other what to do, oftentimes, I think, to pursue their own agendas. But you're not like that. You two have like a laissez-faire relationship. It's pretty special."

With that, she wandered upstairs.

Mo returned to the desk in the library to further design a strategy in Roxie's case. It occurred to him a few minutes later that he'd never inquired about how Abby was doing. *Maybe,* he thought, *I really am one-dimensional when I'm engrossed in a case.*

# Thirty-One

The next day — after he'd thawed and baked bagels (four minutes in the toaster oven) for Shayne and himself, and bid her farewell as she returned to school — Mo went to the courthouse. Following a misdemeanor trial and a civil motion, he headed to the detention center.

He and Roxie had adopted a routine. Their first few minutes together were spent in light banter. Then they slowly slipped into business, like a car going from first gear into drive.

Roxie made no mention of her recent encounter with Jimmy Wolfe.

Mo broached the idea of throwing suspicion upon a wide sample of residents who participated in the Capps Cupcake Competition. While none of them were actually guilty of the crime, it would create doubt, he said, and increase the likelihood of an acquittal or a hung jury.

"I thought the purpose of a trial was to get to the truth," Roxie said sarcastically.

"Only on episodes of *Perry Mason*," Mo explained, referring to the old television show starring Raymond Burr.

"It isn't the defense's job to show that someone else committed Trudy's murder," he continued. "It's perfectly acceptable to point the finger in other directions to shift suspicion away from you. It happens all the time."

"Isn't that unfair?" Roxie inquired, taking the ethical high ground. "After all, none of them is guilty."

"We aren't claiming they're guilty," Katz countered. "We're simply planting a doubt as to whether *you* did it. The standard is *beyond* a reasonable doubt. So long as that bar isn't reached, you go free. And, if only one juror remains unconvinced, the jury hangs."

"Can't you do that by just poking holes in the prosecution's case without casting dispersions on others?" she asked, unconvinced.

Mo knew she meant "aspersions" but it was a common error and he didn't correct her. He simply said, "We're not going to lie, if that's what's bothering you. We can't do that. However, if the prosecution puts a witness on the stand and if that witness had a personal vendetta of some sort against Trudy, we can point it out to the jury.

"Give me an example," she insisted.

"Let's assume the prosecution calls witness X who testifies that she overheard you say that you'd like to see Trudy dead," he began.

"That's entirely possible," Roxie commented. "I said things like that about more than one person when I was angry at them, and I was often angry at Trudy."

"But suppose witness X owed a large sum of money to Trudy," Mo continued, disregarding her comment. "We could use that fact against witness X to challenge her veracity and to suggest *she* might be the murderer."

"What if they launch another investigation against that person?" she asked.

"That'll never happen," Mo assured her.

"How can you be so sure?" she asked. "There are plenty of cases where innocent people get convicted of crimes they didn't commit. Sometimes people even admit to crimes under duress that they never committed in the first place. I don't want us winning my freedom at the cost of ruining someone's reputation or jeopardizing someone else's freedom."

Mo replied, "When a defendant is acquitted, the police rarely open new investigations to consider other suspects. They chalk it up to one more instance where the bad guy gets off for a crime he really committed."

"So if I'm acquitted, I'll carry that stigma with me for the rest of my life," she said in disgust. "Every time someone looks at me, they'll see a guilty person whose attorney successfully tricked a jury into an acquittal."

She lowered her head and muttered, "I'll be forever known as the female O.J. Maybe I should change my plea, admit to the crime, and take my chances in front of the judge at sentencing. What do you think?"

Mo's eyes were gazing vacantly around the room.

"What is it?" she asked.

"Nothing," he answered, wiping thoughts from his mind like he was pressing the delete key on a laptop.

*If Roxie was really guilty, she would have jumped at a strategy that cast blame on others. Instead, she's hesitant. She doesn't want to implicate innocent parties. Does she know the real killer?*

Roxie seemed to read his thoughts. "If we adopt this strategy," she said, suddenly sounding enthusiastic, "who exactly would you point the finger at?"

"We'll have to wait to see who's on the prosecution's list of witnesses," Mo said. "In the meantime, we can be proactive and anticipate who they might call and begin to look into their background."

"Okay," she said reluctantly. "How do we proceed?"

"I want you to make a list of the people who knew both you and Trudy and who are likely to be called as witnesses against you," he instructed. "Keep it small. We'll look into the background of the people on the list and prepare a line of questioning that casts a shadow on each of them."

"Keeping it small will be a challenge," she said thoughtfully. "There's a plethora of people who would happily testify against me. Some despise me. Others just want to see me suffer. And a few would like to get their hands on my house."

Mo handed Roxie a pen and legal pad. Rather than immediately scribbling names on the paper, Roxie sat staring at it.

"This is really quite devious," she said. "We're creating a bunch of red herrings, like in a crime fiction thriller. You'll feed them to the jury to distract them. And it'll let me get back at my enemies."

"Well, it's not exactly fiction," Mo cautioned. He was reminded of his previous conversation with Curtis about diverting attention from Roxie by suggesting the murder was committed by a disgruntled contender for the Capps cupcake crown or an angry victim of Trudy's blackmail. "We're not going to make up stories about these people. We're going to study their background and draw inferences from actual facts."

Roxie nodded, and without further ado, quickly began writing on the pad.

A few minutes later, she handed the pad and pen back to him. The list contained five names:

*Helena Delacroix*

*Dayton Longmire*

*Lucy Dallas*

*Cilia Roosevelt*

*Lance Dobbs*

Roxie began providing background on the people on the list.

"You met Helena. She's a crafty one. Dayton is her financial advisor. Very shifty character. Lucy Dallas is bad news. Her good looks disguise a true malcontent, a poisonous and venomous sort. She's always spreading gossip and rumors. Cilia is one of those sycophants who's willing to do anything to get ahead. She's in government, so God help us all. As for Lance, he's a newcomer and started *Enough Is Enough!* Sad story there, his daughter being one of the victims of Rose Bud and all. Aside from that, he's got an eye for younger women. And the police suspect him of being Rose Bud even though he's totally innocent."

Mo ripped the list from the pad and tucked the paper in his pocket thinking as he did so that she sounded definitive when she dismissed Lance Dobbs as a suspect in the Rose Bud case. *Why was she so positive of his innocence?* he wondered.

Roxie's mates were gathered in the quad when she returned to her cell. It was not unusual for the girls to inquire about each other's meetings with their attorneys. It was like sharing secrets after a date.

"How'd it go?" asked Robyn.

"Same ol'," Roxie replied.

"Are you being square with Mo?" Sam asked.

Roxie was wise enough not to trust anyone. This was particularly true in a jail setting where lying, stealing, and cheating were prerequisites for admission. *If trusting people on the outside was tricky, what sense would it make to trust someone inside these walls?* she asked herself.

Yet she liked these two women. Who knew, maybe she'd confide in them some day.

"I don't know that I want to share information with you," Roxie said. "What I tell Mo is my own business."

"They say you should always tell your attorney the truth," Robyn advised. "If you lie or mislead your attorney, you're just hurting yourself."

"She's right," Sam said.

The women inched forward. "We've been watching you, Roxie," Robyn said, lowering her voice. "Something's afoot. Tell us what it is."

The two women moved even closer to Roxie. They wanted in.

"I shouldn't do this," Roxie sighed. "I don't trust people as a general rule and I surely don't trust the people in here, regardless of which uniform they're wearing. But, for some strange reason, I think I might be able to trust you."

They clustered around her as though they were each going to kiss Roxie's cheek.

The temptation to share her secret plot with someone else was too strong. Half against her better judgment, she surrendered.

"I'm trying to catch Rose Bud," she confided. "He's the one who murdered my friend, Trudy. I'm using Mo to set a trap. You both must promise to keep my secret. No one else can know. Not even Mo."

Robyn and Sam swore fidelity to the plot, though it was questionable whether they could really keep a secret.

*M*o phoned Curtis after emailing him the list of names that Roxie had provided.

"You won't believe who dropped by," Curtis said as soon as he answered the phone.

"Hi, Mo!"

Mo immediately recognized the voice as that of Mai Lin. Mai and her husband David Reese had forged a bond with Mo during the Daingerfield Island case in 2017. Afterwards, he hired her as a research assistant when he became U.S. attorney.

"I just quit," she said, referring to the U.S. Attorney's Office. "It's not the same without you."

"Well, okay," Mo said, somewhat surprised. "Let's get together and talk about your future plans. In the meantime, I'd love for you to work with me in private practice. If you have time, you can work with Curtis on a consultant basis."

"I'm in," she replied without hesitation.

Mo wasted no time proceeding with the issue at hand as though she'd been a member of the team all along.

"I'm interested in two things," he began. "First, any items that discredit the people on this list: prior convictions, professional controversies, investigations, rumors of impropriety, problems with personal relationships. I need ammunition to attack their credibility if they provide damning evidence against Roxie.

"Second, I'm interested in anything that points to the complicity of people on this list in Trudy Vine's death: arguments with her, rifts, personal grudges, threats, competitions. I need material to deflect guilt from Roxie and insinuate that each of the people on the list could be the guilty party."

"Is that all of it?" asked Curtis, who suspected there was more to Mo's request.

"Not entirely," he admitted. "I think there's a reason she's given me this particular list of individuals. There's a pattern here and I'm not 100 percent sure what it is."

"You have doubts, don't you?" Mai asked. "I mean, about her guilt. Despite the fact she's told you she's guilty, you don't believe her, do you?"

"A few things don't add up," Mo acknowledged.

"It's crazy to say it, but maybe she's playing you," Curtis suggested.

"There *is* something off about this case. She admitted guilt too easily. She's up to something."

"Why not drop her?" Mai asked. "Withdraw from the case and be done with her."

Mo shook his head. "No. She's not a force of evil. I'm sure she's a force for good and I'm going to play along.

"The very first day I met her, she lied to me that she'd poisoned Trudy. She also manipulated me into feeling sorry for her by creating a scene with one of the deputies. I don't know what she's trying to do. Yet I believe whatever she's doing is done with good intent. I just have to figure out her game."

# Thirty-Two

That night, Ryan Long sat at Whiskey & Oysters. The place was only half full and no one was seated within earshot. He'd selected a table in the rear of the dining room.

He identified Lucy Dallas the moment she stepped into the bar and restaurant. She was tall, statuesque, and shapely; her hair was golden and her complexion glowing. Ryan thought, *what man wouldn't want to grope this woman in an elevator?*

He signaled to her across the room. She approached the table and they introduced themselves to one another. A waiter appeared. She didn't have to look at the menu; she ordered based on the name of the restaurant. He ordered a second espresso martini.

She settled into the chair opposite him. A whisky on the rocks appeared within a couple of minutes and the oysters would follow shortly.

"I've never had one of those, though my friends drink them all the time," she said, referring to his drink selection.

They engaged in idle chitchat until Tom Mann arrived. Ryan was already regretting the invitation for the journalist to join them. Having taken one look at her, he'd have preferred for this conversation to remain one-on-one.

Lucy was caught off guard when Tom arrived.

"I've invited a journalist friend of mine to join us," Ryan explained as Tom pulled up a chair between them. Lucy reluctantly extended her hand.

Ryan noticed the two rings on her fingers and multiple silver, gold, and bronze bracelets that adorned her wrists, as well as the shiny gold nail polish that accentuated her nicely manicured hand.

The waiter arrived with Ryan's drink. Tom demurred when

asked if he wanted to order a drink. "I'll stick with water," he said, reaching for an untouched glass on the table.

When the waiter departed, Tom turned to Lucy and said, "I understand you're acquainted with Mo Katz. What can you tell us about his assaulting you in an elevator at the courthouse?"

Lucy looked at Ryan, clearly annoyed. "If I'd known I was going to be ambushed by a reporter like this, I never would have agreed to meet in the first place."

Ryan was taken aback. "I thought you'd appreciate my inviting a reporter to join us. The allegations against Mo Katz are sensational ones to say the least and you should expect reporters to inquire about them."

"I'm not looking for any notoriety," she said.

Turning to Tom, she explained, "I reached out to Mr. Long because I learned he's inquiring about the former U.S. attorney. I haven't filed any sexual harassment action. I'm certainly not prepared to go public with any allegations, if that's what you're expecting from me."

The waiter returned with oysters. Tom asked for directions to the restroom and excused himself. Lucy asked for another whiskey on the rocks and Ryan ordered appetizers.

Their meeting turned cold and awkward.

"You should have checked with me before inviting a reporter," she chided him. "I have a reputation to maintain. I feel blindsided."

"It wasn't my intention," Ryan apologized. "It was wrong of me." He feigned remorse simply to appear vulnerable. In truth, the thought of hurting Mo Katz was no longer the most important thing on his mind.

Tom returned to the table but didn't sit down.

"If the two of you don't mind, I've got a story to file," he said.

Then, addressing Lucy, he added, "If you decide to pursue a case, let me know. Otherwise, I'm not taking anything about this meeting to print. It's just salacious gossip at this point and that's not the mission of *The Chronicle*."

Of course it *was* the mission of his paper, which traded in innuendo. He simply felt a need to tread lightly with this one.

Tom left as the appetizers arrived.

Ryan steered the conversation to other topics and all seemed forgiven. Later, he asked Lucy if she'd like to go to his apartment for another round of drinks. On the way, she told him her close friends called her Lucky.

# Thirty-Three

Lance Dobbs was at Elaine's restaurant with Mallorca Cannon, one of the members of Henry David McLuhan's writing workshop. Lance loved coming here for literary events staged by Jeffrey and Cynthia Higgins. Tonight, however, it was only for wine, cheese, and pita bread.

*Ironic, isn't it?* he asked himself. Here he was, the founder of a victims' rights group founded after his daughter's murder, enjoying an evening with a young woman to discuss literature. A woman half his age, if truth be told, and the approximate age of his daughter.

Mallorca's presence, the way she carried herself, and even her very essence reminded him of his daughter.

How he missed his little girl. *If only I could hold her again.*

"Have you spoken recently to the police about your daughter's case?" Mallorca inquired.

She felt a sexual tension lurking in the background. Sentimentality and sexuality created a potent mixture. She worried where it might lead before this night ended.

"I haven't," he replied, assuming Mallorca had asked the question out of genuine concern. "My relationship with the Alexandria police hasn't been a good one."

"Why's that?"

"My daughter and I quarreled before she moved to D.C. I didn't want her to go, you see. When the police learned about our arguments, they suspected that I might have had something to do with her death."

"You're kidding!" Mallorca responded, aghast. *But maybe I shouldn't be shocked*, she thought immediately afterwards. *Maybe this is the way serial killers conduct their business.*

"You have no idea how it made me feel," he confided. "First, I lost my only daughter. Then I'm suspected of playing a role in her death. I'm divorced. I'm all alone now. That's made the whole thing harder."

He ripped off a piece of pita bread, dipped it in a bowl filled with seasoned oil, and tossed it into his mouth. He washed down the bread with a healthy gulp of wine.

"Lina's mother — my first wife — died in a car accident. My ex didn't get along with my daughter. She felt she had to compete with her for my affection. I really don't want to get into it more than that. Suffice to say it was a dysfunctional relationship."

Mallorca finished her glass of wine. She wanted to leave, but before she could make a move Lance signaled to the waiter and said, "Instead of getting another glass, let's get a bottle."

After ordering the wine, he said, "It's a good thing I founded the nonprofit. At least one good thing came from her death. It's proven to be a life raft for me."

A thousand questions raced through Mallorca's mind. "Where were you when your daughter was murdered?" she asked.

"I was here in town," Lance answered. "She and I had dinner at Chadwicks and I walked her home. We argued. I wanted her to return home, *our* home."

"Do the police know that?"

He lowered his eyes. "Of course. That's why I'm on such bad terms with the police. They considered me a suspect for the longest time. I think maybe they still do."

She swirled the wine in her glass and asked, "Were you in town when the other two murders occurred?"

He raised his eyes to meet hers. "Call it bad luck but, yes, I was in Old Town on both of those dates, once for house hunting and the other time when I was setting up my corporation. In both instances, I didn't have alibis that satisfied the police or the special investigator who's been brought into the case."

He was silent for a moment, then added, "In fact, sometimes I think they're still watching me."

*A* few blocks away, Senator Don Lotte was surveying the artwork at the Nepenthe Gallery accompanied by Helena Delacroix.

Helena and the senator met on a dating app. Helena was intrigued by the absence of a photo and ambiguity in the man's professional background.

*"Attend too many state fairs and eat too many corn dogs on the trail,"* read the description of his job, which she concluded was an obvious clue he was a member of Congress.

Helena and Don also wrote in their profiles that they loved long walks along quiet streets, visiting art galleries and museums, drinking fine wine and enjoying gourmet dining, traveling to exotic places, and dancing.

All of which was to say that they were both lonely and in need of a good time, preferably with someone financially independent and emotionally grounded.

Don divulged on their second date that he was married and a U.S. senator.

She feigned surprise but had already googled him. He preferred discretion, he said, which was fine by her…for the time being. Someday she might be interested in being Mrs. Lotte but she was willing to let things evolve organically, which meant she'd give him six months to leave his wife and propose to her.

Tonight, she sensed he was full of anxiety.

She tucked her arm in his and he patted her wrist. They were both staring at a large canvas depicting a blurry wet street in the heart of New York City filled with yellow taxicabs, black umbrellas, and tall buildings.

"Why are you distracted?" she asked. "What's bothering you?"

"I'm getting dragged into possible court proceedings involving a brilliant intern of mine, Patricia, who was killed in Old Town," he acknowledged.

"What kind of court proceedings?"

"Her family is threatening to file a civil case and take my deposition if I don't settle up with them," said the senator. "I really don't want to submit to a deposition."

"How can they hold you accountable for what happened to her?" asked Helena. He shrugged. She then asked, "Were you sleeping with her?"

"Well, it just sort of happened a few times. Once or twice, three times, at the most."

Helena abhorred competition and was glad the intern was out of the picture. "It'll be all right," she assured him. She released Don's arm and stepped forward to study the painting up close.

The price tag read $26,000.

"I can always provide an alibi if you need one, you know," she said, looking at the picture. Even though they hadn't known one another at the time of Patricia's murder, Helena was willing to demonstrate her fidelity to Don if necessary.

He took note.

Before the night was over, the New York streetscape was wrapped and placed in the back of Don's Volvo. They'd drop it off at her place. She had the perfect place to hang it.

*Deputy* Sheriff Davis's brother Freddie shuffled along King Street. He wasn't dressed properly for the cold weather and clutched his shirt collar as though his hand was a makeshift scarf. He crossed the street, ascended a series of stone steps, and settled along the garden wall at the foot of Ramsay House, the city's visitor center.

His watery, bloodshot eyes darted in all directions.

Everything looked slightly out of focus, like a blurry canvas. Across the street, he saw the Burke & Herbert sign on the corner and the dining tables placed along the sidewalk that slanted toward the Potomac River.

A woman passed. He had spotted her earlier in the day down by the river. She was alone at the time and still appeared to be so. She was dressed in raggedy clothes and carried a grocery bag.

She stopped and looked in his direction. Their eyes met. He looked away toward the visitor center. When he finally dragged his weary eyes back to where she had been, no one was there.

He issued a sigh of relief. But suddenly she appeared at the entrance to the garden and mounted the stone steps, moving right toward him.

"What were you looking at?" She demanded.

*Where the hell did she come from?* Freddie asked himself. Then he sputtered, "I wasn't intending anything."

"I saw the way you were looking at me," she said. "It gave me the chills. If you don't tell me who you are, I'm going to call the police."

Freddie stood and took a step toward her. As he did, a wave of recognition hit him. *Could it be?* She looked like a well-known grifter who'd departed Old Town several years ago. *Was she back?*

"Cybil Shawl?" he asked, with a slight hesitation in his voice. "Is that you?"

He hadn't seen her for the better part of a decade. Actually, he thought she'd died. Once a fixture in the city's subterranean culture, she vanished one day into thin air.

The wave of recognition suddenly hit the woman as well. She nodded.

"Hello, Freddie."

"What brings you back here?" he asked.

"I've come to pay my respects," she said.

"Did someone die?" he asked.

"Yeah," Cybil replied. "The woman who died of poisoning. We got history."

"I don't know anything about her," he said. "My sister is warden in the jail where they're holding the suspect. She's a weird one, my sister says. Paid her to help con Mo Katz into taking her case. They pulled some kind of bait and switch."

"Is that so?" Cybil chuckled. "What else did she tell you?"

"Says she's dangerous," he said. "She has a cabal in the jail with a couple of other women, Robyn and Sam. She holds her cards close."

"OK," she said, then added, "Are you doing all right?"

Freddie smiled. "I am. I got a woman attorney doing some pro bono stuff with me. She knows it's hard to make it with a felony conviction on your record. She's helping me find my way. She's all about self-motivation and advancement."

"Who is she?

"Just — just somebody," he said cautiously. "She's handling something big for a special prosecutor type with the state. She cares more about me than my own sister does."

"All right, then," Cybil said. "You take care of yourself and stay out of trouble. Let that woman help you. Respect her. And don't go telling anyone you saw me today. You've got a loud mouth, Freddie, so keep it shut about me, okay?"

He nodded his assent.

*A* short distance away, Dickie Lewis strolled up Ramsay Alley behind the visitors' center. He'd been released from the jail after being charged with a misdemeanor for breaking into Friendship Firehouse. His suitcase had been returned to him and he pulled it behind him. The back doors of restaurants and shops opened into the stone-paved alley.

Workers stood against the brick walls smoking cigarettes and checking phone messages. Most spoke Spanish. Even though the weather was cool they mostly wore shirts, some vests, all happy to be outdoors cooling off from hot and stuffy interiors. Empty crates and trash cans filled with rubbish cluttered the narrow sidewalk.

Cars tucked against the curb, all pointed in the same direction on the one-way alley. Music played from someone's phone. The clatter of dinnerware and the chatter of dinner conversation wafted through the air. Around the corner, a police siren blared.

Dickie had enjoyed himself at the Friendship Firehouse the other night. He intended to return tonight. As he walked up the alley, he surveyed the contents of the crates and trash cans. He saw a potted plant and grabbed it.

No one expressed disapproval so he put it in the backpack hanging from his shoulder.

A girl turned the corner and headed toward the Torpedo Factory. She sported a pair of black boots and a long yellow flowing dress with an ornate red bodice decorated with tiny glistening mirrors. Her long hair dangled over her shoulders and back like seaweed. She had an earring in her nose.

They smiled at one another as they passed. He assumed she was an artist heading to her studio and wondered whether she was signaling with her eyes for him to follow her.

He stopped at the end of the alley. He was afraid to turn around, so he just froze in place for a long second. Finally his reluctance faded and he swiveled his head around. She was merrily prancing down the stone alleyway. He took a step in her direction.

As Tom Mann entered Josephine Brasserie & Bar across from the Alexandria courthouse, he thought it could have been the opening line of a bad joke. "A journalist, an author, and a private investigator walk into a bar…." Except here he was, joining Henry David McLuhan and Curtis Santana to talk about what, exactly?

Tom had left Ryan Long and Lucy Dallas after receiving a call from Curtis.

There was no question in Tom's mind that Ryan wanted to nail Mo Katz and that his motivation was less than pure. Tom didn't want to be any part of it. He didn't mind bringing down public officials; he just didn't want to be a part of someone else's agenda.

He'd been around long enough to know how the game was

played. Nobody really worked for the common good, whatever that was. Everyone had an agenda. And the bottom line was winning, regardless of merit, right, or righteousness. In Tom's mind, Ryan was one of the best in the game, which meant he was also one of the worst.

Plus, Ryan seemed overly anxious to be alone with Lucy Dallas, and Tom picked up a vibe that three was a crowd.

"So why're we here?" he asked upon joining the others.

Curtis filled him in about Henry David's writers' workshop. "We believe the manifesto you might receive was written as part of the writing workshop," Curtis explained to Tom.

Tom thought about Jimmy Breslin, the *New York Daily News* columnist who'd received letters in 1977 from the Son of Sam who terrorized New York City that summer. One of the letters read:

> *"Don't think because you haven't heard from (me) for a while that I went to sleep. No, rather, I am still here. Like a spirit roaming the night. Thirsty, hungry, seldom stopping to rest. I love my work. Now, the void has been filled."*

That was nearly 50 years ago. Tom, working on his high school newspaper at the time, was fascinated by the link between the murderer and the newspaper columnist. He got a chill down his spine as he realized that he was in a similar spot right now.

"What do you want from me?" he asked.

"We'd like you to appear as a guest at my workshop," Henry David answered.

Tom's eyes crawled from Henry David to Curtis.

"Rose Bud's getting his inspiration in the classroom and sharing it with you in the hope of getting you to publish his manifesto," Curtis said. "If you're in the classroom, his temptation to reach out to you in person is going to be too great to resist. You should do it."

Dayton Longmire walked north along the promenade from Robinson Landing. The frigid water of the Potomac River glistened to his right. In the distance, he faintly heard the sound of trucks traveling across the Wilson Bridge. Couples and small groups filled the walkway. Open parks and beckoning restaurants were ahead of him and to his left.

While Dayton avoided eye contact, he had an acute sense of his surroundings and the people with whom he was interacting. He possessed a preternatural ability to absorb the thoughts of those around him. And, while he wasn't looking directly at them, he sensed they were staring at him.

He had short cropped dark hair and a white beard. His face was long and drawn; his lips puckered; his brown eyes looked like glistening rocks on an exotic seashore. He was slender, with a big head, so he rendered a caricature-like appearance.

Dayton had mismanaged the portfolios of a small group of close friends who had invested their life savings in his venture capital firm. He pulled a Bernie Madoff on them. He wasn't proud of it, but he didn't have much choice. He'd made a series of business blunders and he had a luxurious lifestyle that had to be maintained.

He stopped in front of the building where Mo ran his law practice. He cupped his hands, raised them to his face, and expelled hot air into them as though blowing into a horn. Then he rubbed his palms together for warmth. He planned to step inside, unburden himself of his troubles, and seek counsel about the best way to proceed.

Dayton's troubles had been exacerbated by the unexpected death of Trudy Vine. She had been one of his clients. Under normal circumstances, he would not be talking to an attorney now. But he figured it was only a matter of time before the police came knocking on his door. Since he had swindled her, it was fair to inquire whether he had killed her to cover his own tracks.

Dayton approached the doorway when he heard a voice call his name. A Volvo along the curb chirped at the same instant, flashing its lights. He turned to see Helena waving at him. She was standing next to the car holding a man's arm as he pressed the fob.

Dayton recognized Senator Don Lotte, a conservative from Idaho or Utah or one of the Dakotas. He wasn't especially well versed on politicians but recognized Lotte because one of the senator's aides was a victim in the Rose Bud killing spree.

Helena avoided introductions as the couple approached.

She knew Trudy had employed Dayton as a financial advisor. She couldn't put her finger on why it was, but she didn't quite trust him.

"Are you going to be handling Trudy's estate now that she's been unexpectedly taken from us?" Helena asked Dayton.

*It was really none of her business*, thought Dayton, though he was hardly surprised by the question. After all, Trudy's investment portfolio was rumored to dwarf the value of her multimillion-dollar home near Windmill Hill Park.

"To be determined, to be determined," he smiled. He separated from the two of them, having lost the momentum to enter Mo's law office.

"You're…you're….hurting me," she whispered an hour later.

His grip relented.

She stumbled out of the room, stepping over the rose petals scattered across the tiles in the bathroom and the carpet in the bedroom.

"What is wrong with you?"

# Thirty-Four

*Diary entry from December 14.*

What happened last night?

I wanted to exercise control and dominion over her, as I had done with the others. Yet, at the last minute, I pulled back.

I don't know how I feel about that.

On the one hand, I'm relieved…sort of. By which I mean I wasn't caught for any kind of transgression.

On the other hand, I'm not relieved at all. It's pent up and waiting to explode. I need release.

Plus I'm a little disappointed in myself.

After all, I get a thrill from it all.

It's catapulted me into a higher stratosphere where my focus is crystal clear.

They call me a depraved lunatic but I don't feel that way at all.

I am cleansed and renewed each time I act.

Are they closing in on me?

I doubt it.

It felt good contacting the newspaper reporter and requesting that he publish portions of my manifesto. And I used my brain power in composing an entire piece based on a single word: "disenfranchised." That was no mean feat.

Yet I have strayed off the path.

Trudy Vine figured me out. As a result, she had to be silenced. I had no choice. She would have gone to the police, eventually.

Funny, isn't it?

The last person she visits ends up the first person accused of killing her. I could not have written that plot line if I'd tried.

*But it's brought Mo Katz into the equation.*

*That can't be a good thing. I fault Roxie Neele. She deliberately brought him into the mix.*

*Granted, his role is to defend her and not to solve the crimes. He hasn't been anointed by anyone to find me. The guy who is leading the investigation — the private investigator — isn't making any headway.*

*Still, I know a little about how the criminal justice system works. In building a defense for Roxie, Mo may stumble upon clues as to my identity.*

*Once the manifesto is published, I'm going to get away from this madness.*

*No one will notice my disappearance.*

*Time will pass.*

*The crimes will remain unsolved.*

*Eventually, they'll become a fleeting memory.*

*Maybe The Chronicle will write a 20-year retrospective in 2043 about the unsolved murder cases that once haunted and confounded Old Town.*

*I may feel unfulfilled today but maybe it's all for the best. They'll kill me if I end up in jail.*

*Fortunately, my gut tells me that I'm never going to see the inside of a jail.*

# Thirty-Five

As she lay on her bunk in the jail, Roxie recalled Trudy Vine's last visit to her house.

Trudy arrived with a box in her hand, a fact Roxie inadvertently shared with Mo. Fortunately, Roxie reflected, Mo didn't pick up on it.

The box contained three cupcakes. Originally there had been six. Trudy said she'd eaten three of them by the time she got to Roxie's house.

Roxie remembered the bottom of the cardboard box had smudges where the cupcakes had originally been placed, something like footprints.

Roxie made a separate batch of cupcakes when Trudy arrived. Trudy never ate a single one of those cupcakes. She did, however, eat a fourth cupcake from the box as she stood in the kitchen.

The cupcakes were a gift, she explained, a daily gift from an admirer. She couldn't stop eating them. They were addictive.

"Who's wooing you with pastries?" Roxie asked mischievously.

"Someone is trying to get nice with me, hoping a daily bribe of delicious cupcakes will buy my silence."

"Silence?" Roxie inquired, intrigued.

"Yes, I've drawn a connection between someone and the women who've been assaulted and murdered this past year."

"What sort of connection?"

"This person purchased flowers, incense, and candles at my pop-up," Trudy explained, referring to the stand that she ran on alternating Saturdays near the waterfront.

Like everyone else, Roxie had heard about the "calling cards" left behind by the killer, including roses, which had earned the killer the Rose Bud nickname.

Rather than purchase those items at a store, where the transaction could be traced and an identity easily revealed, Rose Bud had apparently purchased from street vendors using cash. A quick transaction without a traceable receipt carried a high likelihood that the vendor would never suspect those items would turn up at a crime scene.

"Who is this person of interest?"

"I can't tell you a name, but I'll give you the initials," Trudy said coyly. "D.L."

"Don't play games," Roxie chided. "You have to share the name and tell the police. Right now. Without further delay."

"He's too slick," cautioned Trudy. "If I go to the police, that culprit will slip right through their hands. I've got to do some more investigative work on my own. Maybe trick a confession out of the slime bag."

"What if another woman is victimized?" Roxie replied. "What about your own safety? You mustn't delay. Time is of the essence. You have to report this to the police today. And if they question your veracity, then share your information with Curtis Santana. He's been hired to help crack the case. He'll believe you."

Trudy frowned. "He's not my favorite. I don't have anything against him personally but I'm no fan of Sherry's."

"That's no reason to delay," Roxie scolded. "And quit eating those things!"

Trudy had finished the fourth cupcake and was reaching for the fifth. Only one remained in the box.

"Do you trust what's in those things? If the person who gave them to you is a killer, who's to say they aren't poisoned?"

Trudy burped. "They're *so* delicious!" Then she added, "Well, if I drop dead tonight, you'll be right. And it'll be your job to bring the culprit to justice." They both chuckled. "But seriously, mark my words. This one's slick and will easily slip out of the hands of the law. I'm going to have to devise a failsafe plan if justice is going to be done."

"Are you going to give me a name instead of those stupid initials or am I going to have to stay up all night trying to figure it out?" Roxie implored.

Trudy acquiesced and shared the name.

Roxie recoiled in horror. "For fuck's sake," she whispered.

Then Roxie had a thought. "The reason you haven't gone to the police is because you're blackmailing him, aren't you?" Trudy said nothing. Roxie continued, "You're up to your old game. When are you ever going to learn a lesson? He's not someone to play around with. He's liable to kill you if your surmise is right."

Trudy paid no attention and began nibbling on the sixth cupcake. "Why have you been so good to me?" she asked Roxie. "It's undeserved after what I put you through."

"Yeah, or so it would appear," Roxie conceded. "I had to put aside a lot of negativity to reconcile with you. But it was worth it.

"I suspected you had issues when we fought one another. You reminded me of myself. I used to suffer from a similar sort of self-abuse. In my case, it was drug and alcohol addiction.

"I didn't decide to help you because I'm a good person. I did it for me. I figured if I helped you, it was a roundabout way of helping myself. And it worked. I got cured."

Trudy laughed. "Who knew? I cured you."

Roxie said. "If you shatter, I'll lose a piece of myself. And, if that happens, who knows, maybe I'll slip back into the addiction that's waiting around the corner each morning when I awake."

They hugged.

"You saved my life," Trudy confided.

"And you saved mine. Just make sure nothing happens to you."

*R*oxie tucked a pillow behind her head. She'd intended to contact the police and give them the name that Trudy had shared with her. A series of unexpected events intervened, however, beginning with Trudy's death and culminating with Roxie's own arrest.

As a result, her plan shifted. Her present intent was to employ the services of the unwitting Mo Katz to expose the culprit and ensure that justice prevailed.

Her meditation was disturbed by an announcement that someone was there to see her. She rose from her bunk and sauntered to the attorney-client visiting room. Was Jimmy Wolfe back? Mo?

Although Roxie expected the unexpected, she was still surprised when she entered the room.

Cilia Roosevelt rose from one of the small plastic chairs to shake hands. Cilia looked very professional in a matching blue jacket and skirt, white blouse, and black and white bolo tie accentuated by a striking silver and turquoise clasp.

"You look like you're all duded up for a court hearing," Roxie observed. "You must be an attorney. Do you work for Mo?"

"I most certainly do not work for Mo Katz," Cilia laughed. She straightened her jacket and both women sat down. She introduced herself and explained that she worked for the Commonwealth of Virginia as part of a white-collar crime unit in the AG's office.

"I'd like to discuss your dealings with Mo Katz and whether he's engaged in any unethical conduct in your case. Your cooperation with our investigation into Mr. Katz could prove vital in obtaining a reduced sentence to the charges you're facing."

"Who sent you?" Roxie asked. "And don't tell me you're not at liberty to share that information with me. If you expect me to cooperate with you, I need to know to whom you're reporting."

Just then the metal door sprung open with a clang and Deputy Marcia Davis strode into the room. Cilia turned, wrinkling her brow.

"She's wearing a wire," Marcia said to Roxie. She quickly stepped forward and pulled open Cilia's suit jacket. Two more deputies entered the room and observed as Marcia pulled at Cilia's sleeve, exposing the wire.

"Stop it!" Cilia screamed.

"You can't conduct your business this way," Marcia shot back. "You come in here claiming that Roxie's attorney is crooked. Meanwhile, you're wearing an illegal wire. What's that make you?"

It didn't take long to break her. After all, Cilia Roosevelt wasn't a hardened criminal. She was simply an insecure subordinate eager to advance her career by doing her superior's bidding. As she sat alone with Deputy Davis, she thought maybe that had something to do with why Ryan chose her for this assignment.

"I shouldn't have done it," Cilia said contritely. "I knew all along that it was wrong. I doubted whether it was part of a law enforcement operation."

"I believe you're genuinely remorseful," observed Marcia, "and, for that reason, this incident won't be reported. It stays within these walls. I'm not reporting it up my chain of command."

Marcia's decision was a calculated one. If she took it up the chain, she'd be reprimanded for permitting a recording device to be brought into the cell during her watch. Plus, someone would want to know how she knew Cilia was wearing a wire in the first place. She was reluctant to admit her loudmouth brother was the snitch. In fact, she didn't like publicizing the fact that she and Freddie were related by blood.

"Out of curiosity," Marcia asked, "who put you up to this?"

Cilia told her. "Ryan Long."

After Cilia left the detention center and sensing opportunity, Marcia called Long. She described the encounter in the jail. "Your tactics are way out of line," she accused him. "What are you trying to do?"

"I'm investigating her counsel," Ryan confided. "I have authorization from the highest level. Mo Katz is corrupt. I appreciate your discretion so as not to interfere with an ongoing inquiry."

"It'll cost you," she said. "My silence, that is."

"Okay," he said after a moment's hesitation.

His willingness to submit to her demand confirmed Marcia's suspicion that Ryan's investigation wasn't sanctioned by higher-ups. He had gone rogue.

Once she had laid out her terms and Ryan agreed to them, he asked: "Out of curiosity, was Roxie Neele present when you discovered the wire?"

"No," Marcia lied. "It was detected when Ms. Roosevelt sought admission to the jail."

She smiled slyly to herself. Ryan was afraid Roxie would share the episode with Mo and that he, in turn, would take action. There was no downside to lying. Cilia wasn't going to share the truth with Ryan. She probably had gone underground to avoid any contact with him. And, despite her personal feelings toward Roxie, Marcia felt responsible for the safety of the women under her watch. Ryan Long gave her the creeps. If she acknowledged that Roxie had seen the wire strapped to Cilia's arm, Marcia was pretty sure Ryan would find a way of hurting Roxie.

The last thing anyone needed was another Rikers Island.

Marcia visited Roxie's cell. A short while later, Roxie instructed Robyn and Sam to contact Mo's office.

# Thirty-Six

The call interrupted his work, but Curtis was glad he took it. In fact, he'd had a premonition he'd be back in touch with those two women. "Appreciate you," he said as the conversation with Robyn and Sam ended. Tucking the phone in his coat pocket, he initiated tonight's business, paying a house call.

A knock on his door precipitated Dayton Longmire's decision to destroy the paperwork. Whoever was on the other side wasn't here on a social call, he felt sure.

He started to the door, then pivoted 180 degrees and dashed to the back door. It opened but the storm door jammed. He slammed the metal frame with his palm and kicked the bottom of the door with the tip of his shoe, hard. The storm door wouldn't budge.

Another rap on the door.

"Dayton, it's Curtis Santana," called the voice on the other side of the door. "Sorry to drop by unannounced like this but I was in the neighborhood. I'm in your writing class. We've been paired by the professor. Is this a bad time? I can come by later."

A second later the front door opened.

"Hey," Dayton said. "Sorry about that. I actually avoid answering doors these days. You can't be too careful." They shook hands and Dayton invited Curtis to step inside.

"No, no, I don't need to be invited in," Curtis apologized. "I emailed but you must not have seen it. You would have been perfectly within your rights to refuse to open the door. Maybe we could go out and grab a beer?"

Thirty minutes later, they were seated at the Blackwall Hitch bar overlooking the Potomac River pier.

While waiting for their drinks, Dayton quickly scanned his emails. He didn't recognize Curtis from the class. However, his anxiety eased when he found the communication from Professor McLuhan about matching an online student with an in-person student to create a collaborative atmosphere.

He also found an email from Curtis about meeting one another.

Still, a strange mixture of relief and paranoia filled him.

On Curtis's part, the meeting was a fishing expedition precipitated by two factors. One, Dayton's name was on the list that Roxie provided to Mo, and two, Curtis had seen him hesitate outside of Mo's office acting as though something was compelling him to enter. If Helena and Lotte hadn't happened upon the scene, Curtis felt Dayton would have stepped inside. *Why?*

"What did you think about that recent writing exercise where we shared our thoughts about being disenfranchised?" Curtis asked. "It resonated with me. I've been on the outside most of my life."

"I thought it was a waste of time," Dayton replied. "I didn't sign up for stream of consciousness exercises. I'm looking for structure. If this continues, I'm dropping out." Then, to be polite, he asked, "What did you write about?"

"Death," Curtis replied. "It's the ultimate form of disenfranchisement."

Dayton laughed.

"Like those young women who've been killed in Old Town over the past year," Curtis continued. "Same with Trudy Vine. They're here one minute and then they're gone. At best, they're a memory."

Dayton kept perusing emails as Curtis spoke because it enabled him to avoid eye contact. "I don't think death is a form of disenfranchisement," he said. "I think you misinterpreted the word. Plus, those women are all very much part of our discourse. People are trying to solve the Rose Bud murders. And there's a suspect in the Vine case, so it'll go to trial and be a subject of discussion."

"Did you know her?" Curtis asked.

Dayton lowered the phone and raised his eyes. "Who?"

"Trudy Vine."

"Yeah, she was a professional acquaintance."

"How so?"

"In financial matters. I do a lot — sorry — I *did* a lot of her investments. I handled her inheritance, invested it in various stock and bond accounts, and got her interested in a few REITs, stuff like that." Curtis appeared baffled. "Real estate investment trusts," Dayton explained.

"Oh. Are you still going to do that for her beneficiaries?"

"It remains to be seen. She has children. They've already been in touch with me. I'll have to see how it goes."

"I hope you don't mind my asking," Curtis said. "I'm not trying to pry into private financial affairs or anything like that."

"No problem," Dayton said. "What do you do when you're not attending writing workshops?"

"I'm a private investigator," Curtis answered. "I was out of the business for a few years, accompanying Mo Katz to the U.S. Attorney's Office when he did a stint there. Now we're both back in private practice."

"Do you work with Katz?" Dayton asked in surprise.

"Yeah. Why do you ask?"

"No reason really," Dayton replied. "Just curious. I mean, he's representing the woman accused of killing Trudy."

"Do you miss her?" asked Curtis.

"That's an odd question," Dayton replied, suddenly annoyed. "We were professional acquaintances. What's your game, anyway, Mr. Santana? I don't think it's coincidental that you dropped by. First you asked if I knew Trudy. Then you want to know what I did for her. And now you're asking whether I miss her. What are you really after? I hope you're not implying that I had anything to do with her murder."

"Sorry," Curtis apologized. "As you said a minute ago, they

155

already have a suspect in jail, Roxie Neele."

"Roxie isn't guilty," Dayton announced. "I've known about her for years and I've formed opinions about her."

"What kind of opinions?"

"She's no murderer," Dayton answered curtly. Clearing his throat, he added, "And now, if you don't mind, I think our conversation is over."

When Dayton returned to his apartment, he immediately went to the cabinet in his study, the one under lock and key, and checked its contents: two books of financial management accounts, one accurate and the other fabricated.

Fortunately, from the looks of things, no one had meddled with either of them.

He closed the cabinet, placed the key on the tray from which he'd retrieved it, and sat down in a worn leather chair beside a table on which a dimly lit lamp shone. He regretted not having the chance to talk to Mo the other night.

Curtis called Mai Lin from the car. "Any luck?"

"You've got it right," she said. She told Curtis about the two books of financial records. "He was cooking Trudy's books," she said.

"I hope he doesn't figure out you were there," said Curtis.

"Not a chance," she replied proudly.

"He was outside Mo's door last night," Curtis said.

"Maybe he wanted to confess," Mai said. "After all, if he cooked the books, he's a suspect in the case, isn't he?" Then she added, "I wonder if anyone else knows what Dayton's been doing? If you know that man's secret, you could get him to do anything you wanted done."

# Thirty-Seven

***Diary entry from December 16.***

*I don't like this, not one little bit.*

*I considered burning this diary earlier today. I'm loath to do so, of course. After all, records need to be retained for when I receive the recognition I so rightfully deserve.*

*These scribblings need to be preserved for posterity. They will become more valuable with the passage of time. I just read about an ongoing battle to publish the writings of one of those school shooters. Can you imagine: People fighting over the right to publish my work!*

*Despite my mounting anxiety, I'm not going to destroy anything. I just have to be smart and stay one step ahead of the competition.*

*Curtis Santana is interviewing people. Where did he get their names? What's he after? And what are they telling him? For the longest time, he was a nobody doing nothing. Now suddenly he's making moves. Is he getting instructions from Katz?*

*Some of the malcontents that he's interviewing are my subjects. I've discovered their weaknesses and I've threatened to expose them. In exchange for my silence, I demand their fealty. That paradigm has enabled me to maintain command and control.*

*If someone learned of my little mousetrap, that someone could disrupt and disturb my universe. That would not be good.*

# Thirty-Eight

Henry David enjoyed class.

"There are lies everywhere, all the time, at all levels," he lectured.

He'd decided to teach remotely today. Some students sat in the classroom, watching him on the big screen, as did the guest speaker. Others were on the screen, their images in rectangular boxes next to his own.

"Parents lie to children," he continued, "and children lie to parents. We lie to one another and to ourselves. The media lies to us as do our political institutions and even our houses of worship.

"We all project a false reality just like the one I'm projecting on this screen. No one is exactly who they claim to be. We all delude ourselves."

He paused and studied the faces on his computer screen. Some of those in the room appeared to agree with him, while others were doubtful.

"But that's okay," he said cheerfully, "because it's what holds us together. The lie's the glue. Without it, we unravel. With it, we hope, which may itself be an illusion."

"All of which is a way of introduction for today's special guest, newspaper reporter and editor Tom Mann."

Tom waved from his seat. Everyone laughed politely. "Fake news" had become a permanent and accepted part of the public discourse. And to many people it seemed to apply to much of the journalistic trade. Public trust in the media was low. Most of the students didn't even read *The Chronicle* or any other newspapers, for that matter. Newspapers were for the 50-plus generation, particularly those who'd come of age reading about Watergate.

True, readership surged after Tom had begun reporting about

Rose Bud, but that phenomenon would recede after the murderer was caught and brought to justice.

Tom rose and stepped to a podium in the front of the room, placing his open iPad upon it.

"I don't share that view," he said. "I don't believe that the lie serves any useful purpose.

"You have to seek truth and expose the lie. That's the journalist's true mission. That's my mission. That's the standard to which most journalists aspire. The term 'fake news' is nothing more than an attempt to discredit the press to allow politicians to get away with their own lies."

But the students in the class weren't there to listen to him pontificate on journalism, not once they knew that this was the guy covering the murder spree.

"Are you going to print Rose Bud's manifesto?" one of them interrupted.

"Do you think you're being manipulated by a murderer?" asked another.

"What ethical considerations will you undertake in reporting about Rose Bud?" bellowed a third.

Other questions appeared in the chat box. They read:

"There's a rumor that you're thinking about printing Rose Bud's manifesto. Is that true? Are you succumbing to a terrorist's demands?"

"What if Rose Bud is emboldened by seeing his name in print and commits more crimes? Does that make you an accomplice to murder?"

Mann read the questions from the chat box out loud. Then he said, "It's true that I have been contacted by the killer."

*That* was news. Stunned silence greeted him. He continued:

"And I have been asked to print a document that he refers to as his manifesto.

"Right now, my inclination is to print the manifesto if it

means he'll stop his murderous rampage. But I worry it could have the opposite effect. If it compels him to escalate his demands and commit additional crimes, then I've exacerbated a problem rather than ameliorated it."

"Has he actually sent you the manifesto?" asked one of the students in the class.

Mann replied, "I'm trying to figure out a way to communicate with Rose Bud."

"So you have the manifesto in your possession?"

"I'm not going to get into the details of my contact," he replied.

An email arrived in his personal account that didn't simultaneously appear in the chat: "Are you coordinating your efforts with law enforcement?" The sender's address was a few random letters and numbers.

Mann surveyed the faces on the screen, both those online and in class.

"I haven't enlisted the assistance of law enforcement," he said. "That's why I don't want to share details with you. You never know who else is listening. I will tell you that I have no intention of editing the manifesto if it's published, not even any typographical errors.

"When was the last time you heard from Rose Bud?" another student asked.

"Yeah, again, I'm not going to get into any of that. Who? What? When? Where? Why? Those are the cardinal questions of the journalist's trade. But I'm not going there right now. Sorry."

Another email arrived from the mysterious sender. It read: "Dark Star Park, midnight Saturday."

*D*own the street at the Commonwealth Attorney's Office, Dash Low, a senior prosecutor, waited for the third ring before taking a call. She was tall and regal in appearance, with a stern face and harshly chiseled facial features. Long black braided hair with gold and red accents fell to the small of her back.

"Hello, this is Dash Low."

"Dash, it's Mo Katz."

Dash had been assigned Roxie's case, so the call from Katz wasn't unexpected.

Dash once worked with Mo in the U.S. Attorney's Office. Though they never discussed it, Dash knew Mo wasn't impressed with her legal talent. Now she was anxious for the opportunity to show it to him.

She'd been told by her assistant that he was calling. That's why she delayed answering. It was important for him to know who was in charge.

"Mo Katz," she said respectfully. "To what do I owe the honor?"

Privately, she had told others he was a phony, arrogant, and overrated. Privately, she wished he'd asked her to join him in private practice when he departed the U.S. Attorney's Office. Right now, she salivated at the thought of defeating him in the courtroom.

"We're overdue for a pretrial discussion about Roxie Neele's case," he said.

"I'm going to take you down," she suddenly whispered into the phone.

"I'm sorry?"

"You heard me, Mo. I'm going to take you down in this trial," she said more firmly.

Dash hadn't planned the outburst, but she'd had little else on her mind during the past few days. The venom burst from her like blood spouting from a pin prick.

"I'm not on trial," Mo replied calmly. "Let's keep it civil. You do yourself a disservice if you make this personal. And with all humility, I caution you that if you do — make it personal, that is — you'll lose the trial because of it."

"Don't lecture me," she said with hostility. "You're the one representing a killer, not that you care. Roxie Neele took an innocent life. It's all a game to you, isn't it? You probably enjoy freeing felons to walk the street. I don't know how you can live with yourself. You're a man without a conscience. I feel sorry for you."

"The more you obsess over me, the easier it's going to be for me to get an acquittal for my client," he commented.

Mo sensed the confidence in her voice, as well as the delusion. In the moment, he considered something that no attorney in their right mind would broach. In fact, it was grounds for malpractice.

Fortunately, she beat him to the punch.

"Let's dispense with the preliminary hearing and the motions and go straight to trial," she said. "It's Christmastime and the docket's clear. We're ready to go on our side. We'll have the case wrapped up before New Year's."

He couldn't believe his good fortune but disguised his elation by saying, "I don't know. That's crazy talk."

While he was eager to accept, he worried that an enthusiastic endorsement would lead her to withdraw the offer.

"It might advantage your client," she added, changing her tactic in order to sweeten the pot. "The more time passes, the more evidence we're going to amass."

"Hmmm."

"Scared to step into the ring?"

"I'm not scared, but you should be."

"Don't trash talk me, Katz."

"Well," he said, "since you sound serious, I'm duty bound to present it to my client despite the fact I think it's crazy. I'm going to recommend that she reject it, of course. We haven't fully developed our defense. Plus, there are serious questions about the admissibility of the evidence seized during the search of her house."

Dash countered: "We could do motions after the jury is sworn in and then roll into the case."

Mo's phone vibrated. He glanced at the incoming number. His thoughts were momentarily distracted. Then he continued, "That doesn't afford me any time to strategize if the motions aren't successful. I'm all about 'justice delayed is justice denied' but this is downright ridiculous."

Mo referred to the words that appear over the door to the federal courthouse in Alexandria, home of the so-called "rocket docket."

"Let me know your client's decision soonest," Dash said. "There's no reason we can't get started by next week."

"Okay. I'll present it to Roxie. But, as I said, I think it's nuts and I'll recommend she reject it." He added, "By the way, you didn't send anyone to the jail to question my client, did you?"

"Now you're the one who sounds crazy," she replied. "Of course not."

"I didn't think so, but just checking," he said.

"Did something happen at the jail?" she questioned.

"No," he lied.

"Okay," she concluded. "Let me know what your client wants to do."

Dash issued a sigh of relief when the call ended. The last thing she wanted was an incident that might cause Mo to reject her offer. In spite of what he said, she knew he relished the thought of going to trial now. His phony reluctance didn't mask his arrogance. But she was onto him, and this time she was sure she could outdo him in the courtroom.

# Thirty-Nine

While walking toward the jail in the Eisenhower Valley, Mo glanced at the missed call notice that had arrived during his conversation with Dash. He recognized the area code for Madison, Wisconsin.

Part of him didn't want to return the call. He wasn't anxious to hear more of Martha's biting commentary. On the other hand, it could be a call from Abby or from a doctor about her condition. Against his better judgment, he returned the call.

"Hi, Mo, it's Mai."

"Where are you?" he inquired in great surprise.

"Madison," she replied. "I flew out here to stay with Abby. I'm no longer at the U.S. Attorney's Office, so I'm untethered. Plus, my consultant work for you can be done remotely."

Mo smiled.

Mai, Curtis, Sherry, and a few others were members of an inseparable team. The nucleus holding them together was built of mutual respect, admiration and love. Sure, there was professional rivalry between them, but never animus, only support and kinship. Other members of the group included Mai's husband, David Reese, and, of course, Abby.

Spite had no place in their house.

"I'm staying in her room," Mai explained. "They have a little suite for us. Katie's here too. I'm taking her to a park this afternoon. Shayne's mother is providing her with special tutoring since she's not in kindergarten now."

"How is Martha?" Mo asked reluctantly.

"She's fine," Mai said. "If there was any tension between Martha and Abby, it's been eliminated by this injury. They are getting along like two sisters who need each other. Right now, it's Abby who needs the tending. Martha is a great nurse."

"Thanks for all you're doing," Mo told Mai. "Is Abby there? Can you put her on? And what about your own family?"

She addressed his last question first. "David obsesses over things and sometimes that drives me nuts. I needed a break, to be honest. Otherwise I don't know if our relationship could survive."

She reflected an instant and added, "He's a great father, however, and he's better at parenting than me. In a way, I'm being selfish by leaving my husband and son to fend for themselves in my absence, I suppose."

"I think you're making a sacrifice for Abby and I'm grateful," Mo interjected.

"Abby's in physical therapy," Mai continued. "The injury was a lot more serious than first believed. Don't ask me to explain, but she tore or ruptured some important ligaments in her leg. I mean, you don't know how complicated the human body is until you injure it. She's healing but it's going slowly."

"And how are you doing?"

"It's like a girls-only holiday. Abby, Martha, Katie, and me. It's all good."

Mo felt a wave of relief. With Mai on the scene, worrying about Abby was off his plate and he didn't feel so bad by not being in constant contact.

"Abby said to say hello," Mai continued. "She hasn't called because she knew you'd be *in the zone* for Roxie's trial."

She didn't tell Mo that Abby was still a little angry at his inattentiveness toward her. Saying *in the zone* was code for being oblivious to other people, i.e. Abby.

Mai didn't share a couple of other things.

The real reason she was in Wisconsin was because Abby begged her to come because she and Martha were not getting along.

"Well, you're a real sweetheart," Mo said.

"Yeah, I know," Mai agreed without hesitation. "Good luck with Roxie. Let me know if I can help."

"I'll set up a Teams meeting whenever I get together with Curtis so you can be part of the conversation," Mo said.

"Thanks," she said. "I'm privileged to be part of the trial prep." Then she asked, "Where are you, and what are you doing?"

"I'm walking to the jail to visit Roxie," he said. "I just passed Henry Street. I have some unfinished business to tend to with my client."

# Forty

"You're really all about deception and half-truths," Mo said.

He and Roxie sat in the tiny plastic chairs in the attorney-client meeting room. He'd played along with her antics from the start, never having bought into what she was selling. Truth be told, he had given as well as he'd got. He'd performed his own brand of deception. But now was the time for reckoning.

"From the first day I visited you, you've played some elaborate game with me," he continued. "You tried to trick me into representing you. You misrepresented your role in Trudy's murder. And you misled me about the nature of the people on the list you gave me. Why did you do all of those things?"

"The best offense is a good defense," she replied.

"That's not a good enough answer. Nobody professes guilt when they're innocent. That's just plain nuts."

"Maybe we should go with an insanity defense," she snorted.

"That's hardly an answer either."

Roxie scrunched her face. "Okay, maybe I went about it the wrong way."

He shook his head, seemingly in disgust, rose, grabbed his coat and scarf, and headed to the phone from which he would inform the sheriff's deputies that he was ready to depart. The deputies would automatically release the latch on the two heavy metal doors that sealed the chamber's occupants from the outside world.

And he would be gone from her life forever.

"Wait!" she protested. "Hear me out. Please!"

He held the phone in his hand, his back to her.

"D.L. Those are the initials that Trudy gave me. Those initials identify Rose Bud. She told me the day she died."

She spoke so fast it was as though her words shot out of a gun.

Mo replaced the phone on the wall stand, his back still facing her. "Those are initials," he said.

"I know what they are. It's all she gave me. If I'd had a name, I might not have needed to solicit your help. Those initials are a clue. And you know how to put clues together. If I'd gone to the authorities with initials, they would have laughed at me.

"Furthermore, Trudy led me to believe that Rose Bud's one of *them*. People at the table never think Judas is breaking bread with them. The culprit's a charlatan."

He turned.

She continued, "I went mad when I got arrested. They didn't just have it wrong. They had it backwards. I didn't commit any murder. Just the opposite. I possessed a clue. I knew things about the killer responsible for everything that's happened.

"Then I got to thinking. Other things being equal, I'd be safe inside these walls. Deputy Davis is a bitch but she's protective of her wards. So I decided to use the situation to my advantage, cast a web, and solicit outside help to expose Trudy's killer and Rose Bud's identity. It's all pieces of the same whole cloth.

"I immediately thought of you. After all, I'd never forgotten what you did to me in that assault case."

"What did you expect me to do?" he asked.

"Perform some kind of magic trick that would implicate the true killer and bring him to justice."

"That's crazy."

"No, it's not crazy, and stop saying that! I'm not crazy, Mr. Katz. I made a fortune from nothing. I've anonymously given back to my community. I am a force for good."

She rose from her chair and stood in the center of the chamber, a single light beaming down on her from an incessantly humming fixture.

"If this is a game, let's make it a real contact sport. Let's figure out how to expose the son of a bitch. There's nothing I'd like to do more than put Lady Justice front and center."

Mo returned to his chair and dropped his coat and scarf on the seat. "The prosecution made me an offer," he said abruptly. "They want to go to trial immediately."

"This is perfect!" she said. "You have to accept her offer. Let's go to trial, expose Rose Bud, and prevent any other woman from suffering at the hands of that monster."

"It's a gamble," Mo said. "A jury could find you guilty."

"That'll never happen, Mr. Katz. You're too good. I'll be acquitted. And somehow or other you'll capture Rose Bud."

*"D.L.?"* Curtis asked, his voice steeped in frustration. He sat with Mo in the law office on Wales Alley; Mai was on a Teams call on the large screen in the conference room.

"What are we supposed to do with that?" asked Curtis. "It's not a clue. It only adds to the confusion. Are they initials for a first and last name? Or a nickname? Two letters in a last name?"

Seated on a sofa in Martha's living room, Mai wrote the initials in large capital letters on a legal pad and studied them pensively.

She said, "Most of the people on the list that Roxie gave you have those initials, either front-way or backwards or a mixture. Maybe she wasn't providing you with the names of people who might be presented to the jury as a potential witness. Maybe she gave you a list of the prime suspects."

"I've interviewed some of those people already," Curtis noted. "There are things that could connect them to Trudy's murder. But we need a lot more time to connect those dots."

While Mo didn't feel the names provided by Roxie were those of prime suspects, he surmised all along that there was another reason she wanted Mo and his team to look into their backgrounds. Perhaps they would find a common thread connecting those names to Rose Bud, he thought.

The conversation shifted to the message that Tom received during Henry David's writing workshop.

"It seems to have worked," Curtis said. "We think it came from Rose Bud. It could be a copycat but we'll have to take that chance."

"What's the next step?" inquired Mai.

"Rose Bud requested a meeting at Dark Star Park in Rosslyn," Curtis explained, referring to the small park on the edge of the Arlington community. "I don't know whether it's a drop spot or a meeting spot, but Tom's going to go there at the appointed hour."

"Will there be backup?" she asked.

"Light surveillance at a comfortable distance from the site."

"Damn, I wish I was there," Mai said.

Curtis nodded. "It is your sort of gig."

"What if they nab Rose Bud?" she asked, studying Mo's image on her computer screen. "Will you be able to persuade the prosecution to drop the charges against Roxie? How do you prove the poisoning is connected to the murder spree?"

"Good questions," Mo said. "If Rose Bud is apprehended, I hope he'll confess to the poisoning. Right now, we only have Roxie's word for it based on her conversation with Trudy. There is no evidence that directly ties Rose Bud to the poisoning."

"Plus," Curtis added, "you've got Roxie's comment about the initials D.L. What if we apprehend someone with different initials? Does Roxie's statement become exculpatory evidence if the suspect denies culpability and pursues a jury trial?"

"Wow!" exclaimed Mai. "I didn't think of that. Those initials are kind of a double-edged sword, aren't they? On the one hand, they provide a clue as to the culprit's identity. But if a suspect is arrested with different initials, what happens?"

Mo shrugged. "We're getting ahead of ourselves. Let's see where the evidence takes us. Things unfold in their own unexpected ways."

"Are you joining Curtis at Dark Star Park?" Mai asked.

"No," Mo answered. "The smaller the group the better. This is about apprehending Rose Bud. I leave it to Curtis and Sherry."

Before they ended the call, Mo asked how things were going in Madison.

"It's getting better all the time," Mai replied.

As evening fell, Mo headed back home on foot. The air was unseasonably warm, although he occasionally stepped through pockets of coolness that felt like wading into invisible currents of cold water.

Day evaporated into night. The moon and stars gradually made their appearance, having hung out in the sky waiting for darkness to reveal their glow. No single force controlled the zone between daylight and nightfall. The sun king had raced off but the moon had not yet introduced itself in the sky.

Birds that had decided to stay the winter rather than migrate further south grew quiet in the holly bushes in which they sought refuge for the night. Commuters transited from work to home and the night crew prepared to head out to work, repairing roads and cleaning offices.

Dusk was an interloper, disturbing both day and night, belonging to neither, invading each one's space, simultaneously arriving and departing.

Headlights sparkled from the fronts of cars, street lamps ignited, and lights flickered inside homes and shops, some turning on and others off.

While walking, Mo meditated on the case.

He was in a dangerous spot. Trials weren't intended to catch bad guys. Roxie expected him to do the impossible. When the jury suddenly realized the wrong person was in the dock and that the guilty party was running around free there was unlikely to be a eureka moment.

Mo couldn't figure out exactly how to use the trial process to put shackles on Rose Bud. Tumblers spun around in his head while he walked, unable to find the winning combination.

*Had Roxie overestimated his ability? Had he tricked himself by agreeing to commence trial proceedings on such short notice?*

As much as he hated to say it, was he being *delulu*? The term that had caught fire on social media circled in his brain: delusional.

By the time he was home, the streets were blanketed in black. The interior lights of homes emitted warmth and safety. A bus rumbled in the distance and the horn of a Metro train blared as the train arrived at the King Street station a half dozen blocks away.

Fortunately, Ryan Long wasn't sitting on the stoop tonight.

Mo ascended the steps to the townhouse, threw his bag on an empty chair on the porch, and settled into the chair beside it.

No lights were on inside. The house felt cold and he hadn't even opened the door. Abby and Katie were in Madison. Shayne was back at school. There was no one for him to come home to.

He glanced down the street and noticed that his recently restored Karmann Ghia looked amiss. The cloth roof appeared to be ripped. Scratches seemed to stretch across the side panel on the passenger's side.

"Damn," he muttered as he went over to inspect the car.

Someone had vandalized his vintage car and written graffiti on it. "BASTARD" was emblazoned on the trunk in foam letters. An egg had been thrown against the front windshield, the shell lying in the street.

"Hey," said a voice. Katz turned. It was Shayne.

"I thought you were back at school," he replied, caught by surprise.

"I decided to hang out until Abby and Katie get back," she said. "I appreciated our conversation the other night. You helped me, maybe more than you know. The least I can do is stick around until everyone gets back home. I'm sure it's lonely in this house with just you in it."

She looked at the car.

"I saw it like this when I arrived," she said. "I went online while I was waiting and found a place on Wisconsin Avenue that can repair it. If you like, I can drive it back to school and leave it at the shop. They said they'd get to it right away."

"Thanks for the offer, but no," Katz said. "We'll let it sit here for a few days, like a message board. Maybe others want to chime in and express their views."

"Maybe it's just the work of one single deranged person and no one else was going to contribute any additional 'messages' to you," Shayne said.

"Why do you think that?" Mo replied.

"I ran into a woman at the Metro station," Shayne explained. "She looked weird, that's all."

"Weird? How?"

"I don't know," she replied. "I shouldn't have said anything. Maybe it was just my imagination."

Mo made grilled cheese sandwiches for Shayne and himself. As she had learned by now, grilled cheese and spaghetti from a can were the limits of his culinary talents.

They sat at the square table and talked until two in the morning. Mo was amazed at how many of Abby's traits found expression in her daughter. But he shouldn't have been. She had inherited the best of her mother. Silently, he wished Shayne's father had lived to see her grow and mature.

They didn't talk at all about Roxie's case or about Rose Bud, but Mo couldn't stop thinking about them. Maybe he didn't have to turn the tables on the real murderer in the courtroom. Maybe he only had to steal the spotlight. Maybe that would enrage Rose Bud. And maybe that would bring him into the public view if efforts failed at Dark Star Park.

After Shayne retired for the night, Mo found his tablet. He needed to escape from the madness surrounding him and decided to visit the public library catalog in search of a good e-book. He typed in "Agatha Christie."

*A*cross town, a shabby figure moved furtively through the night toward Ivy Hill cemetery, where she would sleep among the dead. Cybil Shawl carried a burlap bag over her shoulder, full of groceries, including a half-filled carton of eggs.

# Forty-One

Dark Star Park perched on a crest at the edge of Rosslyn adjacent to a concrete ribbon of Route 50 that snaked its way along a rivulet cut through the terrain. The narrow park contained three large orbs near one another that looked like giant bowling balls ready to roll down the hill. The orbs formed a perfect alignment for the spring equinox.

Tonight held no such magic. Midnight found the streets surrounding the park deserted. Traffic along Route 50 was sparse, cars coming out of the District of Columbia from the Roosevelt Bridge swirling past the Iwo Jima Memorial with their lights slicing through the night.

The only consistent sound — a dull hum — emanated from a lone overhead street lamp.

Tom edged toward the orbs as he ascended the crest of the park from Rosslyn's high-rise interior.

As he stood next to the largest orb, he spied an envelope tucked in at its base. He opened it and removed three pieces of typed paper. He could read it clearly from the light of the street lamp.

A car swooshed by him along Route 50, its lights cutting a block of space in the dark. He glanced up and caught the headlamps in his eyes and raised the papers like a visor.

The car passed.

He went back to studying the words on the papers, glancing at each page individually before sliding the papers back in their envelope and returning to his car.

Route 50 dipped like a chasm through the terrain where the park was located, a stream of concrete that divided the landscape.

On the other side of the six-lane highway Rose Bud sat on a

bench, watching.

The killer had debated the propriety of being here, concluding it was safe to do so. It seemed unlikely Tom would contact the authorities, and Rose Bud needed to be certain that Tom found the envelope.

The killer sat motionless as a shadow on the bench on Arlington Boulevard as Tom descended one of Rosslyn's hilly streets. Then the shadow rose and walked toward the Iwo Jima Memorial, where a car was parked on N. Nash Street.

Lights sparkled on the other side of the Potomac River and the Washington Monument glistened, its granite tip scratching the sky.

Rose Bud opened the car door. The interior lights had been switched off, so the cabin did not illuminate as the shadow slipped into the driver's seat and released a deep sigh filled with writer's anxiety.

*Will Tom like the prose? Does the Manifesto hang together? Is it coherent? Will Tom print it? How would readers react? Will the paper sell out as a collector's item? Might it be reprinted in a collection of American prose alongside political and literary greats?*

Suddenly, lights emerged in two directions, one in front and the other behind. Two cars coming from opposite directions passed by at the same moment. Rose Bud stopped breathing for an instant.

The cars whipped by and continued their journey.

A quarter mile away, Curtis observed Dark Star Park through binoculars from the 14th floor of a high-rise residential building. The envelope had already been tucked behind the concrete ball when he arrived. Other than Tom, no one approached the park during their watch.

Curtis never saw the shadow on the other side of Route 50. He wondered whether Mai, with her keen eye for detail, would have seen something if she'd been with him.

*I*n the morning, Rose Bud went online and scanned the major stories in *The Chronicle*. The headline under the masthead read:

## TRIAL SET IN VINE POISONING CASE

To the surprise of courtroom watchers and students of the criminal justice system, the trial of Roxanna Neele will commence Tuesday. She stands accused of murdering Trudy Vine. Rarely, if ever, has a date been set so quickly for a first degree murder case, which carries a maximum penalty of life in prison.

"In most cases, this would be grounds for malpractice," commented veteran criminal defense attorney Jimmy Wolfe.

Neele is represented by former U.S. Attorney Mo Katz, considered one of the preeminent criminal defense attorneys in the metropolitan area.

"I guess people are making an exception because Mo Katz is defense counsel," Wolfe said, "although, in my opinion, the man's clearly making a mistake in this case."

Katz had no comment when asked whether the rapid progress of the trial was a mistake on his part or a deliberate ploy to catch the prosecution flat-footed and win an acquittal for his client.

Rose Bud scrolled through the online paper a second time. There was no mention of Rose Bud and the Manifesto. In frustration, he texted Tom from a burner phone: Did you get the Manifesto? When are you planning to print it? Within minutes, he received a reply.

Mann: I got it, regrettably. It's a total piece of garbage. I already threw it out. Did you really think I would expose my readers to a piece of crap like that?

Rose Bud: You're kidding, right?

Mann: I'm as serious as a heart attack. You have a penchant for the over-dramatic. The Manifesto is a joke. You're many things, and none of them are kind. You're a racist. Your idea of the "world order" is absurd. And your emphasis on "me" tells me you're more than an egomaniac. You're a sociopath of the worst kind.

Rose Bud: You'll have blood on your hands!

Mann: I expected you to claim that. Of course, your accusation is patently false. I feel no obligation to publish your work because you're pointing a gun at someone's head. Continue with your ruthless rampage until the authorities catch you and put you in a cage.

Rose Bud: If you're not going to print it, I want it back.

Mann: Get this through your thick head: I've destroyed it. No one is ever going to see it. And, since it was written on a typewriter, I hope you didn't make a photocopy before you sent it. It would be gratifying to know that no one will ever get to read it.

Rose Bud: I'm coming after you!

Mann: Can't wait. So looking forward to kicking your ass, you psycho!

*That* wasn't expected.

Rose Bud sat in stunned silence. Accolades had been expected. Rose Bud had *seen* the Manifesto on the front page of today's edition. Now the masterpiece had been usurped by news about the hapless Roxie Neele.

Worse, it *was* the only copy. Rose Bud had deliberately typed it to avoid anyone finding it on a laptop. The pages hadn't been photocopied. There was no way the author was going to be able to recapture the perfect and magnificent phraseology of the Manifesto.

Rose Bud considered the possibility that Tom was lying.

Most likely, Tom had preserved the Manifesto and intended to publish it at a later date. Maybe Tom was waiting until Rose Bud was caught. *If that's the case, he'll be waiting for eternity*, Rose Bud concluded, having no intention of ever being identified.

"He's pissed," Tom emailed Curtis, who studied the text exchange and wondered whether Tom's response would spur Rose Bud to action.

About the same time, an email arrived in Mo's inbox from Roscoe Page. It read:

I hadn't forgotten your request. It took longer than expected. As happens more often than not, you were right. There are investigations buried in a secret vault in the database. Officially closed without findings, they nonetheless contain some interesting information, the sort of things you'd do anything to keep out of the public domain if it'd been written about you.

You will receive a separate email that'll take you to the encrypted files. Hope you can make use of them in trial.

# Forty-Two

*D*ay one of the trial began on a crisp, bright Tuesday morning. The courtroom was only half full during voir dire, which consumed half a day. Mid-afternoon, Judge Paula Krist swore in the panel and opposing attorneys presented their opening statements.

Occupancy in the room had now swelled to capacity.

Dash, dressed in a white blouse and blue skirt and jacket, methodically presented her case.

The evidence, she said, would show that, while the two women appeared to be friends, a far uglier reality lurked under the surface. In truth, Roxie despised her neighbor.

About six weeks prior to the poisoning, Dash told the jury, Roxie purchased rat poison from a hardware store on Washington Street, some of which was recovered in a cabinet in her house.

In the run-up to the murder, Roxie told two people she intended to harm Trudy. Others would attest to the two women's long-running feud.

Hours before Trudy's demise, Roxie fed her a lethal dose of rat poison-laced cupcakes.

"While Trudy Vine sat innocently in the kitchen of the spite house eating delicious cupcakes, Roxanna Neele gloated, knowing that with each bite of a cupcake death drew closer and closer for the woman she heartlessly detested," Dash said with great effect.

"Roxanna Neele acted with malice aforethought in plotting and carrying out the murder of a woman who considered her a friend," Dash concluded. "The evidence will leave no doubt in your mind as to her guilt. And, when you deliberate at the end of this trial, I trust you will judge her guilty and punish her accordingly."

She sat down.

Mo stood, tall and commanding, and addressed the judge formally. "May it please the court." Then he walked across the room and stopped in front of the jury box, addressing the jury in a soft and confident voice.

"Ladies and gentlemen of the jury, I appreciate your indulgence this morning during the jury selection process.

"We're so busy maneuvering in our respective spheres that we sometimes neglect to treat you with appropriate consideration. We forget to acknowledge that the most important people in the room are you.

"After all, you're the ones who are going to determine the destiny of the woman who sits here accused of murdering her friend and neighbor. So let me begin by thanking you for your service."

As he spoke, he established eye contact with each juror. He didn't linger with anyone in particular, but left the impression that a special bond existed between all of them.

"Last night," he continued, "I was reading *The Mysterious Affair at Styles*, a book by my favorite author, Agatha Christie. The chapter I read last night included a trial scene in which Christie paraphrases the remarks of Sir Ernest Heavywether, the defense attorney, making his opening statement.

*'Never, he said, in the course of his long experience, had he known a charge of murder rest on slighter evidence. Not only was it entirely circumstantial, but the greater part of it was practically unproved.'*

"When I read that, I thought I was reading a summary of today's case."

The jurors chuckled.

"The evidence is so thin you couldn't comb it with a brush or shave it with a razor," he continued. "It's so thin you will be hard pressed to even see it."

Then he turned serious.

"In a typical trial, the prosecution presents evidence intended to show the guilt of the accused. If it so chooses, the defense can present evidence, although, under our system of laws, there's no obligation for it to do so and you can't hold it against the defendant if she doesn't present any evidence at all.

"You are expected to weigh the evidence that's been presented to you and conclude whether it establishes guilt beyond a reasonable doubt. If it does, you convict the accused. If not, you acquit."

Mo stepped back, never turning his back on the jury panel, and looked individually at each of the twelve faces staring at him.

"That's what happens in a typical criminal trial. But this is not a typical trial. It's not typical because two things are going to happen before this proceeding has ended."

He had everyone's attention.

"Roxie Neele is the victim of hyperbole and innuendo, two dangerous ingredients that can combine to destroy any one of us. Despite what others might suggest, she did not poison Trudy Vine."

He clasped his hands behind his back.

"As the testimony proceeds, listen carefully to the witnesses because their testimony will begin to unlock the door to the room where the actual murderer resides.

"Together, you and I will learn who is in that room. It's going to be a challenge. I, myself, don't know for sure who murdered Trudy Vine. I only know that my client didn't do it, so the guilty party is elsewhere, waiting to be discovered. Here, among us." Katz waved his arm broadly to emphasize his point.

"We're going to solve the case of this unfortunate poisoning, but that's not all we're going to do. Together, we're going to solve a series of crimes that have plagued our fair city for the past ten months."

The legs of Dash's chair screeched like fingers across a blackboard as she put her hands on the edge of her table and pushed back.

"I say that because the person who poisoned Trudy Vine is also the notorious Rose Bud."

Dash guffawed. Several jurors gasped. A murmur passed

through the assemblage.

Mo continued, "As we look for motive in this case, assume, if you will, that Rose Bud used poison to silence Trudy Vine because she had discerned his identity.

"If that's true, and it is, then Rose Bud lurks in the shadows in every corner of this case. Let's see if we can clearly mark the killer, figure out who poisoned Trudy Vine, and end the reign of terror."

After the opening statements, court recessed for the remainder of the day.

Everyone piled out of the courtroom. Spectators were abuzz with the promise of great revelations. Mo the Magician was certain to entertain and illuminate the story.

*The Chronicle's* coverage got thousands of online hits. In press rooms throughout the country, reporters were assigned to cover the case.

Retreating to his office in Wales Alley, Mo got to work. He actually was uncertain whether he could successfully accomplish the goal he announced to the jury, but he had an inner confidence that he would find his way.

He pulled out the witness list that the Commonwealth Attorney's Office had provided to him. He cross-referenced the list against the names Roxie had given him and the reports retrieved by Roscoe.

He discovered the pattern and realized the significance behind the names that Roxie had provided.

Before the night was over, he had printed out some of the data Roscoe supplied. It would prove crucial for his cross-examination of at least two of the commonwealth's witnesses.

# Forty-Three

**A ROX BY ANY OTHER NAME**

by Tom Mann, editor and publisher.
© The Washington Chronicle

"That which we call a rose, by any other name would smell as sweet," the Bard wrote in his immortal play, Romeo and Juliet.

Today, Old Town faces its own tale of dueling roses or, in this particular case, our own Roxie Neele and the serial killer, Rose Bud.

If defense attorney Mo Katz is to be believed, the two cases are linked and both will be solved by week's end as a jury hears testimony in the murder of Trudy Vine.

In dramatic testimony before a hushed courtroom yesterday, Katz alleged a link between the death of Vine and the series of murders that have gripped Old Town since February.

Katz represents Neele, accused of poisoning Vine.

Katz claims his client is innocent and he has promised to reveal the true killer in the course of the week.

In addition to solving the Vine murder, Katz promises to unmask Rose Bud, the name by which

Old Town's serial killer has come to be known.

Shakespeare's well-known text about the rose stands for the proposition that names do not affect reality.

In the play, Juliet seems to be saying that it is of no consequence that Romeo is a member of her family's rival house, the House of Montague.

Yet, no one can claim that the name Rose Bud is of no significance in Old Town. It is a moniker that represents a plague on our city for most of the year and casts a pall over the Christmas holiday season.

If, as he claims, defense attorney Katz can solve the serial murders, he deserves the accolades of the city.

But if his promise rings hollow, he should be strung up alongside Neele. Bah, humbug!

*T*he next day, the sidewalk in front of the Alexandria Courthouse swarmed with activity. Large lines of people wrapped around the courthouse square, everyone anxious to get a seat in the courtroom. Food trucks did a robust business selling coffee and pastries. And broadcast vans equipped with large antennas to beam the news to anxious viewers sat at every corner.

Wednesday was colder than the previous day, with the thermostat hovering in the high 20s. Not a cloud in the sky interfered with the sun's bright rays lighting up the city's eastern exposure.

Mo entered the courthouse via a back door to avoid the army of reporters who surrounded the main entrance. His safe passage was assured by Bailiff Dee Shorter.

"Thanks, Dee," Mo said, removing his coat and scarf once inside.

"Anything for you, Mr. Katz," Shorter replied. The bailiff had not forgotten Mo's legal assistance when one of his daughters got a DWI. The young woman was acquitted and now attended medical school at the University of Virginia.

"What's the game plan, if you don't mind my asking?" Shorter asked.

"We'll both be apprised as the trial moves along," Mo answered. "Maybe I'll need your assistance before it's all over," he said, smiling.

Shorter beamed at the thought of aiding Mo to catch a murderer.

In truth, Mo's mood this morning could be described in one word: ebullient.

Last night, when he finally got home after a long night of trial preparation, Abby finally called. Her operation had been a success and she was recovering nicely, she reported. She and Martha had become as close as sisters, just as Mai had said. Rather than being driven apart by rival love for Shayne, they were melding over their love for Katie.

Martha had taught Abby and Katie to play a card game called euchre.

"Cards? Really?" asked Mo, who could not recall ever playing a game of cards with Abby in all their years together.

Before the call ended and they exchanged "I love you's," Abby wished Mo good luck with the trial, which she always described as the place where opportunity met preparation. Mo was prepared — over-prepared, really — for trial. All he needed was the right opening.

"I questioned the logic of helping Roxie, but you clearly knew what you were doing," she said. "I'm very proud of you. Not only are you representing an innocent woman but you might actually be able to nab a bad person who's been doing horrible things. You'll restore peace and calm to our community.

"Everyone in Wisconsin is rooting for you. And I think tens of thousands of people who dream of living in warm houses on quiet streets in caring neighborhoods feel the same way.

"Go get 'em, tiger!"

Helena Delacroix was the first witness for the prosecution.

"Did you have any conversations with the defendant about Trudy Vine in the days preceding her death?" asked Dash Low.

"Many times," answered Helena. "Roxie was obsessed with Trudy, and not in a good way. She told me repeatedly that Trudy was the bane of her existence and that she wished bad things would befall her. Theirs was an age-old rivalry, the origins of which are unknown."

"Were you surprised when Roxie was arrested for poisoning her?"

Helena answered, "Not at all. I expected it."

"Smug" best expressed the look on Dash's face as she completed her direct examination.

"Do you recall visiting me a few weeks ago on Roxie's behalf?" Mo asked as he began his cross-examination.

"Vaguely," she answered.

Dash stared at the witness with a WTF look on her face.

"Roxie asked me to take care of a few odds and ends for her following her incarceration," Helena volunteered.

"Forgive me if I look a little confused," Mo said, "but it's somewhat incongruous that you're running errands for a woman you believe to be a murderer."

Members of the jury nodded in agreement.

Dash stood and addressed the judge. "Is there a question in that statement or is Mr. Katz testifying?"

"I'll put it in the form of a question," Mo replied.

"Ms. Delacroix, why did you perform chores on behalf of the defendant following her arrest if you believed she might have committed murder?"

"I'm not sure," Helena replied.

Mo held a piece of paper in his hand and asked permission to approach the witness. The judge gave a consenting nod.

"Do you recognize this piece of paper?" He handed the paper to her.

"I think so."

"Would you read it to the jury?"

"I'd like to see it first before it's handed to one of my witnesses," requested Dash, who quickly approached and snatched the paper.

"What is this?" She asked, dumbfounded

"It's the note your witness wrote on the day she solicited my assistance on behalf of the defendant," Mo said.

He took the paper back, handed it to the witness, and asked her to read it to the jury. Helena read:

> *Following the murder of Trudy Vine, Roxanna Neele said:*
> *"I loved that woman! I'd never have harmed her!"*
> *Helena Delacroix 12/04*

"What accounted for your change in testimony?" asked Mo.

Helena looked confused. Her eyes darted around the courtroom.

"A couple of weeks ago, you told me that the defendant professed her innocence to you," Mo said. "Yet today you are testifying that she loathed the deceased."

"I don't recall writing that or even visiting your office," she said.

"Are you suggesting you didn't write that note?"

"I'm not saying that. I just don't recall the circumstances under which I wrote it."

"Do you have a problem with memory, Ms. Delacroix?"

"No, no…absolutely not," she stammered.

"You work for the Commonwealth of Virginia providing constituent services for the governor's office from a satellite office in neighboring Fairfax County, is that correct?"

"Actually, it's the state Attorney General's Office."

"I'm sorry," he said. "The Virginia Attorney General's Office. Forgive my error."

The judge suspected it wasn't an error at all and surmised that Mo wanted to draw attention to the witness's employment.

"In the past year, have there been concerns expressed in your performance appraisals about such things as memory loss?"

"How do you know that?" she replied.

"Answer my question. Have concerns been expressed about your memory loss?"

Helena looked past Mo to the prosecutor. "Shouldn't you object to issues that aren't germane to the case? Isn't this an invasion of my privacy?"

Before Dash could speak, Mo continued.

"Recently, there was a request to place you on administrative leave, wasn't there?" He opened a folder on his desk and removed a document, which he held in his hand.

"That was initiated by people who dislike me for no reason," Helena said. "They just want to get rid of me."

Her face contorted as she held back tears.

"I don't want to be let go," she wailed. "I can't afford to lose my job. I have a special needs child who depends on me." She turned to the judge. "Please don't report me to my supervisor."

Mo smiled wanly. "Don't worry, Ms. Delacroix. No one is going to report you for anything. But let's clarify something. Isn't it true that Roxie Neele never told you that she was angry with Trudy Vine? Isn't it true that she only said good things about Ms. Vine? And isn't it true that you made up this story today?"

"I don't know. Maybe."

"Your Honor," Dash interrupted. "I object to this line of

questioning and ask that it be struck in its entirety. I understand the court is giving the defense leeway in this case. But these antics by Mr. Katz are beyond the pale, even for Mr. Katz."

Mo lowered his head and stifled a smile. Outbursts like this one weren't lost on the jury.

"Objection denied," responded Judge Kirst. "You may proceed with your line of questioning, Mr. Katz. I think it goes to the truthfulness of the witness. There's nothing objectionable in my estimation."

"What happened to the effort to force you to take administrative leave, Ms. Delacroix?" asked Mo.

"I don't know."

"It got swept under the rug, didn't it? And it wasn't the first time that concerns have been raised about your performance in the workplace, is it? In fact, someone has been carefully keeping an eye on your job security, isn't that true?"

Helena stiffened, appearing more confused.

Mo knew he had to be careful.

If he attacked the witness, he would lose points with the jury, which he assessed was favorably disposed toward him at this stage of the proceedings. Since Helena actually suffered from memory loss, the confusion she displayed in the courtroom wasn't an effort to be evasive. It was illustrative of her actual state of mind.

"I'm sorry to put you through this," he said. While he was a little sorry, his primary concern was upsetting the jurors. "But I have to ask, who's been protecting you, Ms. Delacroix?"

"I don't know what you're talking about," she answered.

"Did that person tell you to lie today? Did that person threaten to quit protecting you if you didn't do his or her bidding?"

"I don't know," she choked, tears streaming down her face. "I don't know anymore."

"No further questions," Mo said, returning to the defense table.

As she stepped down from the witness box, she spied a pair

of glasses sitting at the edge of the defense table. Recognizing the glasses, she discreetly picked them up and slid them into her pocket without making eye contact with Mo.

*N*ext, the prosecution called Dianna Lox, the police department's ombudsperson.

"What is an ombudsperson?" Dash asked.

"I'm an appointed official who investigates complaints against the police department by private citizens and seeks to resolve their complaints through mediation," replied Dianna.

"Do you know the defendant and, if so, how?"

"Yes, she regularly brought complaints to the department."

"What sort of complaints?"

"Complaints that lacked merit," Dianna answered. "They were outlandish. And she was consistently unresponsive to our efforts to resolve the complaints."

Dash flashed a smile at Mo.

"Was there ever a complaint filed by the defendant with your office that included Trudy Vine?"

"Yes," Dianna replied. "Trudy volunteered her business as a place for first-time offenders to perform their community service hours."

"Describe that in more detail," suggested Judge Kirst. "The jury may not be familiar with our community service programs." The offender program was one of the judge's pet projects.

"Sure," Dianna said, placing her hands in her lap and turning to face the jury.

"Trudy ran Light the World. You could bring an old light bulb to the store and get free LED lights for your home. The business was run by people who'd sustained misdemeanor convictions in court. It was a way for those people to work off their conviction. If they performed a set number of community service hours, say 40 hours, their conviction would be wiped clean."

191

"That sounds like a wonderful program," Dash commented.

"Roxie didn't think so," Dianna said. "She accused the police department of funneling money to Light the World in exchange for it supporting our community service efforts."

"Were those accusations true?"

"Not based on my investigation," said Dianna. "It seemed as though the defendant was jealous that the department had selected Light the World. That's all it was. She wanted to sabotage the relationship."

"Did she ever threaten Trudy Vine?"

"She once told me that Trudy was going to meet a terrible fate if we allowed Light the Word to serve as one of our community service sponsors," answered Dianna.

"Thank you, Ms. Lox," said the prosecutor. "Your witness, Mr. Katz." She expected Mo to avoid the subject; instead, he ran toward it.

Mo stood. "Tell us more about the threat," he inquired. "Did she make her statement in front of others? Was it in writing? Did you report it to anyone?"

"No, only to me. It was a comment. I don't remember when. I reacted by dismissing the complaint. I should have reported it."

"But you didn't report it because it never happened," Mo said. "Isn't that right?"

Dash objected. "Counsel is badgering the witness."

The judge cocked an eyebrow. "Mr. Katz?"

"With the court's indulgence," he said.

To the witness, he said, "I have a copy of the complaint here and it's not exactly as you represent it." He picked up a folder and removed a document. "The initial complaint by the defendant said she was acting *on behalf of* Trudy Vine."

He dropped the document on Dash's desk. She picked it up and scanned it quickly, then put it down.

"Roxie Neele alleged that unsolicited payments were deposited in Light the World's account without Trudy's knowledge. Trudy was told to certify compliance sheets or the department would claim the payments were part of a bribery scheme that she was operating.

"In other words, Ms. Lox, the defendant was trying to help Vine navigate her way through some shady dealings," Mo said. "But you make it sound like it was the other way around."

He took the document from Dash's table and, approaching Dianna, said, "Would you like to see the initial filing? It might refresh your recollection."

"I think that's a gross misinterpretation," Dianna said.

"We'll let the jury decide," Katz said. He returned the file to its folder and placed it on his desk. Then he asked, "Tell us again what the ombudsperson does?"

"I investigate complaints filed by the public against maladministration by the police department."

"So an ombudsperson is different from someone who handles internal affairs, which deals with allegations of criminal misconduct by members of the force, is that right?"

"Objection, beyond the scope of direct and relevancy," Dash said.

"It goes to credibility," Mo replied.

"Proceed," ruled the judge.

"You don't handle internal affairs these days, but you used to, didn't you, Ms. Lox?" Mo paused for an answer; Dianna nodded. "I'm sorry," Mo said. "The stenographer can't record a nod. You have to answer the question verbally."

"Yes."

"You left internal affairs during an investigation into the conduct of Sheriff Chris Malcolm, isn't that right?

She hesitated. Finally, she said, "That's right."

"Why?"

"I needed a change of scenery," she replied brusquely.

"Did the fact you were having an affair with the sheriff play any role in your removal from that position?"

She hesitated once again, then said, "It did not."

"Normally, the fact that the two of you were having an affair would be grounds for either or both of you to be removed from your positions, but that didn't happen in this case. Why was that?"

"I'm not sure what you're getting at," Dianna countered.

"What I'm getting at is that you've been compromised," Mo said.

A hush fell over the courtroom. Was Dianna being blackmailed? Was she dirty? Everyone was on the edge of their seat. Dash might have had grounds to object, but she also remained in her seat, seemingly as mesmerized as the jury in wanting to know more details.

"Someone helped you keep a job with the department," he continued. "You probably thought that that someone was doing you a favor. In fact, that someone was only doing a favor for himself. From that point forward, that person could blackmail you into doing his bidding in exchange for remaining silent about the affair."

"That's not true," replied Dianna.

Mo scratched his cheek. "By the way, are you still seeing the sheriff?"

"No-no," she stammered. "We haven't gone out for the past couple of years."

"You sure of that?" Mo asked.

When Dianna didn't answer, he said, "Let's turn back to that community service program. Who told you to lie today about the Light the World case?"

"I don't know what you're talking about," Dianna said.

Mo didn't take any delight in exposing Dianna on the witness stand. After all, she had lent a helping hand to Sherry when Joey Cook and others were unfairly attacking her. Plus, he didn't want to get too far ahead of himself.

"I think you do," he said. "No further questions at this time,

Your Honor, though I'd like her to remain subject to recall."

The judge excused the witness and then announced, "We'll take a brief recess."

*W*hen court resumed, medical examiner Rodney Brown took the stand. Ancient, wrinkled and stooped, with glasses perched halfway down the bridge of his nose, he personified a generation nearing extinction. Mo knew Rodney from his days as a prosecutor. Brown had seemed ancient then, and *then* was nearly 20 years ago.

On direct examination, Brown testified that Trudy died from rat poisoning and had consumed a healthy dose of cupcakes on the day she died.

"How many cupcakes, doc?" Mo asked on cross.

"Six or more," Rodney coughed.

"And were those cupcakes fed to Trudy Vine by Roxie Neele, Doc?"

"You know the answer to that question, Mo. I can't say one way or the other. There's no way of knowing whose cupcakes were consumed by Ms. Vine. She ate a boatload of cupcakes, that's all I know. I don't know who put the poison in them. The autopsy doesn't tell me that."

"Did you know Trudy Vine died on the day of the Capps Cupcake Competition?" Mo asked.

"I used to love every pastry from the Cupcake Coliseum," replied the coroner. "I cried when Claudia Capps closed that place."

"I think everyone in town shed a tear," Mo replied.

Several jurors smiled.

"But you didn't answer my question, doc."

"What you're really asking," said the wise old doctor, "is whether *anyone* could have fed those cupcakes to the deceased. And the answer to that question is, yup, *anybody* could have poisoned her."

"By the way," Mo continued, "Will a spoonful of rat poison kill you if administered in a single day?"

"Rat poison is a cumulative poison that does not produce sudden death when it is administered. Modern rat poisons have long half-lives. Makes them *safer*."

"And how long would it take for rat poison to kill someone?"

"It's likely that the murderer was spiking her food with rat poison for days. She didn't just get sick and drop dead an hour after consuming a cupcake, even if it was laced with rat poison and even if she ate a half dozen that day."

As he returned to the defense table, Mo gave Dash a wink. He wondered how she could have been so vain in her desire to take him down that she neglected to thoroughly consider such a critical piece of evidence.

"How old are you, doctor?" Dash asked, jumping up for re-direct examination.

"Not so old I don't know what I'm talking about," Brown replied. Several members of the jury tittered.

Addressing the judge, Dash said, "The prosecution will offer additional testimony from other experts as to the effect of rat poison on humans when digested in large quantities in a short period of time."

With that, she sat down, avoiding Mo's gaze.

Joey Cook was the last witness of the day. He wore his dress uniform, an impressive display of gold buttons on a double-breasted royal blue jacket replete with ribbons and medals displayed above the left breast pocket.

"Did you visit the defendant on the day of her arrest?" Dash asked, anxious to regain momentum in her case-in-chief and end the day on a high note.

"I did," Joey answered proudly. "I had a premonition that she might have carried out the murder. There was a lot of talk about her at the station. People said she was evil and lived in a tiny spite house. She was rumored to hate Trudy Vine.

"I felt it was my sworn duty as a police officer to question her about the case. So I visited her …"

"Stop right there," Mo said, standing slowly as though there was no urgency whatsoever in his movement.

He was damned if he was going to allow Joey Cook to help Dash rejuvenate the case.

"Judge," he continued, "I don't know whether Officer Cook administered Miranda warnings to my client prior to her arrest. Nor do I know the sequence of events preceding and following this 'visit' to the defendant. I'd like to voir dire the officer in a separate hearing outside of the jury panel."

The judge looked at her watch and said, "I agree. Given the hour, court is adjourned for the remainder of the day."

She asked the jurors to reconvene in the jury room at 10 o'clock the next morning. "As for counsel, we'll resume here in the courtroom for a brief evidentiary hearing." She pounded her gavel bringing the day's events to a close.

# Forty-Four

*O*ld Town awoke to reports of the prior day's trial proceedings. But breaking news quickly superseded those details following an alert that Rose Bud's fourth victim was reportedly coming out of her coma.

**ASSAULT VICTIM RECOVERING FROM HARROWING ATTACK**

by Tom Mann, editor and publisher.
© The Washington Chronicle

An unnamed victim of a vicious attack believed to have been perpetrated by the serial killer known as Rose Bud is miraculously recovering from her injuries, according to hospital officials who are treating her.

"This is a totally unexpected turn of events," said one of the doctors treating the victim at Inova Alexandria Hospital.

"We're cautiously optimistic that she'll regain consciousness by Christmas," the doctor reported.

*T*oday was the winter equinox. Clear skies prevailed for a third straight day. The world sat in perfect repose. Equal amounts of light and dark would consume this day. Going forward, the light would claim an incremental advantage over dark with the dawn of each day, mounting its campaign through winter to spring.

When Dash Low arrived at the courthouse Thursday morning, reporters swarmed her to ask questions whether the new development would result in a trial delay. "I don't see why it should," she answered dismissively to the throng of reporters who surrounded her at the entrance to the courthouse.

"Roxie Neele is accused of a separate crime," she answered crisply. "There is no correlation between the poisoning of Trudy Vine and the Rose Bud murders. I don't for one instant believe Mo Katz is going to uncover Rose Bud's identity in the course of this trial.

"It's a publicity stunt, that's all it is. Mo Katz misses his glory years as U.S. attorney. He can't accept the fact that he's fallen back to earth. He'll do anything to try to recapture the spotlight."

The jurors assembled in a room adjacent to the courtroom where the attorneys argued whether Joey Cook should be permitted to testify.

Judge Krist asked Dash to proffer Joey's testimony.

"The officer will testify that, upon his arrival and prior to the arrest, he asked the defendant whether she played any role in the death of Trudy Vine," she said.

"He will testify under oath that she said, 'I've already cleaned the mixing bowls. The poison's been washed away. You won't be able to find sufficient evidence to convict me.'

"Officer Cook then placed the suspect under arrest and called for backup. She was transported to the station. She refused to repeat the statement after being provided her Miranda warnings.

"The Commonwealth argues that she was not under arrest at the time that she made the statement and that Miranda does not apply. She was inside her house and could have asked the officer to leave. Her statement was voluntary and it is admissible."

Joey was then summoned to the courtroom and took his seat in the witness box. The jurors remained sequestered in the jury room.

The oath was administered. The judge nodded to Mo to conduct his examination.

"Why did you go to the spite house?" Mo asked.

"To arres…" Joey gulped for air. "To speak to Ms. Neele about the case."

Mo had already caught Joey in a lie. He was about to say "arrest." Nothing was more fun than examining a witness after he'd lied.

"Were other officers with you?"

Joey hesitated. "I arrived alone," he said.

"According to the media reports, a slew of officers appeared at the spite house dressed in full military gear."

"They arrived afterwards," Cook said. "I called for backup after she confessed to me. She did so voluntarily. I had no idea what she was going to say. I'd only visited her out of a whim."

"Were you assigned to the case?"

"No. But I felt an obligation to interview her. Given my training and experience, I had concluded I was the right officer to handle the case at this important preliminary juncture."

"You have a penchant for arriving at crime scenes unannounced, don't you?" Mo asked.

"Baiting the witness," Dash objected. "Argumentative."

The judge waved her arm. The arm of her robe danced like a kite. "Overruled."

"Just the other day, you were in the middle of another crime scene with Sherry Stone," Mo continued. "Why do you race to crime scenes like that?"

"I'm an LEO 24/7."

Lest anyone misinterpret Joey's words to suggest he was sharing his astrological sign, Mo asked, "You're referring to yourself as a law enforcement officer when you say LEO, is that correct?"

"Duh," Joey replied. "Of course I am."

"But you're really someone other than that, aren't you, Officer Cook?" Mo asked derisively. "You're a disgraced LEO trying to regain his reputation. Isn't that who you *really* are?"

"It's not like that," Joey said. "Some people in this case might be trying to grab the spotlight, but not me."

Dash perched on the edge of her chair ready to jump up and object. Something held her back, namely Joey's performance. She decided to let him face the barrage of Mo's questions and then make a critical decision.

"If I have fellow officers who will testify that you told them ahead of time that you were going to pin the murder on Roxie Neele to advance your career, would they be lying?"

"Who said that?"

"Answer my question."

"I never said that to anyone," Joey said. "If Shay or O'Toole or anyone else says otherwise, they're lying."

"Speaking of moral turpitude, did you recently file an action against Deputy Chief Stone for harassment?"

"I withdrew it," Joey said.

"Why?"

"I didn't want to provoke the ire of the top brass," he said.

There was a palpable air of untruthfulness about Joey Cook. Katz felt it would accrue to his client's advantage.

"Thank you, Your Honor," Mo said with a smile. "I have no objection to this officer testifying."

"The witness will be allowed to give testimony," the judge said. "The jury can assign whatever degree of credibility it chooses to what he has to say."

Dash rose. She'd heard enough. "Thank you, Your Honor, but upon further consideration, the prosecution has decided not to proceed with the officer at this time. We're prepared to call another witness."

The jury was recalled to the courtroom and the trial resumed.

*D*ominique Lotte was the next witness.

Under questioning from Dash, Dominique explained that she went to a hardware store on Washington Street six weeks prior to Trudy's murder to purchase a holiday wreath to hang on the front door of her and her husband's townhouse.

"I wasn't sure they'd have any, since it was really early in the season, before Thanksgiving, actually," she said. "Fortunately, however, they did."

Mo scribbled a note and handed it to Curtis, who was seated behind the railing. Curtis departed the courtroom.

"While I was there," Dominique testified, "I ran into the defendant and heard her say, and I quote, 'I'm looking for something to permanently get rid of a particularly loathsome varmint who's become a major nuisance in my life.' I watched as she purchased a large quantity of rat poison."

"Did you comment to anyone about what you'd heard her say?" asked the prosecutor.

"Yes, I told the man at the counter that I hoped she wasn't buying it to kill someone."

"And why did you say that?"

"She was filled with spite and hatred. It sent a chill up my spine. I didn't think she was talking about rodents."

When Dash concluded direct examination, Mo turned and looked for Curtis in the back of the courtroom. Not seeing the PI, he asked for a brief recess.

"Denied," announced the judge "No delays. We're adjourning early this afternoon."

Roxie tugged on Mo's sleeve, and he bent down to hear her whisper, "Don't bother questioning her. I said those words, or something close to them. I was referring to rats, the kind with tails, but it doesn't matter. The jury'll believe what the jury believes."

A noise came from the back of the courtroom. Mo turned expectantly. His eyes alighted on Curtis waving his phone.

"Are you sure everything you've testified to this morning is true?" he asked the witness.

"Absolutely. Every word."

Mo walked to the railing as Curtis stepped toward it. The phone changed hands. Mo touched the screen and, leaning over, displayed a photo to Dash.

"What is this?" she cried, surprised and befuddled.

"A door." Mo replied quietly. To the judge, he asked, "Permission to approach the witness?"

"Permission granted."

Mo went to the witness stand and placed the phone in Dominique's palm.

"Do you recognize this photo?"

"It's my front door."

"Do you recognize anything strange about it?"

"I do not. We're very proud of our home. It's immaculate, inside and out."

"There's no wreath on the front door," Mo observed.

"I haven't had time to hang it yet," she replied quickly, defensively. "I've really been a wreck since the poisoning. I mean, there I was, six feet from the murderer in a hardware store."

Mo took the phone back and swiped his finger across the screen studying the other photos that Curtis had just taken.

"But it looks as though you had time to hang bows on holly bushes and place candles in all of the windows," he commented. "Isn't that right?" he asked, showing her the photos.

"Our lawn crew did that," she said.

"They came inside your house and put the candles in the windows?"

Dominique Lotte sighed.

"Here's the deal, Mrs. Lotte," Mo said. "I've got the owner of the hardware store lined up to testify. He's going to testify that my client purchased rat poison. But that's not all. I'm going to ask whether he remembers you. I'm going to ask him whether you purchased a holiday wreath. And I'm going to inquire whether you made a comment to him about hoping she only intended to kill rats.

"And do you know what I think he's going to say?"

"Objection," voiced Dash. "The defense is testifying. He's badgering my client. He's out of line."

Katz disregarded the objections. "He's going to say you didn't buy a wreath. In fact, he's going to say it was too early in the season for him to carry Christmas wreaths. He doesn't sell them until *after* Thanksgiving."

Lotte turned to the judge, her eyes watery. "It isn't true, what I said," she admitted. "I just happened to be in the store, that's all. I didn't buy anything. And I didn't say anything. I'm so embarrassed."

"Perjury isn't something to be embarrassed about, Mrs. Lotte," Mo said. "It's a crime. Truthfulness is the foundation of our criminal justice system. You destroy the sanctity of the institution when you lie."

Dash rolled her eyes. She was too frustrated to object.

Mo continued, "If you've lied about what you purchased at the store, do you expect the jury to believe any of your testimony at all? Are we supposed to engage in selective perjury? Are we to believe some of your testimony and discount other parts?"

He turned and faced the jurors as he addressed the witness. "Why did you go and make a statement to the police in the first place if it was going to include an element of falsehood?"

"I didn't," she answered. "The police found me."

At that point, Mo ceased his cross-examination.

Dash tried to rehabilitate Dominique Lotte.

"Did you or did you not hear the defendant say she wanted to purchase something to dispose of a loathsome neighbor?" she asked.

"Objection," Mo hollered. "That's not what the witness said on direct examination. It's not even close. First the witness commits perjury and now the prosecution twists the words of a perjurer to fit her own narrative. This is an outrage. I move for a mistrial."

The judge instructed the court reporter to read the prior testimony, and the reporter intoned:

> "While I was there, I ran into the defendant and heard her say, and I quote, '*I'm looking for something to permanently get rid of a particularly loathsome varmint who's become a major nuisance in my life.*' I watched as she purchased a large quantity of rat poison."

"I apologize, Your Honor," Dash said, recognizing her error. "It wasn't my intention to mischaracterize the witness's testimony."

"We stand in recess," the judge said. "You" — she pointed to Dash and Mo — "my chambers in five."

Ten minutes later, the attorneys were admitted to her chambers. The court reporter was turned away, being told it was a private conversation that needn't be part of the record.

Judge Krist removed her robe, opened a window, and settled on the sill with a cigarette in violation of a city ordinance prohibiting smoking in public buildings. Dash stood silently against a wall. Mo sat in the center of the room.

As the judge lit her cigarette, Mo began, "Mrs. Lotte never purchased any wreath at the hardware store. She was there spying on her husband, who's having an affair with Helena Delacroix. They were there together buying mistletoe or something.

"I would lay this all out in court but I actually subscribe to a certain amount of discretion."

"I didn't know the word existed in your vocabulary," Dash interjected.

"Actually, I do practice it," he replied, "particularly in a case where the senator's being a prick about dividing marital assets in their divorce case." He looked at the judge and said "Sorry" for using crude language in chambers. Then he added, "The last thing I want to do is help him in the divorce case. He might gain an advantage if he can show she's been stalking him."

"Very admirable of you," Dash commented sarcastically. "Of course, you pretty much trashed the ombudsman the other day. Too bad she's not getting divorced."

"Children, children," the judge admonished.

To the prosecutor, she said, "I'll give you the benefit of the doubt that you innocently misquoted the witness but it was sloppy and unprofessional at best."

To Mo, she said, "You made some wild promises in your opening statement. I'm not seeing any clear path to identifying Rose Bud or connecting this case with those murders. I hope you weren't misleading me and the jury and I trust you know what you're doing."

To both of them, she said, "I'm not declaring a mistrial. The prosecution's faux pas hardly rises to such a level. But I am cautioning both of you to be on your best behavior. You're beginning to sound like two feral cats."

As they left chambers and went back to the courtroom, Mo thought about Dash's carelessness. She hadn't prepared for trial, pure and simple. The prosecutor's disdain for him had led her to make mistake after mistake, a series of self-inflicted wounds.

And Dash could only think to herself what a sanctimonious son of a bitch that Mo Katz was, while she was blind to the fact that she should have heeded his advice when they first spoke about the case.

Ralph Howzer, owner and operator of the hardware store on Washington Street where Roxie purchased the rat poison, testified next. He provided the receipt for the poison and, when shown the bags of poison retrieved from her spite house, testified that it was the same brand he sold, though he couldn't be sure if those were the identical bags he'd sold to Roxie.

On cross-examination, Mo asked, "Did you ever hear the defendant utter any statement about what she was going to do with the rat poison?"

"No, I did not. I assume she was going to use it to kill rats."

"Do you happen to have surveillance cameras in your store?"

"Yes, I do," replied Howzer. "People come into the store and steal things off the shelves. Not my usual customers, you understand, but it happens. It's become a real thing, theft.

"I monitor the cameras from the counter where my cash register is located. If someone steals something, I confront them about it."

"Do you provide notice that there are surveillance cameras?"

"No."

"And is there a camera at the counter?"

"No. I'm only concerned about the theft that takes place in the back of the store out of eyesight."

Mo returned to the defense table and sat down.

"Is this witness excused?" asked the judge.

"Yes," Dash and Mo answered together. As Howzer stepped down from the witness box, Mo scribbled another note and handed it to Curtis.

The remainder of the day's testimony went smoothly, which meant uneventfully, including various witnesses who provided the details of Roxie's arrest, the chain of custody established for the evidence seized at the spite house, and the collapse and death of Trudy Vine at the waterfront as witnessed by several horrified onlookers. Court recessed mid-afternoon.

In the evening, Mo huddled with Curtis, who was in the office, and Mai, who was on the big screen in the conference room.

Mo was clearly frustrated.

Tom Mann had planted the story about the victim's recovery in the hopes that Rose Bud would visit the hospital. Sherry had doubled security. Yet, despite the news alert in *The Chronicle*, no suspicious characters had taken the bait and come to the hospital.

"Rose Bud is being cautious," Curtis observed. "He may be onto us."

"I think he's paranoid by nature," Mo replied. "He's careful about every step. Maybe something else spooked him, something outside of our control."

Their conversation then focused on the courtroom testimony.

"What was with your question to Mr. Howzer about the surveillance camera?" asked Mai.

"I couldn't figure out how the prosecution found Dominique Lotte," Mo replied. "If you recall, she said that she never went to the police, that the police found her. Since she hadn't purchased anything, the only logical explanation is that a video surveillance camera was set in the store. Dominique must have been on the video. And the surveillance had to be hidden or she wouldn't have lied."

"Shouldn't the police have provided that evidence to you?" Mai asked.

"Yes."

"Did Dominique lie about Roxie's statement?"

"No. Roxie told me that she said it. I attacked Dominique simply to raise a doubt as to her credibility."

"Mo, that's cruel," Curtis chuckled.

"What about the other witnesses?" Mai asked. "Especially the ombudsman and that other woman, Delacroix."

"Both witnesses' testimonies are pertinent," Mo explained. "Delacroix should have been removed from her job years ago. She suffers from a mild case of dementia. Someone managed to hide her infirmity and keep her in her job. She's beholden to that person. That's why she lied under oath. She was following instructions from someone to cast aspersions on Roxie.

"The other is Dianna Lox. She was pulled out of internal affairs because she had an affair with the sheriff in violation of department policy. She should have been fired. But she wasn't, again because of the intervention of a third party. Like Dominique, Dianna is beholden to someone. That's why she also misrepresented the facts during her testimony."

"Who is the intervener?" Mai asked anxiously.

"Our murderer," Mo said.

"And do you honestly believe that person is also Rose Bud?" asked Curtis.

"Absolutely," Mo said.

Curtis said, "I visited Howzer, like you asked, Mo. He gave me the surveillance film."

"What's it for?" Mai inquired.

"To identify the murderer," Mo said. "I think he got the idea to use rat poison to kill Trudy based upon her offhand comment in the store."

"You mean to say you think he was *inside* the store?" Mai exclaimed.

"Assuming it corroborates other evidence, then my answer is yes," Mo replied. "Life is full of irony."

"What's the other corroborating evidence?"

"Material that I asked Roscoe Page to gather for me," Mo said.

That was news to them. Yet, based on past experience, Mai and Curtis knew Mo held his cards close, even from them. Until he was absolutely certain of something, he always maintained a level of separation.

They also surmised that the material from Roscoe was hacked from a law enforcement sensitive database and that Mo was protecting them from any blowback.

"What's next?" asked Curtis.

"We're going to lay a trap," Mo answered.

They watched the surveillance tape from the hardware store, after which Curtis called the Alexandria jail.

That night, a mobile phone rang. Robyn and Sam were on the other end.

"I've got some important news to pass along," Robyn said when the phone was answered. "The sheriff is going to testify tomorrow in the murder trial. Mo Katz plans to attack his credibility using a report he found. We're hoping you can do something to stop it."

"How do you know this, and who told you to contact me?" asked the party on the other end.

"Roxie spilt the beans," Sam said. "She confided in us after she met with Katz."

Added Robyn, "You know how information travels in a jail, particularly about Sheriff Malcolm. Although some people don't like the man, he's been good to us."

Sheriff Chris Malcolm was rumored to provide special treatment to his stable of female prisoners in exchange for sexual favors.

"I'm not a magician," said the voice on the other end.

"That's not what we heard," said Robyn. "We were told you can make stuff disappear before it sees the light of day."

"Maybe you can make the report vanish during the trial," added Sam.

"What report are you talking about exactly?"

"There was an investigation conducted of sheriffs accused of some sort of improprieties," explained Robyn. "Apparently, it was damning toward Sheriff Malcolm. We don't know the details."

Detailed or not, her explanation stunned the person on the other end of the call.

"How did Mo Katz get hold of any documents related to an investigation?"

"From what we understand, Katz hacked into some database," Robyn said.

"Please help the sheriff," Sam pleaded. "We got ourselves a good thing here and we don't want to lose it."

"Plus, we want to see Roxie fry," said Robyn.

# Forty-Five

*Diary entry from December 20.*

Tonight I received a phone call from two of the girls in Chris Malcolm's penthouse. They're worried the sheriff is going to be exposed for running the best little whorehouse in Old Town.

They mentioned a report about the sheriff that uncovered his unsavory little operation. What they don't know is that I'm the one who wrote that report. After I drafted it, I shared it with the sheriff. In agreeing to bury it, I was able to secure the sheriff's eternal gratitude…along with his willingness to do my bidding whenever needed.

I've used the sheriff to get serious criminal offenders on work release and to warehouse other offenders who committed minor crimes…all to advance my own ends.

It's the same MO I've successfully used to get other government officials in Alexandria and throughout the Commonwealth of Virginia to do my bidding.

It's what I did to Helena Delacroix, Dianna Lox, Dayton Longmire, and others.

I can't permit that report to become public.

It's not because I want to protect the sheriff or his girls. It's all about self-preservation. That report is the tip of the iceberg. If it is released, my MO is exposed. That can't happen.

Rose Bud hesitated. *His* MO! Was this a bluff? He quickly calculated the connections among Mo Katz, Roxie Neele, and the two jailbirds, Sam and Robyn.

It was possible, though unlikely, that they were in cahoots with one another. The report existed in a database. It was password protected. To protect the contents from being divulged, the standard PW wasn't used. So even if Katz was cagey enough to find it, how did he open it?

Rosebud ran through a series of scenarios. One was to play the odds and do nothing. Another was to check the database in the morning. And a third was to initiate a plan tonight to prevent the report, if it existed, from seeing the light of day.

Earlier in the day, Rose Bud had resisted visiting Alexandria Hospital, fearful that Katz had set a trap. A few days ago, after he'd learned that Tom Mann had destroyed the manifesto — or at least claimed to have destroyed it — he had similarly shown restraint, again sensing that Tom might actually be working with the police or Curtis Santana.

*Had he been overly cautious in both of those instances?* he wondered. *Should he have gone to the hospital to check on the patient? Should he have confronted Mann?*

Now, weighing the options, Rose Bud concluded that decisive action was finally needed.

# Forty-Six

Day four of the trial opened with Sheriff Chris Malcolm taking the stand.

Normally, the judge would be hearing motions on a Friday, but being near Christmas, things were slowing down and she had a clear docket. Given the tremendous interest in the case, she decided to proceed with the trial. The courtroom was packed to capacity.

Tom Mann assumed his customary seat in the front row. His reporting had transformed the trial into the most sensational story of the year. He relished his additional role in helping to trap Rose Bud.

Other prominent figures in the assemblage included author Henry David McLuhan, state auditor Ryan Long, and Assistant Commonwealth Attorney David Reese, who silently resented Dash's prominent position in the prosecutor's office.

"Sheriff, are you acquainted with the defendant in this case and, if so, how?" Dash asked.

"Yes, in fact she's known to everyone in law enforcement, from what I understand," he answered. "Neighbors have filed complaints with my office, the police department, anyone who wears a badge. She's been cited for badgering people, maintaining an unsightly building opposite her house, assaulting neighbors, and causing a general commotion everywhere she goes."

He stroked his thick mustache thoughtfully. "Since her arrest, she's been impossible in my jail. She's managed to anger her cellmates, insult my deputies, and create enough chaos to transform her wing of the prison into a ward in an insane asylum."

"Have you spoken to the defendant about her case?" Dash asked next.

"No, but I've overheard her screaming invectives about the victim in this case, Trudy Vine."

"What sort of invectives?"

"That Ms. Vine deserved to die and that someone should have mixed nails and razor blades in with the rat poison."

"*A*re you sure you heard those things?" Mo asked on cross-examination.

"Yes, absolutely, no doubt about it," answered the sheriff.

Mo held a manila file open in his hands.

Beads of sweat formed on the sheriff's forehead as Mo studied the file. Jurors perched on the edge of their seats. And a hush descended over the courtroom.

Twice before, Mo had presented incriminating evidence to witnesses. On both occasions, the information damaged the witness's credibility and cast doubt on the veracity of their testimony.

Suddenly a fire alarm sounded. A loudspeaker issued a recorded warning.

**"A FIRE HAS BEEN REPORTED IN THE BUILDING. A FIRE HAS BEEN REPORTED IN THE BUILDING. EVERYONE IS TO EVACUATE IMMEDIATELY.**

**DO NOT USE THE ELEVATORS. I REPEAT, DO NOT USE THE ELEVATORS.**

**EXIT THE COURTROOM AND PROCEED DOWN THE STAIRS AT EITHER END OF THE HALL."**

Strobe lights ignited.

Mo placed the manila file on the defense table and proceeded to the exit.

Bailiff Dee Shorter was at Mo's side. "Judge asked that I escort you and Ms. Low through the back door, across chambers, and down the rear staircase," he said out loud. They exchanged a glance.

Then in a whisper, Shorter continued, "Just like you predicted."

They both stole a glance at the security cameras strategically located in the corners of the courtroom.

Before today's proceedings commenced, Mo predicted that an intervening event would prevent the contents of the folder from being admitted into evidence. Swatting incidents such as bomb threats or fire alarms were the most likely possibilities, he said.

For that reason, he had asked that the surveillance cameras be checked to be sure they were in working order.

Shorter now escorted Mo, Dash, the sheriff and the judge through a maze of halls and corridors. Roxie was directed down another staircase in the back of the building by a deputy sheriff.

Members of the public formed lines and piled out in orderly fashion through the lobby and to a staircase located beside a bank of elevators.

Within minutes, people flooded out of the building and ran into the crowd of reporters and pedestrians milling about the courthouse. Like a stream rushing into a river, the mass swelled as more and more people were thrown into the courtyard in front of the building. Bodies pressed against one another. The throng pushed out into the street.

Police cordoned off the streets around the courthouse. On the opposite side of the street, protestors railed against Roxie when she appeared outside, her wrists and ankles shackled. No one had bothered to provide her with a coat to insulate her from the cold. She stood shivering in the blouse and skirt she wore in court, changing from her prison garb in a dank cell each morning.

In the anonymity of a crowd, threats were thrown at her. "Poison the rat!" "Burn her!" "Fry her bony ass!" Each insult was hurled by an otherwise compliant taxpayer who supported the rule of law.

Meanwhile, Mo, Dash, Sheriff Malcolm, and the judge stood in an alley behind the courthouse surrounded by deputies and bailiffs. They were all bundled up in their winter coats.

Someone hurled a tomato at Roxie. Then someone pelted her with an egg. An officer with a bullhorn half-heartedly implored the crowd to stop.

Mo left the circle safeguarding him and ventured out into the street. "Get her into the courtyard," he demanded, chastising the officers. "You've had your fun. Now get her away from this crowd before a brick is thrown and someone gets seriously hurt. NOW! Or else I'll sue each of you separately along with the department if someone's injured."

He was fearful of gunshots ringing out.

Mo removed his herringbone coat and handed it to Dee. "Make sure she puts this on before she freezes to death," he said.

As Dee wrapped Roxie in Mo's coat, other officers took her to a protected area removed from the boisterous crowd.

Twenty minutes later, the all clear was announced and people filed back into the courthouse.

Although the elevators were operating, Mo opted to walk up the staircase from which he'd descended a short while ago. When he arrived in the courtroom, he opened the folder he'd left on the table and found that it was empty.

Roxie returned. She removed his coat and placed it on a chair beside the railing separating the judge's bench, jury box, and prosecution and defense table from the spectator seating.

Her blouse was stained from a rotten tomato and egg.

"I see they got you," he said.

"It could have been worse," she replied as she took her seat. "They could have hit your coat." She nodded and added, "Thanks. Next time, though, I'd appreciate a smaller cut. That coat of yours was about 20 sizes too big for me and weighs a ton."

Dee appeared and gave her a once-over. "Do you want to change?" he asked.

"No, she's fine," Mo said. Before Roxie could voice her disagreement, she went, "Oh!" and echoed his reply. "I'm fine, I'm fine."

Five minutes later, everyone resumed their seats in the courtroom. As the jurors filed into the box, many of them nodded sympathetically toward Roxie. Mo had instructed her to remain standing until they were all seated.

Mo now stood and waved the manila folder.

"Your Honor, someone pilfered the document inside this folder," he said. "It must have happened during the fire alarm. Fortunately, the cameras in the courtroom recorded everything that happened as we filed out of the room. I am asking for a brief recess to study the film."

"This court stands in recess." The judge pounded her gavel.

Mo and Dash returned to chambers with her and the bailiff.

"Did you orchestrate this?" the judge asked Mo.

"I didn't pull the alarm, if that's what you're asking, judge," he answered. "But I did expect someone to pull a stunt like this. So, if that's what you mean by 'orchestrated,' then I'm guilty as charged."

"Did the file contain incriminating information about the sheriff?" asked the judge.

"Someone thought so," Mo replied. "It was a bait and switch on my part. The folder contained a blank piece of paper. I assume there's something incriminating out there on just about everyone. Looks as though I was right."

Everyone took a seat in front of a computer set up on the conference table in the center of the room.

On the screen, they could see Dayton Longmire as he stepped through the gate separating the courtroom pews from the bench, opened the file, removed the paper, folded it without looking at it and stuffed it inside his jacket. Then he proceeded out of the room.

*Dayton Longmire!* "That's not who I was expecting," Mo said.

"And exactly *who* were you expecting?" asked Dash.

Mo stood and paced the room. "How many cameras are set up in that courtroom and where are they positioned?" he asked.

"Are you going to answer my question?" Dash demanded.

"Let's look at the CCTV," Mo said, hoping the closed circuit television existed. "The film will answer your question for me."

*O*ver the next hour, a swatting spree quickly unfolded. First a bomb threat was lodged. That was followed by a report that a heavily armed person dressed in military fatigues had entered the courthouse. And online messages were posted about killing Mo and the judge.

The city seemed to have come unhinged. The streets around the courthouse were closed. A helicopter hovered overhead. And a bomb threat was called in to the hospital where the latest victim of Rose Bud's rampage lay recovering.

In the midst of this madness, a news bulletin announced that someone walked into the Alexandria police station and confessed to being both the serial killer and Trudy Vine's murderer.

# Forty-Seven

**LEWIS ADMITS TO POISONING, SERIAL MURDERS**

by Tom Mann, editor and publisher.
© The Washington Chronicle

Richard "Dickie" Lewis has confessed to poisoning Trudy Vine and to committing a series of strangulations dubbed the Rose Bud murders.

Lewis turned himself in at the Alexandria police station during the fourth day of the Vine murder case trial, where Roxanna Neele stands accused of the crime.

Lewis, in his late 20s, is unemployed and has no fixed address. He has a misdemeanor charge pending for breaking and entering.

Alexandria prosecutor Dash Low had no comment when asked whether the murder trial would proceed against Neele now that Lewis has confessed to the crime.

Defense counsel Mo Katz has called for the dismissal of the case.

On Friday, the trial proceedings against Neele were interrupted by a fire alarm that resulted in the evacuation of the Alexandria courthouse. No fire was detected and the police suspect the alarm was a hoax.

The alarm set off a wave of false reports at the courthouse, including a bomb threat and reports of armed terrorists entering the building. All of the alarms proved unfounded.

After the second false alarm and subsequent evacuation of everyone in the courthouse, Mo, Dash and Curtis retreated to Mo's office. A laptop was set up on the long table in the center of the room. Dee Shorter had just emailed copies of the additional tapes of activity in the courtroom from a variety of different CCTV angles.

"Dickie didn't kill anyone," Mo said as they huddled in the conference room.

"Maybe he's looking for attention just like the crazies calling in bomb threats and reporting armed vigilantes in the courthouse," Curtis speculated.

Mo shook his head in disagreement. "He thinks he's protecting Roxie."

They turned their attention to a film showing the assemblage at the courthouse where people formed lines to file out of the courtroom.

Dayton stood in the queue. A hand reached out and grabbed his shoulder. The index finger pointed toward the defense table. The third finger of that hand wore a black onyx ring with a diamond cut in the center.

Reluctantly, Dayton stepped out of line and approached the bench. He stopped at the defense table, opened the file, removed the "document," and returned to the line, eventually filing out of the room.

Then they reviewed the film showing activity in the hall outside the courtroom, where Dayton handed the folded paper to another person. That person wore a black onyx ring with a diamond cut in the center.

"Ryan Long!" Dash said incredulously. Like others, she associated the ring with the person. Now the film showed Long standing beside Dayton and holding the fake document.

Turning to Mo, she asked, "What do you make of this?"

Mo's face showed no surprise. He placed three papers on the conference table as though he was laying down aces in a card game.

"According to this paper," he said, pointing to one of the documents, "Long made a personal plea to Helena Delacroix's supervisor to keep her in her position. When that failed, he threatened to expose the supervisor for fraud. As a result, Helena kept her position even as her mental condition continued to deteriorate.

"Similarly, Long assisted Dianna Lox at the police department, where she was transferred from internal affairs to the ombudsman's office," he continued, pointing to another file. "Again, he accomplished that by threatening to expose people in her chain of command with one form of malfeasance or another.

"Finally, Long squashed an investigation into the sheriff's performance that would have ended his job if it'd been publicized," he concluded, pointing to the third file.

"O-ka-a-y," Dash spoke slowly. "But what does that have to do with Trudy's poisoning or the Rose Bud murders?"

"Long persuaded all three of those individuals — Helena, Dianna, and Chris — to lie at Roxie's trial. He desperately wanted Roxie to be convicted."

"Why?"

"Because he poisoned Trudy, who suspected him of being Rose Bud."

"Rose Bud!" Dash exclaimed. "Ryan Long!"

Mo nodded. "He constructed a network of sycophants over whom he exercised dominion and control. They were all afraid he'd expose their vulnerability so they acquiesced to his demands. His power was real. And it was frighteningly horrible. Just look at how he was able to persuade law-abiding people to offer false testimony in a criminal case."

Dash was stunned. "When did you first suspect him?"

"The night he appeared at my home, threatened me with an investigation into one of my old cases, and offered to drop the investigation if I was willing to abide by his whims when he needed a favor."

"*You* have secrets?" She arched an eyebrow.

"He thought so."

"And the connection between Trudy's murder and Rose Bud's identity?"

"That was provided to me by Roxie. Trudy was too scared to say his name out loud so she only gave Roxie the culprit's initials."

"R.L.?" Dash asked suspiciously.

Mo said, "No, D.L. His full name is Damian Ryan Long."

Dash spent a moment in silence digesting the information. Then, looking at the screen, she asked suspiciously, "How did Long know the document was in the file?"

"We had a couple of the inmates from Roxie's cell block call Long last night."

Dash shook her head and sat back heavily in her chair staring at Mo. "Anything else I should know?"

Curtis, who had stood by silently, now chimed in. "Long participated in a writing class with Henry David McLuhan. We're working with Tom Mann to expose Long as the author of Rose Bud's manifesto. A few nights ago, Tom established contact with Rose Bud to drop off his manifesto, which was deposited at Dark Star Park in Rosslyn."

"Damn you, Katz!" Dash burst out, half in anger, half in awe. Then she smiled in resignation. "You don't have authority to do these things, but it sounds as though you've wrapped him up pretty good."

Anticipating her next question, Curtis said, "We don't know the connection between Damian Long and Dayton Longmire, but we suspect we'll find a similar form of blackmail consistent with the other relationships. Dayton's been involved in some shady stuff."

Dash reflected in studied silence connecting the data points in her mind. As a state investigator, Damian Long would have known about Helena's on-the-job problems, Dianna's internal investigation and her own indiscretions, and the sheriff's improprieties. Damian also possessed the know-how to access personal information about Dayton, who was a state employee.

"Why didn't you share this from the beginning?" she asked, offended at having been excluded from Mo's investigation.

"If I'd come to you earlier, Long would have claimed I was trying to retaliate against him. My only recourse was to build the case on my own.

"Plus, I didn't have enough to go on, not until the pilfering of the document earlier today.

"And, lest you forget, we've been courtroom adversaries. I wasn't sure it would all hold together, at least not until now."

"I'm impressed," admitted Dash. "Now all we have to do is tie all of this in a bow, present it to a judge, and issue a warrant to arrest Damian Ryan Long.

"In the meantime, I'm going to dismiss the case and release Roxie from custody. We'll need to get a statement from Dayton. And we need to have a heart-to-heart with Dee, Dianna, and Chris."

Then she added, "I guess I made the right call after all, fast-tracking the case for trial."

"I'm *sorry?*" Mo replied. "What are you talking about? *Making the right call*. What right call?"

"All along, you thought I had jumped the shark and had taken this case to trial out of spite, didn't you?" she asked. "After all, I do envy you. But that wasn't my motivation.

"Freddie Davis called. He's one of my snitches. He shares information with me, mainly gossip picked up from his sister. Anyway, his sister said Roxie was playing you. Freddie suspected it had something to do with finding Trudy's true murderer and figuring out Rose Bud's identity. That was confirmed by the scuttlebutt he picked up from a couple of women he visited in the detention center."

Incredulity flashed across Mo's face.

"Don't look so surprised," she laughed. "I never trusted Joey Cook. I'd spoken to Rodney about the effects of rat poison. Roxie wasn't guilty and I knew it. But if there was a chance that Rose Bud could be apprehended, I was willing to break the rules and see if you could make a believer out of me."

"I had no idea," Mo admitted.

"Next time around, don't assume that people who're jealous of you are your enemies," she said. "You might find they're actually your greatest admirers. Now let's catch ourselves one badass."

*W*ithin an hour, the case was dismissed, the jury disbanded, and Roxie released. Dickie remained in custody although he wasn't formally charged with any offense. And a rumor circulated that an arrest warrant was being drawn up against some unknown party.

# Forty-Eight

While the group conferred, Damian arrived at Alexandria Hospital.

Patients had not been evacuated because the threat was not deemed credible due to the rash of false reports about the Alexandria courthouse. Rather, the detail of armed guards outside the room of Rose Bud's victim was increased.

"I'm with the state Attorney General's Office," Damian said as he approached a guard, pulling out his identification.

"No one's allowed in or out," the heavily armed officer replied.

"I'm here on official business," Long said insistently as he attempted to brush past the guard, but the man stood his ground.

"Sorry, sir. I don't make the rules. I only carry them out."

"I understand," Long acquiesced. "How's the victim?"

"Not well, sir. That report about her making progress was intended to draw out the murderer. You know, sir. He'd want to silence her."

Long nodded. He turned to leave.

The officer added, "That's not all, sir. Word is that they also played a trick in the courtroom earlier today."

I don't have the details. All I know is it was instigated by Mo Katz, the attorney in the case. That man's a fox, I swear. Anyway, he reportedly left some documents in the courtroom and someone lifted them while the courtroom was being cleared."

"Do they know who did it?"

"No, sir," the officer reported. "They're supposedly reviewing the surveillance tapes tonight. But from what I understand, it's not that Lewis kid. He's a nutcase anyway. I think it's some other weirdo."

# Forty-Nine

Roxie returned to her spite house, walked around the exterior, and studied the two signs. First was the one she placed in the yard to balance the signs she considered pretentious.

It read:

> *In This House We Believe:*
> *Only My Life Matters*
> *Privilege Determines Right*
> *Humans Are Aliens*
> *Science Is B.S.*

Elsewhere was the sign planted by one of her detractors, which read:

> *A Spiteful Person*
> *Lived in This House*
> *Now she's in jail*
> *Because she's a louse*

Roxie pulled the first sign out of the ground and ripped it in half. She walked to the back of the house and opened a trash can filled with bags of dog droppings, empty beer bottles and cans, and other rubbish that passers-by had dumped into it.

An awful odor emanated from the can.

She threw the sign on top of the trash heap, closed the lid, and returned to the front of the house.

Roxie studied the house lovingly. Everything about the place looked fresh and new, invested with meaning and purpose. She recalled once being released from the hospital after being plagued by

COVID-19 and looking at her surroundings with new appreciation. She felt the same way now.

*It's good to be back*, she thought to herself.

Suddenly, across the street, she heard a crash. The edge of the roof of her dilapidated house on the other side of the street had shrugged, tipping slate tiles onto the ground accompanied by a hefty batch of bricks from the side of the house. She looked at the scaffolding and thought to herself: *That needs to be fixed or next time someone's going to get injured.*

Then she turned her focus back to the matter at hand.

*Much work needed to be performed in short order*, she told herself. Throughout the city, stores, arts centers, clinics, and other venues desperately awaited their annual infusion of cash, some to sustain their very existence. Holiday checks had to be delivered.

The case hadn't gone exactly as she'd hoped, but she had no regrets about summoning Mo and using him to gather sufficient clues to force Damian Long to climb the gallows. She knew she never could have accomplished it on her own.

And while she didn't have first-hand knowledge that Mo and Curtis had met with Dash or that an arrest warrant would soon be issued for Long, she knew something was afoot.

A tear formed at the corner of her eye when she thought about Dickie. "That fool," she whispered.

She searched the flower pot on the front stoop and found the key to the front door and removed it from the soil and opened the door. Grains of earth clung to her thumb and fingers and the base of the key.

She raised her hand to her nose and smelled the fresh earth.

"Aromatic," she commented aloud before wiping her hand on her pant leg.

Prison was hell, despite the congeniality of her cellmates Robyn and Sam. The smell of jail stuck to her like an unpleasant cologne; not only was it still on her clothes, it was in her body fibers and her soul. She still felt light-deprived too, recalling day after day of the fluorescent glows that substituted for sunshine streaming through window panes.

Roxie went inside and sat in the kitchen, put her elbows on the table, and rested her chin on fisted hands. Her head dropped a notch. She began to cry uncontrollably. Eventually, the crying stopped, she swallowed salty phlegm in her throat, and the sniffles subsided.

As she inhaled, her chest heaved.

"Spite house," she whispered, patting the table as though it was the mane of a favorite colt. "I'm back in spite house."

Eventually, she rose and surveyed the house. Cobwebs needed to be swatted down in corners. A few dead bugs lay on countertops and along floorboards. She went into the bathroom, spat, and flushed the toilet.

The plumbing worked fine!

She surveyed the windows. None had been broken in her absence. She smiled. At times, not only did she think bricks would be thrown through the windows but she honestly expected the place to be burned to the ground.

That was particularly true when she'd been escorted out of the courthouse during the false fire alarm. The menacing crowd had frightened the bejesus out of her.

*W*hile Roxie ruminated, a few neighbors gathered on the street corner.

They murmured to one another that Roxie Neele had returned to the spite house. Except now the tenor of their conversation had changed. Rather than disparage her, neighbors expressed sympathy and support. Instead of tomatoes and eggs, they carried flowers and freshly cooked meals.

Instead of torches, they held candles and lanterns.

The procession inched forward. Roxie was owed an apology. The time had come to reassess what she meant to the community.

# Fifty

Mo was preparing to leave when Jimmy Wolfe appeared in his office.

"Not now, Jimmy," he said wearily.

"You'll want to hear this," Jimmy said. Mo politely shoved past him on his way to the door. "It's about Trudy. I thought you should know."

Mo stopped in his tracks. "What are you talking about?"

"She was the victim in the old Neele prosecution. The one you handled. The one you prosecuted against Roxie."

Mo halted; his mind slipped back in time. The case was *Commonwealth v. Neele*. The victim's name wasn't mentioned, as was the case in any criminal prosecution. Mo had met the victim for the first time on the day of trial. He hardly remembered her name, if he'd ever known it at all.

"It was her," Jimmy said. "She was married to a guy named Trey Elliott at the time. Then she divorced him and married Carl Vine."

Katz stared at the veteran defense attorney. The timing for their encounter seemed off. A manhunt was underway to find Damian Long. Why was Jimmy sharing this news now?

"I'm not sure why Roxie withheld such critical information," Jimmy continued. "I even visited her in jail, begging her to tell you the truth. I suspect she was hedging her bets. If she'd been convicted, she could have filed a grievance against you alleging a conflict of interest.

"You prosecuted Roxie for assaulting Trudy and now you're defending Roxie for killing Trudy. How's that going to sound in the press? It's not good for your reputation."

Listening to Jimmy, Mo heard the voice of desperation. Jimmy hadn't come here tonight to do him any favors. Jimmy was jealous of Mo's courtroom success. He despised the fact that Mo had won.

Mo was reminded of the possible conflict of interest in his representation of Roxie. If that didn't present an ethical dilemma — and it didn't — then this wasn't a problem either.

"It's not a conflict of interest, Jimmy," Mo said. "I checked. The two crimes occurred years apart. There's no correlation between them. Plus, the charges against Roxie are being dropped. She's not guilty of any crime."

"You better hope so," Jimmy replied. "It's going to look bad for you if you get an ethics complaint filed against you. I'm just trying to be helpful, you know."

Mo's phone rang.

Jimmy continued, "If you want, I can tidy up the final details of the case for you. Hand me the case. That way, you won't be accused of any conflict of interest. Otherwise, I'm duty bound to contact the state bar in the morning and ask them to examine your role."

Before Mo could answer, the call went to voicemail. Another incoming call rang. He answered the second call.

"Hello."

"We're home!" exclaimed Abby.

Mo smiled. "Wonderful! Hang on one sec."

Placing the phone over his chest, he said, "I appreciate your concern for my reputation, Jimmy. You're a great friend, coming down here and all. I don't need any help now that the case has been dismissed, but I'll keep your kind offer in mind. And thanks for offering to contact the state bar on my behalf."

Then he turned away from Jimmy and pressed the phone to his cheek. "It's great to hear your voice. I can't wait to see you and Katie."

"I can't wait to see you either," Abby said. "I missed you. A lot."

When the call ended, he listened to the message he'd missed, which had stopped mid-sentence.

# Fifty-One

Curtis stood in Damian Long's study when the search warrant was executed 30 minutes earlier.

Wearing a pair of blue latex gloves, he rummaged through Long's things. He spotted a copy of Unabomber Ted Kaczynski's "Industrial Society and its Future" manifesto on the floor. Glancing up, he spotted a newspaper column tacked to a wallboard from June, the month Kaczynski died in prison. The article recited some of the words of the manifesto.

> "In order to get our message before the public with some chance of making a lasting impression, we've had to kill people."

A chill ran down his spine. He pulled out his phone, called Mo, and, receiving no answer, began to leave a message. "Damian's hero was..." He stopped.

He'd found the diary sitting in a drawer buried beneath a stack of T-shirts and underwear.

He grabbed the document and turned its pages, scanning the entries quickly.

*Diary entry from February 13.*

*I'm not much of a romantic. Maybe that's part of my problem. I have to go online to figure out how to set a mood.*

*This Valentine's Day I'm going to make my move. I'll blindfold her and envelope her in a warm embrace. We'll make sweet love. Afterwards, we'll lie in bed, our heads against the headboard — the one we pounded against the wall incessantly! I'll have an ashtray on my chest, we'll smoke cigarettes.*

### Diary entry from February 15.

*I don't know what happened.*
It started out like I imagined it would. Then something went inexplicably wrong. I wasn't prepared for that. Once it veered off course I didn't know what to do.
She started to laugh. At me. A mean laugh. Mocking. Wicked. Condescending.
Stop it! I insisted. Don't ridicule me. Shut up!
If she'd reacted the way she was supposed to, this never would have happened.

### Diary entry from June 4.

*That bitch, clawing at me like that.*
She invited me over to her apartment after work. I asked if I could get there ahead of her and cook dinner. She welcomed the idea and willingly surrendered her key.
I didn't bother making dinner. I knew in advance what was going to happen. I'm clairvoyant, you see.
When she arrived, I caressed her face and lovingly placed the blindfold over her eyes. I have to admit she seemed a little nervous, even though she didn't resist.
As I squeezed my hands around her soft throat, the blindfold fell to her shoulders. I watched as she stared back at me in disbelief, incredulous as to what was happening.
Controlling a person's life is empowering. When they realize you are squeezing the life out of them, their incredulity is replaced by panic, but by that time it's already too late.

*Diary entry from November 1.*

*Last night was devilishly divine.*
*I dressed as Hemingway, complete with white beard. She called me daddy. The girl was effed up. We laughed and laughed. When the night was over, I laughed last.*
*I felt less a novelist than a playwright, a master of the three-act play.*
*The first act was the seduction, getting her in my grasp, innocent and helpless, believing that everything is okay. Believing in tonight, tomorrow, and the day after that.*
*(What a sap.)*
*Act two was the murder, the instant when romance and enjoyment turned to disbelief and horror. No more tomorrows.*
*Act three was the signature line: staging the candles, incense, bubble bath, and rose petals. Ah, those ubiquitous rose petals!*

Curtis leafed through the rambling messages, all written in cursive. He felt the weight of the pages in his hands. It was the definitive evidence to convict Long of the string of murders that had plagued Old Town since Valentine's Day.

Finally, he turned to today's entry, the last one.

*Diary entry from December 20.*

*Roxanna Neele should never have been charged with murder. I assumed I had sufficiently covered my tracks so that no one could credibly be accused of the crimes. When Joey Cook fabricated a confession and pinned it on Roxie, I was incredulous.*
*Frankly, I was a little jealous too.*
*Regardless, I expected the charge to be dismissed in a day or two.*
*Then Roxie retained Mo Katz and the case got assigned to Dash*

*Low.*

*What a fiasco.*

*To think that my life has been upended by a rogue cop inventing a phony confession to resuscitate his career and a prosecutor whose ambition to take down Mo Katz seems to have blinded her to the cardinal rule to be prepared for trial ahead of time.*

*It just goes to show that spite, jealousy, and insecurity can propel people to act in ways that logic and rationality do not.*

Curtis didn't have time to meditate on the irony of that last statement, but he couldn't ignore it. Damian *personified* malice. That this monster should talk disparagingly about how spite poisoned others was the greatest hypocrisy. No one better characterized spite than Rose Bud himself.

Curtis handed the diary over to the forensic team. The incriminating evidence would be tagged, bagged, and preserved for trial. As soon as Damian was apprehended, the scourge would end.

Curtis called Mo a second time. The phone was busy. He texted: "I found Long's diary. It's enough to bury him for the rest of his life." His phone vibrated.

"Santana."

Dash was on the other end. "A woman named Lucy Dallas is at the station to press charges against Damian Long. He apparently choked her the other night. It has the hallmarks of an assault perpetrated by Rose Bud."

Curtis replied, "I'm on my way over. The search produced a handwritten personal diary. Everything is in it. We just have to catch the bastard."

En route to the police station, Curtis called Tom Mann.

# Fifty-Two

Mo stopped at the townhouse, which bustled with activity.

Katie was playing outside in the yard, if that's what one could call a postage-stamp-sized square of sod in back of the dwelling. Chefs Abby and Martha were experimenting with recipes in the kitchen. Shayne was working in the office on a school project.

Martha's husband, Gus, who'd driven the family van nonstop from Wisconsin, was sacked out on a sofa in front of the television. A breaking news bulletin was reporting the dismissal of charges against Roxie Neele in the Trudy Vine case.

Two of Martha and Gus's children were running around the house like gerbils.

Martha gave Mo a big bear hug. "Abby's told us all about your big case. It's all over the news. We have a celebrity in the house. It sounds like you've done a great job."

Gus stirred. "It's all over the news," he repeated, rousing himself awake. "You've done a good job!"

Abby gave him a long kiss. She wore a knee brace over her pants; a crutch leaned on the wall beside the refrigerator.

"Are you hungry?" Martha asked. "I'll bet you haven't had a good meal since Abby left. With the trial, it's a wonder if you've been eating at all. You look a little emaciated if you don't mind me saying. Don't worry. The cavalry has arrived. We'll have you back to a fighting weight in no time."

"The cavalry has arrived," Gus repeated. "We'll have that emaciated look gone in no time."

Mo thanked them, kissed Abby again, and made a hasty retreat from all the commotion. As he stepped onto the front porch, two cruisers pulled up. "Deputy Chief Stone recommended we keep an

235

eye on your house now that your wife's home," an officer said as she alighted from one of the cruisers.

As Mo expressed his thanks, Mai suddenly appeared beside him. "You can't leave without saying hello to me!"

"You were so sweet going out there to help Abby," he thanked her.

"Actually, I'm the one who's grateful," replied Mai. "Martha turned out to be a gracious hostess and we all had a lovely time. By the way, I'm proud of the way you've been handling Roxie's case. Good luck in tracking down Long."

He thanked Mai again, took the officers inside to meet Abby, Martha, Gus, Shayne and the kids, and then drove to the spite house.

*D*amian Long stood draped in the cold shadow of the house undergoing repairs across the street from the spite house. He watched as the damaged Karmann Ghia pulled to the curb and Mo stepped out.

Damian had received a news alert a moment ago. Tom Mann identified him as a person of interest in the Rose Bud case. The Manifesto had been found along with his personal diary describing the murders, according to *The Chronicle*.

It never occurred to Damian that he was writing a confession when he scribbled his diary entries. Maybe that's what Henry David intended all along if he suspected Rose Bud was in his class. They had all conspired against him.

Damian held a Molotov cocktail in one hand and a box of wooden matches in the other. If this was the end, he would go out in a blaze of glory.

Spite house would burn.

*I*nside, where Roxie had the furnace cranked up to over 70 degrees, Mo relayed Jimmy's recent visit.

236

"I really don't care about Jimmy," Mo said. "He's always been envious of my success, as though my victories somehow diminished his own. But that case has always bothered me. As I told you before, I've always wondered what happened."

Roxie gazed at him in silence, then finally opened up. "You were convinced I was guilty," she began. "You were also convinced that the witness who appeared and testified on my behalf was lying. Except she wasn't. She was telling the truth.

"I never assaulted Trudy Vine, whose last name was Elliott at the time. She really paid Cybil Shawl to beat her up. She was totally messed up, psychotic actually.

"I took pity on her after the trial and kept an eye on her. After a while, I befriended her. Slowly, over time, she told me about a scam she ran to shake down citizens in the community.

"She would concoct a crime, appear the victim, and accuse someone of perpetrating it. I wasn't her first victim nor was I the last. In addition to claiming assault, she'd accused others of robbery, vandalism, and even a hit and run."

Mo appeared perplexed. "I never heard of those cases."

"They never got to court, Mr. Katz."

"But she brought your case before a magistrate."

"The magistrate was on the take," she explained. "You see, Trudy never expected her cases to go to trial. She had a perfect scam going. She would create the hoax, the magistrate would issue a warrant, and Trudy would recycle a portion of the blackmail back to the magistrate.

"She approached me in court that day and asked me to settle the case. If I would pay her $10,000, she would walk away. I refused. I forced her to go to trial. And I would have prevailed if it hadn't been for you."

"The appeal," Mo said. "You won on appeal because she never showed up." He evaluated what he'd just said. Then it dawned on him. "You paid her."

"That's right," Roxie admitted. "First I paid her, then I befriended her, and finally I cured her. Or at least I thought I did."

"Thought you did?"

"She had found a way to return to her old tricks. In her final escapade, she accused Long of being Rose Bud. It was a surmise on her part. She ran a concession stand, and beginning back in February he purchased his romantic wares from her — the candles, incense, and, of course, fresh roses.

"She blackmailed him in exchange for her silence. They met up from time to time. He'd pay her. All the while, he was thinking of a way to eliminate her."

"When he heard you ask for rat poison in the hardware store, the lightbulb must have gone on," Mo said, picking up the thread. "He bought some rat poison himself. He must have accelerated their meetings to every other day. He was paying and poisoning her at the same time. The final dose must have been in a box of cupcakes she brought to your house."

Roxie said, "She hadn't confided in me until the day she died. When she dropped dead, I was scared out of my mind. I was certain that Damian Long was going to kill me next.

"Then I got arrested by stupid-ass Joey Cook, who wanted to look like a hero. That fool got shot up seeking notoriety and would have been killed if it hadn't been for Sherry Stone. Anyway, like I told you, once I was in jail I hoped I was in a safe place. And, as it turned out, I was in the enviable position of being able to bring Long to justice."

Mo mentally answered other questions for himself. He saw no need to raise them with Roxie. Even if he did, she'd probably only provide a half-truth.

For instance, he figured Roxie lied when she said Trudy only provided her with the initials D.L. As she now relayed the story to him, it sounded as though Trudy mentioned Damian Long's full name when she shared her suspicion that she knew the identity of

Rose Bud.

Roxie only provided Mo the initials D.L. because they were the same initials as many of the people who had been blackmailed by Damian. When Roxie gave Mo a list of "suspects," she was actually giving him a list of victims. She hoped he'd find incriminating evidence if he dug deep enough, and that was exactly what had happened.

As to the damage to his car, Mo suspected Roxie employed Cybil or some other street person to scuff up the car to further spur him into action.

"Why do you play these games?" he asked. "The half-truths, I mean. You pretend to be an uncaring person. You exist behind a veil. Is living in a spite house supposed to convey to others that you don't care about them? The more I get to understand you, the more I realize that you only pretend to spite others. You actually care about people."

Suddenly, a thunderous crash could be heard outside, followed immediately by a gripping scream. They both rushed to the front window. A fire was burning across the street.

Roxie said, "It sounds as though the day of reckoning might be at hand."

*A* moment earlier, Damian had lit the Molotov cocktail and cocked his arm like a quarterback to hurl it across the street from his position at the house under construction.

At that very moment the side of the roof gave one last shrug and a huge avalanche of slate tiles cascaded down, accompanied by a hefty batch of bricks that jumped from the concave wall.

Damian glanced up at the thundering pile of debris seconds before it slashed his eyes, crushed his forehead, broke his teeth, and demolished his face.

His blood-curdling cry echoed in the night as he fell to the ground, buried in a mountain of bricks and slate, his hands grabbing the sides of a face pummeled by sharp rock and heavy stone.

The cocktail in his hand ignited his clothing. He tried to leap out of the flames that engulfed him. Feeding off dry leaves and papers strewn about the sidewalk, the fire grew with each second that passed.

In under a minute, Damian was transformed into a human torch.

# Fifty-Three

Damian "Rose Bud" Long was rushed by ambulance to the Alexandria Hospital. His face and arms looked as though they'd been in a high-speed blender.

Some of those who saw him prayed he wouldn't survive. Others wished he would.

The fire department put out the blaze, which had spread down the street igniting trash and the few remaining dry leaves of autumn.

Mo had called in the emergency. He and Roxie had run out and were able to partially snuff out the flames that engulfed Damian's battered body before the emergency medical team arrived. But once first responders and firefighters pulled up, they stepped back to the curb. After Damian was transported to the hospital and the fire was extinguished, they returned to Roxie's house.

"I need to calm my nerves," Roxie said. She made tea. She poured a splash of bourbon in both their cups before placing one in front of Mo. He curled his fingers around the warm cup.

"I don't feel sorry for him in the least," she said. "Those bricks and pieces of slate were fated to crush him. He killed innocent women, blackmailed vulnerable people, and poisoned my best friend. He was a despicable monster."

Mo said. "I feel the same way." He debated telling her about his recent encounter with Damian at his home.

"Don't tell me," she said. "I can see it in your face. You want to share something with me. Don't! Keep it to yourself. Sometimes the less we know about one another the better.

"Before the roof fell on Long, you started to ask why I engage in half-truths. I do it to protect myself from getting hurt by other people. I like to keep it that way.

Surveying her tiny house with contentment, she said, "The spite house is the right fit for me. I could live in a mansion if I wanted, but then the fun would end. People would identify me as some sort of grand philanthropic dame. I prefer this. It allows me to lead an enigmatic life and remain hidden in plain view.

"There's something to be said for going small."

After they finished their tea, Mo suggested that Roxie return to Harvard Street with him and spend the night with his family.

"Don't worry about me," she replied with a look of utter calm in her green eyes. "I'll be fine. You did a great service. You put the forces in motion that exposed Long as Rose Bud and brought him to a fateful spot earlier tonight."

"Good enough. We'll check on you tomorrow then," Mo assured her.

In the morning, Roxie crossed the street and inspected the damage to the crumpled building. No one had placed any flowers or candles where Rose Bud had fallen. Only a pile of rubble marked the spot, like an untidy tombstone in an untidy graveyard.

As she assessed the situation, a woman dressed in shabby clothes passed on the sidewalk.

"Hey, Cybil, come here," she hollered, spying the raggedy bundle of garments toting a bag. "I own this dump. I'm going to need someone to house-sit this place for me during the renovation. I'd even pay to have someone inhabit the joint."

Cybil shuffled over and smiled. "I know such a person." She studied Roxie. "Why do you do these random acts of kindness? You go out of your way to help people, like you're doing now for me. Just like you did for Trudy."

"I'm not helping you," Roxie said. "I'm helping *me*."

Cybil laughed.

"Check with me in about a week," Roxie said. "I'm sure a building inspector is going to require the roofline to be repaired before anyone can move into the place. There's going to be a lot of noise and commotion. But as soon as that's done, you've got your own quarters. And I'll pay you a thousand a month to occupy it and keep an eye out."

Cybil held out her hand for them to shake on it. "Deal," she said.

"What's in the bag?" Roxie asked.

"Groceries," Cybil answered. "I always carry food with me. You never know when you're going to have your last meal."

Roxie looked in the bag and noticed fresh bread and eggs. "Come inside. I've brewed some fresh coffee. Let's have a proper English breakfast."

Arm in arm, the two women trundled to Roxie's spite house.

*Mo* awoke after 9 a.m. and went downstairs, drawn by the smell of coffee, pancakes, and bacon, which, as he entered the kitchen, were spread on the square kitchen table, along with fruit, scrambled eggs, toast, bagels, sausage, and grits.

Conversations emanated from all corners of the house.

He joined the one with Gus expounding on the Green Bay Packers. Critical as he was of Aaron Rogers' departure, Gus expressed nothing but sadness that Rogers sustained a season-ending injury on his first series of downs as the new quarterback for the New York Jets. "He never should have left Wisconsin," Gus lamented. "But it wasn't fair what it cost him."

Gus and Martha's children — Terry and Tammy, otherwise known as TNT — were running under, around, and through the furniture.

There was also some trash talk between Gus and Shayne about the Georgetown women's basketball team and Milwaukee-based Marquette.

At the opposite end of the room, Martha and Abby, new Best Friends Forever, discussed their plan to visit Mount Vernon in the coming days.

And Katie frolicked and dashed in and out of conversations with the adults and mischief with the other children.

Mo grabbed a cup of coffee and a bagel and settled into the day's conversations.

*In* the evening, another meal was prepared but it wasn't spread on the table. It was packaged into baskets to be carried down the street.

The entire Harvard Street group trooped to Roxie's house. Mo called Sherry and she and Curtis joined the party as it rounded the corner onto Prince Street.

As they approached the spite house, other neighbors were seen departing their homes or pulling up to the curb in their cars.

"Who are all these people?" Katie asked curiously. "And where are they going?"

The sidewalks were suddenly filled with people carrying food baskets, house plants, lit candles, bottles of wine, pies, and gifts wrapped in bright colors with red bows. The crowd had grown twentyfold from the group that had gathered on the street corner the night of Roxie's release.

Bundled in coats, hats, scarves, gloves, and boots, and carrying a moveable winter holiday repast, they were all headed to the spite house to pay homage to the extraordinary woman who occupied that residence.

Leading the parade was Alexandria Town Crier Benjamin Fiore-Walker dressed in his trademark livery of black gentleman's coat over a red waistcoat, white britches, and black tri-corn hat with white trim.

Mo recognized trial witnesses, jurors, and courtroom observers. Dickie Lewis was headed over, accompanied by Deputy Davis and her brother, Freddie. Sheriff Chris Malcolm was in the company of ombudsperson Dianna Lox and prosecutor Dash Low. Author

Henry David McLuhan was walking with members of his workshop. Even Tom Mann was running over, carrying a large cake.

"It seems the devils who cluttered the streets only yesterday have been replaced by the angels of our better natures," Sherry said as she wrapped her arm around Curtis and leaned into him.

As guests arrived at the house, they were welcomed by Robyn and Sam, who had been granted home detention under Roxie's supervision.

Someone had written on the sign in front of the residence. It now read:

> *A Wonderful Person*
> *Lives in This Spite Haus*
> *I Thought She Was Evil,*
> *Turns Out She's Santa Claus!*

Joy and good will permeated the street.

People streamed into the narrow abode, filling the residence with more bodies than it could possibly hold.

People just kept entering. No one left. The walls should have been bulging but they weren't. Somehow or other, there was room for everyone. And no one complained about being in close quarters.

"*A* toast!" someone exclaimed. Above the din, a chorus proclaimed: "To Roxie with the moxie!"

"To Moxie Roxie!"

"To our blessed Roxanna!"

"To Rock Anna!" toasted Dickie, gleefully.

Accolades followed, including the revelation that she was responsible for the holiday donations that were now filling the coffers of businesses and nonprofits throughout Old Town.

No one could see Roxie, which was hardly surprising. She was tiny and the room was packed with tall people. To see her would be like spotting a blade of grass in a forest filled with oak and evergreen trees. Yet her voice rang out.

"I'm overwhelmed and appreciative of your unexpected presence. It's too much, really. I'm filled with joy and wonder and gratitude.

"In this moment when we hold one another close, let's remember two things. The first is that we drove a spike into the heart of evil. For close to a year, a dark force preyed upon us. Now that demon has been arrested. Once again, we are safe.

"The second is that we suffered a terrible loss that we should not forget in the midst of our revelry. Three victims fell to an evil hand and a fourth clings to life. None of them deserved being harmed. We pray for the recovery of the survivor and for the souls of the departed. And we proclaim our devotion to the families who have lost a loved one to senseless violence."

Roxie announced that Enough Is Enough! would receive a $500,000 grant to help families grieving over the loss of loved ones who were victims of violence.

The names of Rose Bud's victims were read aloud: Patricia Sakkara, Rachel Adores, and Lina Dobbs, as well as the name of the woman recovering in the hospital, Omega Song.

No one mentioned Rose Bud's name.

Someone asked Mo to say a few words.

"In many cultures, deceased loved ones remain alive so long as the living recite their names," he said. "To the list, let's add the name of Trudy Vine."

A moment of silence followed.

Then the revelry resumed. Darkness would return in due time but the night belonged to fellowship and good cheer.

In the background, Bruce Springsteen belted out a holiday favorite and everyone joined in singing a slightly revised version of his well-known song: "Santa Claus Is Comin' to Old Town."

A full moon shone over the city this night with orange and red accents forming a halo at the edges of the blue orb.

# Epilogue

*O*mega Song, the sole survivor of Rose Bud's brutal rampage, awoke on New Year's Eve.

Elation best described the reaction of her family gathered round her bedside. Jealousy, however, described the reaction of many of the other patients on her wing. They were upset over the attention lavished upon Omega while no one bothered to visit and shower them with presents.

Enough Is Enough! received matching grants from several Fortune 500 companies, increasing its coffers substantially. While the skeletal staff was ecstatic, other nonprofits resented the windfall the upstart received. They were concerned that Enough Is Enough! would gobble up the limited charitable funds and grab attention that they needed to survive.

Tom Mann was nominated for a Pulitzer for his reporting about Rose Bud. Some of his peers sang his praises, but others were resentful and envious. They claimed *The Washington Chronicle* was nothing but a rag. Tom never won in the end. Other reporters expressed their disappointment while disguising their glee.

On the other hand, Tom published an exclusive article revealing that Roxanna Neele was the elusive benefactress of dozens of local business and philanthropic efforts. According to his article, no one had done more than Roxie over the past decade to advance worthy social causes in Old Town. Not to mention that she had helped uncover Rose Bud's identity. Her misanthropic identity dissolved and she became an Old Town celebrity.

Roxie hired Cybil Shawl to manage her properties, with assistance from Dickie Lewis. It turned out that Dickie was Roxie's son. Cybil and Dickie moved into the house across the street following its restoration, each occupying a separate floor.

Several of Henry David McLuhan's students published in an anthology that briefly became a bestseller on Amazon. The writings by Mallorca Cannon were selected as an NPR Best Read for the year.

Robyn and Sam were released from home detention. The remainder of their sentences were commuted by the governor. They sponsored writing classes at the jail under the auspices of Henry David. Freddie Davis assisted. Fellow jailbirds expressed anger that the convictions were commuted and some taxpayers complained it was a waste of taxpayer money to provide a literary program for inmates.

In societal news, Helena Delacroix and Don Lotte were engaged following a settlement with Dominique in which she cashed in handsomely. Helena stepped down from her position to assume a new job assisting older employees dealing with memory loss and other infirmities.

Dash Low won commendation for her adept handling of Roxie's trial and was elected commonwealth attorney. Some courthouse observers were jealous that Dash had moved up the ladder so quickly.

Ombudsperson Dianna Lox, who, unbeknownst to everyone, was an attorney, was appointed Dash's chief deputy. There was plenty of resentment toward Lox, who was considered an outsider.

Cilia Roosevelt was named the new ombudsperson, which had a lot of people rolling their eyes since she had worn a wire when she interviewed Roxie in the jail. But one thing no one could deny was that Cilia never returned to work for Damian Long after the wiretap incident. She resigned her position and secretly contacted the FBI to report the incident.

During a separate review of Damian's emails and other records, the $5,000 transfer to Deputy Davis was discovered, resulting in the deputy's removal from her job. Her brother Freddie avoided talking about his sister out of embarrassment over the fact that she'd accepted a bribe to remain silent about Cilia's wiretap incident.

At Jimmy Wolfe's request, the state bar examined and found no conflict of interest or other ethical issues related to Mo's representation of Roxie. As it turned out, Jimmy regularly contacted the bar raising questions about Mo.

But in a manner of turning the other cheek, Mo nominated Jimmy for the Virginia State Bar's prestigious Green Award — in memory of Warren Cyprus Green, a revered defense attorney from Richmond. When Jimmy was selected as the 2024 recipient, Mo bought two tables for the event.

David Reese departed the Commonwealth Attorney's Office and joined the new firm of Katz & Reese, Attorneys at Law. Mai Lin ran the office and Curtis handled investigatory work.

Sherry Stone was sworn in as chief of police for the City of Alexandria.

Although Martha and Gus returned to Wisconsin with their children, Martha conversed with Abby on a near-daily basis. At the same time, the two mothers constantly complained about the other's method of caring for Katie and Shayne.

Shayne enrolled in a program at Georgetown called Reconciling Adoption and Identity to help adopted children who struggled with identity issues.

In early 2024, the Virginia State Police identified a suspect in the Colonial Parkway murders; he'd died in 2017.

Damian Ryan Long expired from the crushing blow he sustained.

# Author's Note

This book is dedicated to David Clark.

David and I have remained steadfast friends for half a century, beginning in the fall of 1972 when we met at Windham College (now Landmark College) in Putney, Vermont. Five years later, David was a member of our wedding party when Robin and I got married in Garrett Park, Maryland. As the years passed, we've kept in touch through correspondence and our occasional visits to his farm in Westminster West, Vermont.

David attended an inaugural book party for *Daingerfield Island* in 2017 in Putney and has remained a loyal fan of the series. Two years ago, in 2022, he joined me at our old college campus when I signed copies of *Gadsby's Corner*, book five in the series.

Thank you, David, for your friendship all these many years. Book seven is for you.

While I reminisce about Putney, I would be remiss if I didn't mention two wonderful individuals with whom I worked on *The Windham College Free Press*: Julie Bettin and John Cahan. We'd pull all-nighters before the publication of each issue, ending up at the printer's shop excitedly waiting as the paper came hot off the presses in advance of our delivering copies to campus. My love for writing began in our tiny newsroom. Those times with Julie and John were some of the most enriching experiences of my college years.

And a special shout out to three other Windham College alumni who joined John Cahan at my book signing at The Ivy in Baltimore, including Susan Apgar, William "Skipper" Marquess, and Karen Wise.

# Acknowledgements

Since beginning the series in 2017, I've interacted with thousands of new and returning readers. I'm enriched by each encounter. Thank you for your friendship and support.

Since *Spite House* is the seventh book in the series, I'll use Lucky 7 to pay tribute to some of those who've been instrumental in the creation of this book and the series writ large.

1. The Crew. Once a manuscript is written, you need a *reality check*, i.e., objective readers to critique your work and offer blunt advice and course corrections, and I was blessed to have the Fab Five in that role: Margaret Chapman, Karen Hansen, Molly McClintock, Julie Poling, and Katherine Ward.

Alex White edited the first draft and my wife, Robin, refined the story before it went to Charles Rammelkamp, my editor, who, as he's done since book one, provided crucial edits and insightful suggestions on what to leave in and what to take out.

Ace Kieffer designed the layout and my son, Alex, created the cover art, as they have done for the entire series, giving the books a familiar visual theme. Bookmobile/Itasca Books Distribution Services in Minneapolis printed and distributed the paperback and managed the e-book, and my thanks go to Mark Jung, Julie Poling, Chloe Johnson, Annie Klessig, Althea Faricy, Rachel Holscher, Nicole Baxter, and Chris Doughty.

I'm also grateful to Amy Bertsch, public information officer at the Alexandria Sheriff's Department, and Emily F. Hedrick, ethics counsel with the Virginia State Bar, for helpful advice with *Spite House*.

2. Locales. Brendan O'Leary owns the spite house on Prince Street that I reference in the first chapter and use as the model throughout the book. I appreciate his collaboration in letting me use his home in my book. Also thanks to Kathy — who's lived in the spite house for the past seven years — for showing me around the place. It's a wonderfully cheerful and cozy little spite house!

Carrie Garland consented to the use of Nepenthe Gallery and Lisa Katic to the inclusion of Wine Gallery 108 as a rendezvous destination for the fictional characters Helena Delacroix and Senator Lotte. Additional thanks go to Jeffrey and Cynthia Higgins for permission to set a scene in Elaine's on Queen Street; Danielle Anderson for permission to use Whiskey & Oysters on John Carlyle Street; Jared Barker for Josephine Brasserie & Bar on S. St. Asaph Street; Trae Lamond for Chadwicks on Union Street; and Rob Puzio for Blackwall Hitch on the waterfront behind the Torpedo Factory. It's fun mixing fictional characters with real places. (By the way, *Nepenthe* is a Greek term that means "a place of no sorrow." It's a perfect motto for a spite house!)

3. Stores. Where would I be if there were no stores to visit to promote and sell my books!

In Old Town, thanks to Beth Lawton and Kellie Sansone for keeping my books well stocked on the shelves of Made in ALX on Montgomery Street in Old Town North and for hosting my semi-annual writing workshops.

Ellen Klein at Hooray for Books! has welcomed me to her store on King Street throughout the years, as have Don Alexander and Rachel Baker at The Company of Books in Del Ray, and Heather Guiles and Margot J. at the Barnes & Noble in Alexandria's Potomac Yard.

Special thanks to Melanie Fallon and the wonderful folks at Ramsay House/The Alexandria Visitors Center for carrying my books and allowing me to occasionally drop by and sign copies for local residents and out-of-town visitors in the garden adjacent to the visitors center. Ajalynn Flores Richard helped arrange my pop-up at the Fort Belvoir Exchange in Southeast Fairfax County where I'm able to discuss my series with fellow veterans. And thanks to The Old Town Shop and the Gadsby's Tavern Museum Society for carrying copies of *Hazel Falls* and *Gadsby's Corner* during the year.

Other Virginia bookstore owners who have welcomed me include David Shuman at Book People in Richmond; Allen Robinson at Books & Other Fine Things in Leesburg; Ralph Tedeschi and Maria Kelly at Turn the Page Bookshop in Williamsburg; Victoria Mitchell at Dog Eared Books in Hampton; Ellen Woodall at Blacksburg Books in Blacksburg; and the awesome staff at The Winchester Book Gallery in Winchester.

Out-of-state bookstore owners and operators who've hosted me for recent book signings include Hannah Fenster at The Ivy in Baltimore; Thomas Martin and Tess Jones at The Bookplate in Chestertown, Md.; Jinny and Janice at Old Fox Books & Coffeehouse in Annapolis, Md.; Susan Sawin at Island Books in Duck, N.C.; Lisa Driban and Jennifer Blab at Hockessin Books in Hockessin, Del.; and Melinda Hall at Wall of Books in Cornelius, N.C.

In addition to the Barnes & Noble at Potomac Yard, other Barnes & Noble staff who have hosted me in Virginia include Tania Ellison in Manassas; Scarlet Rose in Fairfax; Megan Vu in Ashburn; Cristina Knighton in Woodbridge; and Christine Smith in Williamsburg. Outside of the Washington metro area, I arranged visits to BN stores with Rebecca Ely and Sara Hassan in Exton, Pa.; Brenda Freeman in Frederick, Md.; and Heather Schweitzer, Jim Reynolds, and Jon Elliott in Valley Forge, Pa.

4. Friends. I appreciate everyone who's supported my writing over the past year. There are a lot of people to thank. The problem with a list is that I'm going to forget someone important. So here's an incomplete list of folks who were especially kind to me this past

year:

Linda and Conn Anderson, Peggy Baldwin, Pat Ballard, Tammy Barker and Terry Street, Erin Beherns and her family, Gordon Bennett, Becky Bonsall, Leroy Brown Jr., Vinod Busjeet, Julia Cain, Margaret Chapman, David Crawford, Jean Conley, Janet Crawford, Torey Doverspike, Jean Durette, Cedar Dvorin, Paul and Denise Freeland, Colleen Funkhouser, Ronnie Edelman, Linda Ely and Jim Crouch, J. Wayne Esser, Lucy Goddin, Peg Halloran, Scott and Lorrie Hill, Laurie Hughes, Stephanie Jackson, Janina Jaruzelski, Heather Jenkins, Marilyn Jenkinson, Steve Johnson, Robin Jordan, Keri Kelly, John Koenig, Jim Larocco, the Lavey-Eccles family (including their beautiful daughters Sophia and Victoria), Deborah Lessard, and Lois Ligoske.

Also Joan Maling, Pat McCombie, Randy D. McCracken, Donna McDaniel, Don McEwen, Jennifer Medicus, Barry Meuse, Heather Metz, Julia and Mark Miller, Ken Munis, Adrian and Rhiannon Nicotra, the O'Connell family, Lucelle O'Flaherty (daughter of the late great Judge Daniel Fairfax O'Flaherty of the Alexandria General District Court), Roger D. Parks (President of American Advertising Distributors of Northern Virginia), Ralph Peluso, Beth Reddick, Mina Rempe, Robert J. Riccio, Kathy and John Russell, Priyanka Saha, Susan Samuels, James Savage, Tom Scala and his daughter Scarlet (who stole the show at the Sherwood Regional Library book reading), Jim Schuyler, Gordon and Barbara Scott, Jill Sidford, Desameaux "Mo" Shorter, Mary Anne Sprague, Joab Stieglitz, Alfa Tate-O'Neill and her Swiss Shepherd Marco, Jerry Terlitzky, Ed Tolchin, Maggie Tomasello, Carl Turner, Joao Andrez Leon Vazquez, Thomas James Werner, Ben Winn, photojournalist Kesha Williams, and Mary Wadland, publisher of *The Zebra* in Alexandria.

Classical WETA's Nicole Lacroix was my partner at two wonderful readings of *Slaters Lane* at River Farm and at The Landing in Potomac Yard, and Bill Newman joined us at River Farm for his dramatic reading of *Daingerfield Island*. Both Nicole and Bill have narrated some of my audiobooks and they have been dear friends in our joint performances.

Benjamin Fiore-Walker, the city's official Town Crier, allowed me to include him in the scene where townspeople are going to the spite house to celebrate Roxie's release. Ben is a remarkable orator. He's playing a leading role in the city's ongoing celebration of its 275th birthday.

5. The 50+ Club. I'm blessed at 71 years to be actively writing a book series, which I began when I turned 65. During the past year, I've spent a lot of time lecturing fellow baby boomers about the value of writing memoirs, historical fiction, romance, or whatever suits their mood. Writing is a wonderful way to stay alert, engaged, and creative.

I've lectured at several Osher Lifelong Learning Institute programs and my thanks go to Laurie Hester, Phoebe Williams, Ann Covington, and the staff at William & Mary; Peggy Watson and her staff at the University of Richmond; Molly McClintock at Virginia Tech; and Nancy Osborne in Manassas.

Encore Learning in Arlington also hosted me for a series of online lectures. Thanks go to Kerry Fraatz, Jeanne LaBella, and Deb Spero.

The Hollin Hall Senior Center hosted me, and I'm most appreciative to Patti Bruch, Veronica Cartier, Alexa Fuerth, and all of the members of the center's Cozy Mystery Book Club who joined us.

I am also thankful to Jennifer Bennett at Goodwin House Alexandria, Emma Grammer and Jill Arvanitis at The Fairfax, Kimberly Nelson at Greenspring Village in Springfield, Dominique Wallace and Elisabeth Longworth at Ashby Ponds in Ashburn, and the entire staff at The Landing. My gratitude to all of the residents at those venues who attended my readings and shared their literary projects. And special thanks to Sandra S. O'Keefe, onetime librarian at Lloyd House, who acquired a set of Old Town Mysteries for the library at Goodwin House, and Dale Brown, who helps her with the annual fall book sale.

6. Events. Cynthia and Jeff Higgins, owners of Elaine's, graciously offered The Library on the second floor of their beautiful restaurant for the release party of my last book, and thanks to everyone who attended.

I participated in several special events in Alexandria throughout the year, including ones with Alyson Foster and Kristie Leckinger at Lost Boy Cider on Hooffs Run Drive; Javier Groisman and John Johnson at Kilwins on King Street; and Bill Butcher and the wonderful staff at Port City Brewery. A.J. Orlikoff, Jaclyn Spainhour, and the staff at the historic Congressional Cemetery in D.C. welcomed me for a book event. And thanks to Kimberly Adams at World of Beer in Exton, PA, for our St. Patrick's Day book promotion.

Public libraries are a vital resource, and I am grateful to the Sherwood Regional Library in Fairfax County and the Kate Waller Barrett branch library in Alexandria for hosting events. In particular, thanks to Jeff Snavely in Fairfax County and Athena Williams in Alexandria. I'm also appreciative to readers who've donated my books to the public libraries and to Fairfax County Library for including some of my e-books and audiobooks in its online collection.

River Farm, the headquarters for the American Horticultural Society, has been a wonderful venue, including the Spring Garden Market and a Halloween reading featuring Bill Newman and Nicole Lacroix. Thanks to Suzanne B. Laporte, Peter Tajat, Leslie Bauman, and the entire River Farm crew who managed both events.

I visited with three very special book clubs during the year, including the Wellington Book Club, the Navy Officers' Wives Bookclub, and The Zebra book club.

Anita Kerr hosted the Wellington club meeting at her home

and the group included Lainge Bailey, Cydney Hawkins, Karen Keefer, Lauren Hall Keene, Greg Kmiecik, Heidi Marchand, Kathy Shenkle, Marilyn Simon, Pat Suarez, and Katherine Ward. We mourn Greg's passing earlier this year.

The Navy Officers' Wives Bookclub has supported me from the beginning of the series and includes Dana Daspit, Susie Davis, Marlene Ghormley, Caroline Klam, Rachel Messman, Lib Mueller, Anne Smith, Harriet Slezak, and Willie Wright.

Maureen Cooney organized The Zebra book club's meeting at a la Lucia in Old Town where we were joined by Kathryn Craven, Tish Dalton, Candace Harman, Irene Ivone, Mary Nokes, and Wendy Pierce.

7. Family. Last but not least is family: Robin, Alex, Andrew, and Aron. It can't be done without their love. Robin has edited (and improved) my writing, as she did years ago when she served as my editor on the *Marquette Journal*. Alex has created a visual theme for the series with his cover designs. Andrew advises on plots and character development. And Aron has done artwork for several social media campaigns.

I'm sure I've forgotten to mention several people who were instrumental to my success over the past year and for that I apologize, but better to acknowledge many of you than neglect to mention any of you.

I look forward to meeting or renewing acquaintances in the months and years ahead. See you at a book signing!

JW 4/14/2024


Mo Katz and the crew will return in *Tales of Old Town*, a collection of short stories.

# WHERE CAN I BUY OLD TOWN MYSTERIES?

If you enjoy Old Town mysteries and want more copies of "Spite House" or copies of the other six books, contact Made in ALX (www.madeinalx.com).

If you're in Old Town Alexandria, the paperbacks are all available at the Made in ALX boutique at 533 Montgomery Street. If you're dropping by, let me know and I'll rush over and sign your book if I'm able to do so! (Email me at wazwitz@yahoo.com.)

Paperback, e-book, and audiobook editions are also available at Amazon.com, Apple Books, Audible, Barnes & Noble, Google, Libro.fm, and Kobo. My distributor is Itasca Books Distribution & Fulfillment (https://itascabooks.com) and you can always reach out to them.

*Daingerfield Island.* The inaugural Old Town Mystery opens with the discovery of a body floating in the Potomac River off Daingerfield Island, south of Reagan National Airport. Mo Katz unlocks the mystery behind the drowning based upon a photo in a locket worn around the deceased woman's neck. (Daingerfield Island, which includes a marina, is located south of Reagan National Airport.)

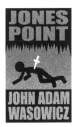

*Jones Point.* An attorney's mysterious murder and a plot to smuggle surface-to-air missiles into Washington, D.C., culminate in a firefight on the Wilson Bridge spanning the Potomac River. Alexandria police woman Sherry Stone is introduced as the newest member of the team. (Jones Point is a park located along the Alexandria waterfront beneath the Woodrow Wilson Bridge.)

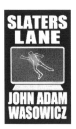
*Slaters Lane.* A senior prosecutor is brutally assaulted on Easter Sunday, setting off an investigation during the early stages of the COVID-19 pandemic. A complex mother-daughter relationship adds to the intrigue surrounding the assault. (Slaters Lane is located in Old Town North and intersects Washington Street.)

*Roaches Run.* A new-age guru's theory about a 12-year cycle of life offers insight into a clash between individuals seeking retribution for past transgressions. An explosion at the Roaches Run waterfowl sanctuary outside Washington, D.C., spells disaster for an unsavory character. (Roaches Run is located across from Gravelly Point north of Reagan National Airport. It is hiding in plain view. Everyone drives by, but no one stops!)

*Gadsby's Corner.* A performance of "Mystery in the Museum" turns deadly when a patron drops dead during the performance of the play. Assistant Commonwealth Attorney David Reese solves the crime with assistance from The Female Stranger, the spirit who haunts Gadsby's Tavern in Old Town Alexandria. (Gadsby's Corner is located outside Gadsby's Tavern in the heart of Old Town.)

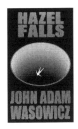 *Hazel Falls.* Years ago, the mysterious case of the Orr sisters mesmerized Old Town — one sister disappeared while the other's body was found at Wilkes Tunnel. Human remains are now discovered on the same day the murderer's conviction is overturned. Is the real kidnapper/murderer still at large? (Hazel Falls is a fictitious place located in the Eisenhower Valley that pays homage to "Hazel," the magnificent subterranean boring device that completed a two-mile journey to protect Alexandria's waterways under the direction of AlexRenew.)